Under the Influencer

Laura Ridgefield

ISBN (trade paperback): 979-8-9955376-0-1

ISBN (ebook): 979-8-9955376-1-8

Cover graphics by Yummy Book Covers

For all librarians, especially my Grandma Emily,
who let me stamp date-due cards at the library and gifted me a
trove of discarded books

Chapter 1

Hashtag Influencer

"**B**ridget, I swear if you do not stop arranging Q-tips and let me shower, I will come in there, strip naked and turn your Insta feed into OnlyFans."

Bridget Kolodziej cracked the bathroom door open four inches, squeezing her face into the gap. Her roommate Tran stood in the narrow hallway, her arms crossed over her scrubs.

"One more angle. Two minutes, tops!"

She closed the door gently on Tran's sigh of disgust, not wanting a waft of air to disturb the vignette she'd created: a flickering wood wick candle, vintage pedestal soap dish with three goat's milk soap balls and the hero item: a clouded milk glass canister artistically stuffed with Q-tips.

"You're pushing it for a roommate who's not actually on the lease," Tran called through the door.

A pinprick of guilt tweaked her as she checked the shot one more time. Quick adjustment of the ring light and *record*. The seconds ticked by as she panned from left to right. Eight... nine...ten. *Stop*. Perfect.

"Done! You can come in!"

Tran opened the door and squeezed into the bathroom as Bridget cleaned up the props. "What was this one for?" Tran asked, her voice muffled as she pulled her scrubs over her head.

"Amazon seller who sent sample product. Thought I'd use it for the Container Corner Ambassador Search audition. Want it?" She handed the container to Tran, who turned it over with a skeptical look.

"As your doctor, I have to say glass in the bathroom is not a great idea," Tran said. "It's cute, but it would look better on your dresser, Miss Influencer."

Translation: stick it in your room where I don't have to see it. Bridget smirked. "Got it, doc."

Leaving Tran to her steamy shower, Bridget bumped open the door with her hip and headed to her bedroom. She stashed the candle, soap dish and her cheap ring light in a bin before placing the milk glass container on her dresser. *It does look nice there.* Catching her reflection in the mirror, she paused to gather her wavy brown hair into a scrunchie and rubbed a finger across her chin to dispel some of the winter's flaky dryness.

She flopped down on her bed with her laptop to edit, but couldn't resist a quick check of her profile: 101,223 followers. Bridget sighed. *Miss Influencer.* If only.

In the two years since she registered @CabinetsCountertopsClosets on the socials, she dreamed of growing her organizing channel to 100,000 followers, getting an agent, making big deals. Deals that would mean she wouldn't have to live in Tran's extra-bedroom-that's-really-a-den. Or even quitting her job to make content full time.

But the harsh reality was, big brands wanted people with millions of followers, not thousands. And smaller brands just wanted UGC –user generated content—paying her a tiny stipend to create videos that they could push out on their own channels.

"Mary D'Esposito" flashed on her phone screen. She bolted upright, her laptop sliding off her lap as her heart beat in her throat. *Calm down. Don't freak out.* Mary had been her sophomore year college suite mate, but more importantly, she was an account supervisor at InfluenCZA, an agency that booked content creators, bloggers, and social media personalities. Bridget had been wheedling Mary for months, trying to sweet-talk her in the hopes of working as an influencer with her dream client, Container Corner.

She muted the tv and answered the phone. *Breathe in through the nose, out through the mouth. Zen. Calm.*

"Hey girl, what's going on?" She cringed as nerves made her voice speed up like a podcast at 2x speed.

"Hey Bridge. I know you've been asking me to consider you for content and we talked about Container Corner–"

She couldn't stop herself. Bridget blurted, "The Ambassador Search! Yes! I've been working on a post to submit and I would love to—"

"No. Listen. Not for Container Corner." Mary paused for a beat. "I have a different project for you. Not exactly what you're currently doing, but it's a paid engagement. A good one. You have a passport, right? Not expired?"

Bridget's brain wasn't working. "Passport? Sure." *Was there an international organizing crisis?*

"You're single so you can drop everything and go some-where"—*ouch*— "and you get decent engagement on your content. You have, what, 100,000 followers?"

"Just hit 100K on Insta, and close to 80,000 on TikTok." The squeak in her voice made her sound too eager. She squeezed her hand into a tight fist then released it. *Calm down.* She cleared her throat. *Professional.* "What's the project?"

"I need you to go on a vacation and post about it as a paid engagement for my client."

"A travel gig?" *Was this a joke?* "So, not for Container Corner?" Bridget tried to hide her disappointment.

Mary ignored her question. "You need to leave next weekend and be gone three weeks—until just before Christmas."

Bridget opened and closed her mouth twice as the circuits between her brain and voice reconnected. "Mary, people follow me because I post videos about cleaning out drawers and organizing closets. Things that don't require me showing my face on camera."

"That's ok! The campaign concept is to send twenty non-travel influencers around the world to live in rental houses. You don't fit the profile exactly, but my motocross star dropped out this morning."

"I don't know, Mare..."

Mary's voice grew more desperate. "Maybe you could do Closets Around the World or something, I don't know! But I need to deliver twenty influencers by tomorrow or my boss will be livid. I could lose the account, Bridget."

She hesitated, "Do this for me and I'll put you on the short list as a Container Corner ambassador."

Bridget felt the adrenaline spike through her veins. "Seriously? That's my dream assignment, and I'd be–"

Mary cut her off. "So you'll do it? Are you by your computer? I'll send you the writeup. The pay is good, so don't say no until you read it all. I need your answer in the next two hours. Call me! Bye!"

Bridget pulled her phone away from her ear as it buzzed with an email notification. Subject: THE GIG OF A LIFETIME.

She scrolled the document as the details sunk in: she'd stay twenty-one days in a HouseHijack (*terrible* name) rental, post sixteen pieces of content, and she'd make $50,000, plus $10,000 to cover expenses. *Holy crap.*

"Tran! *Tran!*"

Bridget tried not to spiral as a wave of panic filtered through her. Travel content meant people doing things like zip-lining, or jeep tours, or sipping poolside drinks with paper umbrellas. People doing spa days or petting marmosets. People who posted photos of deconstructed entrees, smoke-infused cocktails and used words like 'aesthetic' and 'manifesting' and 'my phone eats before I do.'

Not organizing Q-tips on a counter.

The kicker? She never showed herself or anyone else on camera, not even a voice over. Her quick "before and after" videos used catchy music with captions showed nothing more than her hands holding a glue gun, scrubbing a shelf, or pressing contact paper in place. Never her face and rarely her voice, if she could get away with AI narration or subtitles. On-camera influencers had perfect hair, dewy makeup and confidence...none of which were her strong suit. She had more varieties of grout cleaner than she had lipsticks.

"What's up?" Tran appeared in her doorway wrapped in a fluffy white robe, her bobbed black hair stringy and damp.

Bridget handed her phone to her roommate. "If you ever dreamed of kicking me out for a few weeks, today might be your lucky day."

Tran shot her a look of concern before scrolling through the documents. True to form, she got to the heart of things in an instant. "This is huge. Really big, Bridge."

Tran tossed the phone into Bridget's lap. "Does Home-Hackers know you're not a travel influencer? That you organize spice racks for likes?"

Bridget shrugged. "Not HomeHackers...*HouseHijack.* I've

been begging Mary for a shot at making content for Container Corner but she gives me this. But she said If I help her out with this, she will recommend me for CC. Though she obviously thinks I am desperate with zero social life."

Tran appeared to consider that. "Don't sell yourself short. You have book club next month." She narrowed her eyes. "But you *are* going to do this, right?"

Bridget set her phone face down on the desk. "I'd leave in a week and be gone through December 22."

"They're paying you $50,000 for three weeks and change? That's more than half a year's salary! It's a car, a nice one! That's 10 years off your college loans!"

"I'd have to get the time off work." Bridget bit the skin around her thumbnail. "Or I could quit?"

"As long as you find a job when you get back, I say do it. I love you, but I can't be your sugar mama forever." Tran squeezed her shoulder then walked out toward the kitchen.

"Carl owes me comp time for all the weekends and nights I worked in September getting quarterly returns out," Bridget called after her. "December is slow, and I'd be back in time to send out tax forms in January."

Tran returned with a half-full bottle of Moscato and took a hearty swallow before offering the bottle. "Bridge, you hate that job. If you can make more than half your salary with three weeks of work, maybe you don't need to go back. You know Ben, the ER nurse? His aunt Molly in Texas makes almost a million a year doing videos about queso and barbecue." Tran tapped a short, well-shaped fuchsia fingernail on the back of her phone. "Your stuff is good and this is your chance to show it. Where are they sending you?"

"The guy who dropped out was going to Ireland, so it's easier for her if I go there. At least they speak English."

Tran sat down on the twin bed as she muttered something in Vietnamese, the implication clear that Bridget should know more languages. Easy for her to say—Tran was a genius. Besides perfect fluency in both English and Vietnamese, she spoke French, Spanish and had a working understanding of Portuguese and Latin. The woman was an actual brain surgeon. Technically, still a resident on a neurosurgical rotation, but who's counting?

"I need to email her tonight with my decision." Bridget dabbed her thumb with a tissue, having worried it to the point of bleeding. "The worst part? The campaign is called Hashtag #YOLOSolo."

"Yikes." Tran took another long swig from the bottle of Moscato and emptied it. She leaned forward, locking in on Bridget. "Look, I'm going to say this once. Go soak in the shamrocks or discover leprechauns or whatever you do there. Kiss the Blarney Stone or fall in love with a hot Irishman. You weren't going home for Christmas anyway, with your parents going on their cruise. And I'm going to Fiji with the fam. Why would you stay here alone?"

"I'll be someone who posts junk drawer organization videos alone in Ireland."

"You'll be an *influencer getting paid for posting content* in Ireland."

Tran's words hit deep. She'd been chasing the dream of turning her hobby into a career for years. This gig was tantalizing, if terrifying. A flicker of desperation twinged in her brain. *This might be my only shot.*

Bridget picked up her phone and skimmed the contract again. Her eyes zoomed to the grey signature box.

If you sign it, you have to do it. It's not like bailing on plans at the last minute. This is binding. Ironclad.

She held her breath as she typed her name in the electronic

signature box. She faced her phone screen toward Tran. "Press *Enter* for me."

"Yes!" Tran squealed, jumping up from the bed, hitting *Enter* with relish. "Girl, I'm so proud of you! Now, the most important thing—what are you going to pack?"

In the days before her flight, Bridget's life became a whirlwind of itineraries, travel arrangements and shopping. Calls with Mary became a daily—even hourly—thing, with her friend ping-ponging between assuring Bridget that everything would be amazing and sharing her own worries that the entire campaign was going to be a disaster. The HouseHijack campaign was complicated, with several A-list influencers and their agents changing demands on the daily.

Ireland was a new market for HouseHijack, and the previous influencer had rejected all the suggested rental locations before dropping out, so Bridget was left to pick between a meager selection of locations that were in the budget and still available.

One listing ticked all the boxes: small enough to be within budget, close to a good number of tourist attractions, and Bridget would get the whole place to herself. The photographs showed a quaint little cottage in a town called Ballyknockerain. It was barely a speck on a map of southwest Ireland, but close to other picturesque towns, with lots of natural beauty and historic sites to provide options for content.

A tiny bit of her anxiety gave way to anticipation.

Because she was a last-minute substitution, Bridget had missed the onboarding calls, branding meetings and other prep. Instead, Mary and Shawn, her client from HouseHijack, barraged her with a full day's worth of information crammed into a 45-minute tag-teamed conference call.

"Sell the solo-travel lifestyle. Showcase the house and area, and the benefits of renting a HouseHijack property" said Shawn, reading off a set of bullet points.

Mary chimed in, "At least half of your posts should feature you on camera, speaking about your experiences. Demonstrate that solo travel can be fun, easy, and accessible for anyone. Show them they can live the dream of HouseHijack travel without worry."

She could do that, right?

Tran, on the other hand, used every bit of her limited free time to prepare Bridget for the journey. For a girl whose parents came to America from Vietnam with a beat-up suitcase holding the family's only possessions, Tran made up for lost time (and luggage). The pile of suitcases Tran pulled out of their shared storage space was taller than she was.

"Tran, I can't take eight suitcases for three weeks!"

"Half are for you. Half are for me. Fiji, remember? And stop complaining -- it's only two suitcases. The rest are your carry on, your makeup case, and your garment bag. Oh, and your laptop bag."

Bridget leaned against the towering stack of luggage. "Absolutely not. There's no way I'll be able to manage those by myself."

Tran rolled her eyes. "Porters and carts. They call them trolleys." She paused, then slipped out of the room. "Hang on, I've got something for you," she called over her shoulder.

Tran returned carrying a bag from one of the high-end electronics stores on Michigan Avenue. "Since you're not used to filming yourself, I got a going away present for my famous influencer friend." She extended the bag toward Bridget with a little shake. "Go on. Open it!"

"Tran, I can't..." started Bridget. They played this game every time. Tran was generous to a fault and took offense to any thought that her gifts were extreme. She peered inside the bag to see a top-of-the-line ring light, microphone, and selfie stick. "Thank you, you big dork." She gave Tran a tight hug, then extended the selfie stick to its full height. "You want me to be one of *those* tourists, don't you? Annoying everyone by jockeying for position to get the best shots?"

"That would be something to see," said Tran dryly. "The girl who doesn't even stand up for herself in a Starbucks line telling people in Ireland to get out of her way? It's almost enough to make me cancel Fiji."

"Like anything would make you cancel Fiji."

Tran offered to drive her to O'Hare on Saturday afternoon, but the hospital called her in to cover a shift. She left Bridget on her own with a hug and a pledge to cover the Uber.

Bridget felt an unexpected clench in her stomach as the drive cut through Chicago's north side neighborhoods. She cupped her hand against the fogged-up window to better see the Christmas lights adorning the porches and rooftops, trying to ignore scent of the stale heat blasting from the vents. The idea of being away from her city for so long was unsettling.

On the bright side, the first installment check from InfluenCZA had come on time and cleared without issue. Seeing that money sitting in her account was both exhilarating and unnerving. This was the beginning of a whole new life. She simply had to find her way to Ballyknockerain, and not end up in Belfast or Iceland or Palau or something. She closed her eyes and took a deep breath. Pulling her phone out of her pocket, saw a text from Mary.

> Safe travels! Text if you need anything. About half of the content creators have posted their first videos. Can't wait to see yours.

Damn. She'd had every intention of getting Tran to film her as she left the apartment, but in the mad scramble to leave, she forgot. Not the most auspicious start.

She popped in her earbuds and shot a wary glance toward the driver. "Could you turn down the music for one minute? I need to make a quick video."

"Here goes," she murmured. It was a shame her expensive selfie stick was stuck in the trunk, but she held the phone against the headrest and pasted on a smile. *Record.*

"This isn't my usual type of post, but I'm Bridget, the person behind @CabinetsCountertopsClosets. I'm going to be spending a few weeks in Ireland, in an adorable cottage thanks to House Hijackers, and I'll be taking you with me as I document my travels here on this channel. Right now I'm in a car on my way to O'Hare Airport. Next time I post, I'll be on the Emerald Isle. I look forward to sharing this journey with you!"

Maintaining a tight smile, Bridget stared at the tiny camera lens on her phone, trying not to look down as she fumbled for the pause button. She played back the video, her internal monologue critiquing her voice, her bare-minimum makeup, her drab winter parka that had seen better days. In short, everything. She hit post and her stomach clenched again. There was no turning back now.

Next stop, Ireland. So far, zero likes.

Chapter 2

The Hits Keep Coming

Finn Malloy was in a foul mood.

His brother might call that his natural state, but today felt extra dark and particularly grim, and he had earned every bit of it himself.

He'd been working in shipping at Kehoe's Dairy long enough that the job was mindless and straightforward. Moving cases and bottles was loud, cold, and messy at times, but a decent wage if you didn't mind your boots sticking to the floor and your trouser legs stiff with milk each night.

Best of all, it was outside of the eyes of his interfering relations. Growing up as the youngest of five children, every damn person in his family felt it was their God-given duty to meddle in his life. This was the first job in years that hadn't been brokered or arranged by one of his sisters, their husbands, or his uncle. It was blissfully free from coworkers who would report back to his clan on his every move.

He'd been minding his own at the lunch table in the break room when Roddy White started in on Claire McKibbon. You'd think a man twice divorced at thirty-four would show a little more restraint before sniffing after a girl like Claire, but assuming Roddy had sense would be your first mistake. Claire hadn't been working at Kehoe's more than a fortnight, but Roddy made a beeline for her as soon as he saw her bending down to take inventory on the lower shelves.

Finn tried to stay out of it. He kept his head down, focused on eating his sausage roll and crisps. It wasn't his business, no need for him to get mucked up in all of it. And yet, his eyes followed as Roddy cornered her by the lockers, entreating her to step out with him that night.

When Roddy put his hands on her waist, Claire's careful diplomacy took on an edge of fear. "Stop it, Roddy!" she said, twisting to get out of his grip.

Finn didn't even realize he'd dropped his lunch. By the time he closed the distance between them, his arm was already cocked, his stance alone a threat.

All Roddy had to do was let her go on her way. Take his hand off her jumper. Walk out of the room. "Move on, Roddy."

"What are you going to do about it, Malloy?" Roddy's sneer was a lit match to the fuse of Finn's temper.

In mere seconds, Roddy was holding kitchen roll to his face and Finn's knuckles were split and bleeding. After a moment of stunned silence, Finn turned on his heel, picking up his bag and coat. He crossed the warehouse floor to the manager's office, rapping on the glass before opening the door. Tommy Barnes looked up in confusion. "Finn, what—"

"I'll save you the trouble of giving me the sack. I quit."

"Malloy, what are you losing your head about? *Malloy!*" Before his manager could get up from his desk, Finn was out the door. With four jobs in two years, quitting was starting to become a bit of a habit.

"Finn!" Claire called after him as he walked across the dairy floor, stepping carefully around the ever-present puddles of milk and water on the floor. He pretended not to hear her. He needed to get somewhere alone, where he could kick himself in private. The last thing he needed was Claire's apologies for him getting involved. She'd assume it meant something that he defended her. But Finn would have done it for anyone.

He couldn't abide a bully.

Gran's tiny cottage was deep in shadow by the time he returned home, the long winter nights coming on in a hurry. Didn't matter; Finn could navigate home in total darkness on the narrow, winding roads that threaded through the Irish countryside.

The stone house was a true crofter's cottage, though Gran had replaced the thatched roof when Finn was a teenager. Some might call it cozy with a parlor, kitchen, two bedrooms, and a bathroom in between. Others might call it tiny and shabby. Both would be correct. It was the house his mother was raised in, and in turn, Finn and his siblings and cousins spent countless hours playing, exploring, and generally getting into trouble here. As a child, going to Gran's had been a treat, a chance to be spoiled and play with the animals in the barn.

Today, it was a refuge.

With the door shut behind him, Finn finally let himself relax. He pressed the wall switch and the glow from Gran's Belleek porcelain lamp made the house inviting, if still cold. He started a fire in the stove with the few pieces of wood he'd stacked. He'd need to bring in more wood to last the night, but that could wait. For now, he slumped into the well-worn armchair in the corner and let the tension in his body release with a sigh.

Finn contemplated Gran's wooden rocker, standing quiet

on the edge of the braided rug, and felt the familiar sting of grief. "Lost another job, Gran. But don't lose faith in me," he murmured. Gran had understood him better than anyone in the family. The youngest of seven children herself, Gran made Finn her particular favorite, their bond forged in the common complaint of being the youngest child. Instead of living at home, Finn had moved in with Gran during her final year on earth, managing the cottage and everything else.

Without meaning to, his eyes rested on the pile of mail next to last night's supper wrappings. It wasn't hard to guess they were dunning notices. Heating oil. Cell phone. Credit cards. While Gran left him the house free and clear in her estate, she didn't have any to spare for the repairs it needed, including repairs to the roof. Nor the estate taxes. Not to mention two ancient pain-in-the-ass donkeys.

With a groan, he got up to feed the ungrateful animals. If any creatures felt the loss of Gran more than he did, it would have to be those godforsaken donkeys. But Gran had loved them, just as she loved her stubborn grandson.

When he got back inside the house, his brother Cillian was stomping on the entry rug to shake the wet off his boots, hanging his jacket on the coatrack behind the door. *Treats the place like he owns it.* Finn crossed his arms, leaning against the doorway of the kitchen. "Did you even knock before coming in?"

"How are you getting on?" Cillian ignored his complaint and gestured toward the takeaway cartons and unopened post on the table. "You're becoming a hermit, Finn. Don't you want to go out and do something? Anything?"

Finn's irritation flared as he watched his brother sift through the clutter on the table. "If you don't mind, that's my private correspondence."

Cillian picked up a handful of mail, slapping it against the table. "Love letters, are they? This lot will have you out on your ear before too long."

He casually ran his hand along the back of the kitchen chair. "Mairead said you quit up at Kehoe's today. Claire McKibbon was telling the story up one side of town and down another."

And there it was. "Is that why you're here? Then you're welcome to fuck right off." Like clockwork, his family couldn't keep to their own business if their lives depended.

"There's that charming personality." Cillian jostled his elbow, a transparent effort to get Finn to smile. Something that failed miserably. "It is my concern. I'm your brother. And God knows, you're lucky to have me." Cill was known for his easy manner, always with a joke or a wink for a pretty girl. It's what made him successful as a tour operator for people on holiday, especially Americans. Right now, his cheery disposition was only serving to irritate Finn.

Cillian dropped the pile of letters and headed to the icebox. Opening it, he made a clucking noise that would have made Gran proud. "A jar of olives, two takeaway boxes and some cheese that appears to be turning into an antibiotic." He shook his head. "You're twenty-eight years old, Finn. Do you think Gran would want this for you?"

"Don't, Cill," he said through gritted teeth.

Cillian pressed on. "How much do you have with the bank, then? It's November 30. Do you have enough to get through the end of the year, with no money coming in?"

"I'll get by." Finn bit off each word.

"You know, Finn...if you sell the cottage, you could pay off the creditors, set a bit aside. Gran wanted to set you up in life. Sure, she gave each of us a bit, but you got her house for a reason."

"Mostly because she wanted to saddle me with those damn donkeys."

Cill laughed. "I don't envy you them, it's true. But she also saddled you with the inheritance tax."

Like I don't know that. "I've got it down to only 15,000 euro...and that's with all the repairs I've had to make. The way you're talking, you'd think I owed a fortune and should sell it to the first idiot who comes calling. Not likely."

"When's that 15,000 due? First of the year?"

"I'm working on that."

"Speaking of idiots, you give Bernie's offer any more thought?" Cillian asked.

"Bernie Coughlin can kiss my ass."

"It's ready money for the house, Finn. In truth, he's offering more than it's worth."

Finn rounded on his brother. "You think I should sell him Gran's house—my house—so he can rent it out to rich people on holiday, who will sit with their noses in their phones, muck up the floors, break the china and spill their wine spritzers on the floor? And me, living in some economy flat or back with Ma?"

"Who the hell is drinking wine spritzers?"

Finn waved his hands dismissively. "Or mojitos, or Aperol...but it won't be a pint."

"Noted." Cillian sighed. "You know, she didn't leave you the cottage to have it bury you. Don't be so stubborn that you lose it all anyway."

Finn's body tensed. Cillian was precariously close to the line. They'd scuffled as children, but it had been a good many years since Cill had tempted him to settle things physically. Though his brother was a year older, Finn had at least twenty pounds of muscle on him.

"I'll thank you to leave now," he said, forcing his words out evenly.

Cillian paused, and Finn could see him weighing his options. After a moment, he shook his head. "Stubborn fool."

"I'll get another job," Finn said loudly.

"How long will that one last you?" Cillian shouted in return.

Finn slammed his fist on the table, making the plastic containers rattle and tip over. The noise seemed to end the conversation, and both brothers went quiet.

Cillian was the first to speak. "I know why you did what you did at Kehoe's. I'm not going to argue with your reasons. But if you don't get a grip on your finances, you'll be running out of choices. I love you too much to watch that happen."

Cill clapped him on the shoulder, and Finn reached up, covering his brother's hand with his own. It wasn't settled between them, but it was a workable truce.

"Look, I can put you to work doing pickups for holiday-goers in the spring, but it's quiet now. I don't have extra jobs to spare." Cillian scrolled through his phone, shaking his head. "I have a pickup at the Killathay station Sunday afternoon. It's an American, so they'll probably tip. You want it?"

"Fine then." He remembered his manners. "Good of you."

Cillian grinned. "Oh, I nearly forgot. Ma wanted me to swing by and make sure you remembered dinner next Friday. Father Tim is coming round, and she wants us to show out. And since you don't reply to her texts..."

Finn rolled his eyes. "I reply to her texts. Look, she texted me last on...oh." Sheepishly, he clicked on the unread texts and typed a brief reply.

Cill looked over his shoulder. "Who else are you ignoring?"

"Not sure who this is." Finn's brow furrowed as he read his

phone. "Oh hell...it's Claire. She wants me to come by her dad's Sunday at six for supper so he can get me a job."

"There you go, boyo!" Cillian grinned. "Pick up the American in Killathay at 4:30, drop her in Ballyknockerain, then go get your job at six at the McKibbons. Then on Friday, you can tell Ma she finally has more than one good son."

Cill laughed as he sidestepped the half-hearted cuff Finn aimed at his shoulder, adding, "Claire's a fine thing, isn't she? She was telling everyone who'd listen about how you stood up for her."

Finn dismissed that idea with a withering look.

Cillian sighed. "Dodging the same things everyone else chases. Eejit. Come on, let your fancy and successful big brother take you to the pub for a bite so you don't get botulism from your fridge. At least I know you'll be fed twice this week."

Chapter 3

Planes, Trains, and Automobiles

After the stress of changing trains in Mallow early Sunday morning, Bridget collapsed into her reserved seat with a sigh of relief. She pulled out her phone for at least the fifteenth time to check her post, and was relieved to see a steady increase in likes and comments, most from her regular followers.

Getting through customs at Dublin airport, navigating her way to Heuston Station and swapping trains had sapped every ounce of her energy. The "grand soft day" as her taxi driver had called it was now a full lashing of rain against the train windows, blurring out views of the city, then pastures, then mountains.

Between the rhythmic hum of the train and the steady drumbeat of the rain, she struggled to keep herself from dozing on the first leg of the ride by reading emails and triple-checking her itinerary on her laptop. Once in Killathay, her driver would take her to the idyllic cottage, where she'd post her first video by the deadline, and she could get a good night's sleep.

The idea of sleep pulled at her very soul. She put away her

laptop and slid it into its bag, stashing it under her seat. If she closed her eyes for a minute...

She woke to someone tapping her shoulder and a shaky voice saying, "Weren't you getting off at Killathay, dear? We've stopped—you'd better hurry!"

Bridget forced herself awake, groggy and confused. Looking out the window, a steady stream of people walked toward cars behind a Killathay sign. *Shit!* In a frenzy, Bridget struggled to grab her suitcases then lurched her way down the aisle, bumping into every seat. At the doors, she thumped her suitcases down to the platform one at a time. At least the rain had stopped.

Stepping off the train, a man's voice called out behind her. "Young lady, I think you left a bag!"

A bag?

Her laptop!

In a panic, Bridget abandoned her suitcases on the platform. She pushed past the man with a grateful "thank you!" and weaved through the train car back to her seat. She reached under to grab the laptop bag.

She tugged. No movement.

Pulled again. Nothing. *Shit.*

An announcement chimed overhead. "Doors will be closing in two minutes. Please stand clear of the doors."

"Help! I need to get this loose. I have to get off!" She scanned the mostly empty car in a panic. The few passengers still present were not making eye contact. "Please!"

"Oi, Bridget! Anyone here named Bridget?" A man's voice with a thick Irish brogue rang out in the vestibule between cars.

A flush of relief coursed through her. "Me! Yes!" She banged her head on the underside of the table as she tried to gesture toward the voice at the door. "But my bag is stuck on something!"

"For the love of Pete." A pair of faded jeans and work boots appeared at her elbow, and soon a whole body was crouched under the seat in front of hers.

She could see his hands reach behind the seat. "Hold tight," he grunted.

Obediently, Bridget kept her grip taut on the thick woven strap of her laptop bag, willing it to release. She watched through the seat gap as his hands worked to coax the strap out of its tight spot, feeling him tug in each direction.

"Will you let go then?" the man snapped.

Bridget recoiled, wincing as she banged her head again on the underside of the table. "You told me to hold tight!" She sat back on the aisle floor as he continued to work the strap.

"Here, it's loose." With a grunt, he pushed the case toward her, then slid out from under the seats.

As he brushed the dust from the floor off his hands, she took stock of him. A thatch of thick black hair was close-cropped on his head, with thick eyebrows to match. His hands seemed rough, but not dirty. Obviously used to hard work. He wasn't tall, but still cleared an inch or two over Bridget's five-foot-six frame. And he was *solid* under his shirt.

When he finally looked toward her, she saw his sharp, ocean-blue eyes.

He held out his hand to help her up. "I'm your driver, by the way. Finn Malloy. Now let's get out of here before the train —oh, fuck all."

The hiss of the hydraulics cut off his words. Bridget gave him a horrified look as she scrambled to her feet. "No! Stop the train! Make them stop it—my bags!" The lurch of the train knocked her off balance, but Bridget wobbled determinedly toward the vestibule door. Finn caught her hand to pull her back.

"Wind your neck in, there's nothing to be done. We're

down for 40 minutes to Tralee, then the train will turn round and come back to Killathay."

"My suitcases are on the platform!" The exhaustion and stress of the day was giving way to an overwhelming amount of emotion. "All my bags, all my clothes...everything." She could feel the tears welling up.

"Sit," he barked. She slumped down in a seat, despairing as the landscape began to slide by through the window. Her driver gave an exaggerated sigh, pulling out his phone.

"Jimmy? Finn here. Yes, saw your mum at the train station. Good...good. Listen, can you help me with something?"

In a few moments, he ended his call, sliding into the seat across from her. "I've got Jimmy Barnes on the case. He'll stow your bags in the boot of my car. They'll be set until we get back to Killathay around six." With a huff of frustration he added, "Probably won't have you dropped until seven or so." He began texting slowly, using one finger to hunt and peck on the keyboard. "So much for six o'clock," he muttered to himself.

The carriage doors slid open as the conductor began to collect tickets from the handful of passengers that boarded the train in Killathay. When he arrived at their table, Bridget unleashed a torrent of explanations. "Please, I'm so sorry, we were supposed to get off at Killathay, but my bag was stuck under the seat, and this is my driver who helped me dislodge it. I flew in from Chicago this morning, and all my bags were left on the platform. He's trying to get someone to look after them. He said it's 40 minutes to Tralee, and then we have to take the train back, is there anything else we can do?" She barely took a breath as she explained.

The conductor looked at Finn. "She with you, Malloy?"
Finn nodded.

"He's giving me a ride tonight." Bridget offered. Both the conductor and Finn failed to conceal a grin.

"Is he now?" The conductor stifled his smile as he pulled a notebook from his pocket and began to write. "I'll not be charging you for the ticket. Find an empty seat and this time, get off at Killathay, miss. At least you've the sense to travel with this one here. Good man." With a nod to Finn, the conductor continued his way through the carriage.

At least one problem solved. She smiled up at Finn. "Thank you—I think I forgot to say it before. I'm Bridget, by the way."

"I know."

Not much for small talk. "I...thank you so much."

"You probably don't want to be telling people I'm giving you a ride. Means something different here."

Bridget scrunched her forehead in confusion. *Oh.* She blushed furiously when she figured out the sexual context. "I didn't mean–"

He cut her off with a shrug, turning to look out the window. Bridget followed his gaze, grateful for the chance to compose herself. *Not even here 12 hours and already embarrassing myself.* It didn't take long to leave the town of Killathay behind, trading its clustered buildings for stone fences and sheep. The tiny winter sun dipped low in the sky, casting an ethereal glow over the expanse of soft gray-green hills. As the embarrassment and chaos ebbed, so did her rush of adrenaline. She stifled a yawn.

It would be dark by the time she got to the cottage, so her goal of a quick walk-through of the place seemed unlikely for her morning deadline. She needed to pivot. The thrill of travel, right?

With a flash of longing for her high-tech selfie stick, still nestled in her carryon back in Killathay, she fished her phone out of her pocket.

"Be right back." Bridget slipped out of her seat, navigating her way to the vestibule for a bit of privacy. Her reflection in the window showed a hot mess. Puffy eyes and wild hair be damned; it would have to do. *Record.*

"Hey guys! Bridget here! You're not going to believe this. I missed my stop in Killathay because my bag got stuck, so I'm now on a round trip to Tralee, which is like, 40 minutes away. My adventure is a bit delayed, but I'm still looking forward to seeing the adorable cottage I booked through HouseHijack."

She pivoted herself to show the window of the train behind her. "Not a lot to see yet, as it's almost sunset and I've been up for about 40 hours straight, but I've spotted a bunch of sheep and fields and stone fences, and I'm sure things will get a lot more interesting tomorrow. Until then, signing off!"

Her bright, tight smile stayed fixed until she tapped her phone to end the recording. It wasn't Oscar-worthy, and the camera angles needed work, but it would do. She slipped back into the carriage and sat across from Finn.

Snip. Trim. Enhance. Zoom. Caption. Hashtag. Background sound. The mobile version of her editing app wasn't as easy or as quick as editing on her laptop, but it was good enough.

"What're you doing there?" Finn's rough voice startled her out of her concentration. He leaned forward, gaze intent on her screen. She caught a faint scent of sawdust.

"Editing a video—hang on." She focused her attention back on her phone, trying to tamp down her distraction. "Sorry, I have to email this really quick. I'm on deadline." She drafted a terse email to Mary and attached the edited video. *Send.*

In seconds, her phone began to buzz: Mary. *That was fast.* She held up a finger, signaling that Finn should be quiet. With a huff, he turned and faced the window, arms crossed.

Making friends all over the place. She cleared her throat and answered. "Hi! I just sent you my video —you're quick!"

Mary's tone was serious. "I need to talk to you."

Oh no. "Sure, what is it?"

"You know this isn't some throwaway thing, Bridge. Everything you do has to be approved. We went over it in the onboarding."

"I know, I just sent it to you."

"Not that one. The one you posted yesterday. You didn't get it approved by the client *and* you said their name wrong. I warned you -- they follow all our creators and they get to approve everything before you post, Bridget. They raised holy hell with my boss."

Bridget pivoted away from Finn and lowered her voice. "I didn't think I was official yet...wait, I said the name wrong?"

"'HouseHIJACK, not hijackers." Bridget winced. "It's a short-term rental company, Bridge, not a band of terrorists. You probably shouldn't be saying that name anywhere near an airport anyway. Did you never see the movie 'Airplane?'"

"It was just something I did to update my followers."

"If you're going to mention the client and the job—"

She balled a fist against her forehead as she squeezed her eyes closed. "No, you're right. Of course. It won't happen again." *Stupid stupid stupid.*

Mary sighed, the edge of her irritation softening. "You're not the only creator I've had to have a come-to-Jesus call with. The former gymnast you met during onboarding? She created a 'HouseHijack Ambassador' logo and put it all over her feed. And my ice cream taster? He just posted a video getting drunk at the airport. Not great."

"Oh jeez. I'm so sorry, Mare."

"Just another day at the office. Everyone's going rogue and we haven't even started. I'm popping Tums like they're Skittles."

"I'll delete that video right now. I just sent you my first real video for your approval. I shot it on the train I'm currently stuck on. I look like a disaster, but maybe it will be kind of funny? If you don't like it, I can reshoot it."

"You're stuck on a train? Are you ok?"

"Yes, my stupid laptop bag got hooked on a seat, and I'm now going to be probably two hours late getting to the cottage."

"Make sure you don't post it until I tell you it's approved."

"I know. Sorry again."

She hit end on her call and stared off into the distance. *Off to a fantastic start, Bridget. Your first post for the program, and you screwed up the client's name.* Now would be a great time for a giant hole to swallow up the whole train.

She glanced over at Finn, still looking out the window. "Sorry, I didn't mean to be rude."

"Messed up your video, did you?" Finn's voice was short.

Great, he was pissed at her too. It was going to be a long trip to the cottage. Time to eat crow. "I'm sorry, I realize I screwed up your day."

"No difference to me, I charge by the hour," he said with a clipped tone. "You a streamer or something?"

"Or something, I guess. I'm a content creator on an assignment to showcase Ireland for a house rental company. I'm supposed to post videos daily, but I've already screwed up my first one."

Finn turned to her, quizzically. "First one? You've never done this before?"

"I guess you could say that." Bridget smiled ruefully. "I have a lot of followers, but not for this kind of content."

"What d'ye normally do then?"

"I make videos about how to organize your home."

He laughed. "Do you now? Big market for teaching people how to put away all kinds of nonsense they buy and don't have room for in America?"

His face twisted in a sort of smirk, and Bridget froze, a cold knot forming in her chest. She felt blooms of color rising on her cheeks. What was it about Finn that made her so self-conscious? She swallowed a retort, instead focusing on her phone. His snarky remarks reinforced Bridget's nagging self-doubt as they sat together in silence. Impostor syndrome coming in hot.

"Sorry. That was rude."

Bridget looked up to see Finn's intense blue eyes locked on hers. He sighed. "I had an appointment at six, and I took out my frustration on you."

Somehow his apology made her feel even worse. "I'm sorry I made you miss it."

"Not your fault." His voice was gruff, but he seemed mollified by her apology. He turned back toward the window.

Time to stew in her own remorse. She screwed up this guy's evening, made Mary's job harder...not a stellar start to her trip. The hour on the train gave her ample time to catalogue her faults. The combination of physical and mental exhaustion took its toll, and she closed her eyes.

"Better get up, don't want to miss Killathay again and go back to Dublin, do you?" She woke to Finn tapping her shoulder. In the fog of sleep, the words barely registered. She rose to her feet, jostling as the train churned to a stop. Finn had her laptop bag slung across his own shoulder. "Don't be leaving your phone, either."

The clammy air brought her to full alertness as they disembarked in Killathay. Bridget followed Finn quietly to a small car, one of only a few still in the lot. When she saw her suitcases safely in the back of his car, she allowed herself to relax a little. Finn stowed her laptop and got into the driver's seat. Bridget hesitated. As a lifelong city girl, the idea of sitting in front as the only passenger was strange, but Finn's car was tiny. She forced herself to open the passenger door.

The last of the winter daylight had slipped away and the stretch of shops and buildings were quiet. "Is everything closed? I need to pick up some things. Groceries..."

"I'm taking you shopping then?" Finn asked, a note of exasperation telegraphing loud and clear.

"There's supposed to be a store near my cottage? It was in the listing. I could check my binder."

"In Ballyknockerain?" he laughed. "Not likely. There's a pub and a druggist, and maybe a shop or two. Ballyknockerain is a speck on the map."

Bridget was exhausted, hungry, and feeling stupid. She pulled herself together and took a breath. "I'm sorry for the inconvenience, but I need 10 minutes at a supermarket for tonight. I'll rent a car tomorrow. And like you said, you're being paid by the hour."

Finn started the engine. "As you wish, Boss Lady."

The trip to the grocery store took closer to 30 minutes, Bridget emerging with essentials in an assortment of Lidl bags. They set off to the cottage without a word. The road to Ballyknockerain wound perilously along a narrow path, and the swish of the wipers made it hard to see. Finn shifted gears expertly as they coursed through the hillside.

"You're a good driver," she said, trying to break the awkward silence.

"I hope so. Drove for Kehoe's for almost a year." Finn kept his eyes intently on the road.

"Kehoe's?"

"A dairy halfway between here and Cork."

"How long have you been driving people?" Another dumb question.

He made a show of looking at his wristwatch. "About three hours. Lucky you, I'm out of work at the moment, so my brother Cillian put me on this job. He runs the livery service, doing tours and transport."

"A family business, then."

"His business, not mine. I'm just the help." *Well, that touched a nerve.* His bitterness came through loud and clear. Maybe they could play the quiet game until they arrived. She'd get into the cottage, put away her groceries and sleep for about twelve hours. Or maybe fourteen.

After a while, Finn said, "I'm not sure what's down this way, but GPS says it's straight off this road," Finn turned onto a pebbled driveway thick with bramble and overgrown shrubbery.

Finn maneuvered the car slowly down the rough gravel, sticks and twigs popping under the tires. Bridget peered through the windshield to catch a glimpse of the cottage in the glow of the headlights.

"Oh no," she whispered.

The 'quaint cottage with old-world charm' described in the listing was nowhere to be found. Instead, the cottage was straight out of a horror movie with obvious disrepair and neglect. Scraggly bushes clustered around the entryway and even from the car, she could see the paint on the door was peeling.

Finn kept the headlights on high beams to illuminate a path through the rain. Bridget picked her way across the crushed stone, half-dragging her carry-on suitcase as Finn ported her two other bags down the walk. The little arched doorway offered little protection from the rain. At the door, she fumbled for her phone to open the email with instructions.

"He said the key is on the ledge above the door."

Finn grunted, knocking twigs and other detritus off the porch as he set down her duffel and tipped the large suitcase to rest. Bridget reached up to fumble around for the key. She flinched as her hand touched a massive spider web, dropping the slim silver key with a clink on the stone.

Both reached down to retrieve it at the same time, bumping heads so hard that Bridget saw stars.

"You all right?" Finn asked as she rubbed her forehead.

"You have a hard head," she answered weakly.

"You don't know the half of it." He cupped her head with his hand, his thumb grazing the tender spot where they connected. "Tough to tell in this light, but I think you'll be fine."

For the first time, the Irishman smiled. A real smile, with dimples and everything, all the way up to his ice blue eyes.

In one fluid motion, he scooped up the fallen key and unlocked the door. He stepped into the cottage first, and she could almost feel his body tense as he scanned the shadows of the room. Bridget hung back as he felt along the wall for the light switch.

With a click, the room illuminated.

Neither one spoke.

After a few beats, Finn broke the silence. "What you were dreaming of, is it?"

The tiny cottage was not "quaint with old-world charm." "Tired," would be a kindness, and "run down," didn't begin to cover it. With peeling wallpaper, broken chairs in the corners, and a layer of dust and grime on nearly every surface, the room's aesthetic was more dilapidated and abandoned than restful respite. A sharp tang of mildew permeated the stale air. The room was sparsely furnished with a wooden table and two chairs, a faded pink floral sofa, a wide wooden bench and a bookcase with old copies of *Woman's Way* magazines from the 1980s.

In a trance of disbelief, she forced herself to walk toward the shadowy bedroom to peek inside. The mattress was obviously bowed in the middle, coved with a garish threadbare comforter.

Plink. A droplets of water fell from a seam in the roof to a nearly overflowing bucket next to the bed.

Horrified, she backed out to the main room and turned toward the kitchen. The refrigerator motor was audibly grinding, and two cabinet doors hung at odd angles.

Every single atom of her tidy organizer's mind silently screamed. She caught movement in the corner of her eye. A tiny mouse scampered over her shoe and out the door. She jumped with a scream, her elbow knocking into the ancient rusty kettle on the stove. She crossed back to Finn, still standing at the doorway of the cottage, his face inscrutable. The emotions of the day tumbled down on her, panic and exhaustion leading the pack.

This is a mistake. Mary was crazy to think she could do this job. She was an ocean away from anyone she knew and this horrible, decrepit cottage was beyond the pale.

"I can't stay here," she whispered. "I can't possibly stay here!"

Chapter 4

A Host of Problems

Finn dragged his finger across the surface of a bookcase, then wiped the grimy smear of dust on his jeans. Gran would've been horrified at the state of things.

"Hate to see what a bargain holiday looks like if this is the fancy place."

"No...there has to be some mistake." Bridget pulled out her phone. "I saw photos. This is completely wrong. This is a deathtrap."

"Social media is going to have a wild time with this real Irish holiday experience." He swatted a sofa cushion, creating a voluminous cloud of dust that made him cough. "A new meaning to viral post."

"Not funny!" Bridget snapped, frantically pacing in the relative safety of the doorway as she dialed.

"Simmer down. I'm not laughing at you, I—"

She cut him off with a raised hand. *Rude.* "Mary, it's Bridget. This house...it's not going to work. This is not me being a neat freak or particular—it's unlivable! It has *rodents*! It's literally leaking from the ceiling into a bucket, and it's filthy and...

call me back." Her voice scaled higher until the last phrase was almost a shriek.

She turned to look at Finn, her eyes wide with panic. "What am I going to do?"

He had enough problems of his own without taking on this one. *Not your business, Finn.*

She continued to scan the room on high alert. "I can't stay here. No human should ever stay here!"

"It wouldn't be my first choice, that's true." He crossed his arms and leaned back against the doorframe, then jumped forward as it gave a loud crack. "Place is falling down around us."

Her grey eyes were wide and watery as she looked pleadingly at him. This girl with her mess of brown curls and her tiny beauty mark nestled next to her mouth...she needed help. *Bleedin' hell.* He tamped down the urge to fix things for her. He'd already texted Claire that he'd miss dinner, but offered to come by late. If he got involved with this American, there was no way he'd make it to the McKibbons' place at all.

But he was the only soul she knew in Ireland.

He sighed. "Let's get you out of here. I'll take you back to town and help you find a hotel or some place with a room for you, at least for tonight."

Her features relaxed and he could hear the exhaustion in her voice. "Yes, please. Give me a minute, I have to take some photos so I can show Mary why I can't stay here."

Finn hesitated not wanting to leave her alone. *Not your problem.* "I'll take your bags back to the car."

Suitcases re-stowed in the boot, he watched Bridget lock the door and reach up on tiptoe to replace the key on the ledge.

Wasted effort–no one was breaking into a kip like that. She began to make a run for the car in the rain. Without warning, she slipped on the flagstone, pitching sideways into mud and gravel.

"Bridget!" In a heartbeat, he was out of the car and at her side. He bent down to pull her to her feet.

She tried to pull away. "No, I'll get you full of mud. I'm fine."

"Hush. Are you hurt?" he asked, probing at her wrists and palms. Her hands were cold and and flecked with bits of gravel. He tucked his hand inside his sleeve as a makeshift handkerchief, using it to wipe her cheeks clean. In the light of the high beams, he could see a smattering of freckles across her nose.

"Hands and ch-chin." Sure enough, a thick bead of blood was forming on the tip of her chin.

"Hang on." Finn guided her round to the back of the car, pulling a small first aid box out of the boot and a holey blanket. Though the kit was mostly bare, he found a wad of gauze and squirted some antiseptic gel on it. "Press this to your chin and we'll get you someplace to stay." He led her to the passenger door and laid the blanket across her seat. With the gauze pressed against her chin, Bridget sat down in the car looking utterly defeated.

Now what was he going to do with her?

"I can't take you anywhere as you are. People will think I tried to murder you," he said, gazing down at her mud-spattered clothing. "And buried you, by the looks of it."

Only one thing to do. "Look now, I live about a half-hour away in Kildunne. You can clean up at my house while I make some calls for a hotel or something. Unless your boss finds you a new place to stay in the meantime."

Bridget dabbed the cut on her chin, peering into the small

mirror on the window visor. "I don't think that's a good idea. Can't you take me back to the train station?"

"Don't be daft. The station's closed this time of night anyway."

"I'm not being…daft. There's no way I'm going to the house of someone I barely know. I've seen Dateline—this is how people get murdered."

Unbelievable. Here he was, tossing her a lifeline and she was complaining about the color of the rope.

"You don't know your arse from your elbow around here. You've no car, and I won't leave a helpless kitten like yourself alone with your phone on eight percent and you looking like you're about to conk out at any moment."

"I didn't ask you for help," she said petulantly.

"Of course you did! At every turn, Boss Lady!" Finn rattled off her transgressions in a falsetto voice. "My bag is stuck! My suitcases are on the platform! I need food! My cottage is too rustic. Where's the Starbucks?"

She gasped at the last. "I never asked for Starbucks," she said, her voice wobbling.

He took a breath, reining in his temper. "And you go on, never giving one thought about the fact that my 20-minute drive today is venturing on three hours with no end in sight, making me miss a new job."

Her chin began to waver. "You said you were being paid by the hour so it didn't matter." With an air of injured dignity, she added, "I'm sorry I created such trouble for you. You didn't plan for this, and you've gone out of your way to help."

Ah, wonderful. Now she's apologizing. He scowled out the window. "Never mind."

"This was all a huge mistake." The last syllable trailed off into a sob, and the floodgates opened. A full-on crying fit. Just what he needed.

Wordlessly, Finn reached into the spud box and pulled out a wad of paper napkins. "Here now. Stop your crying. We can't have you in this state." He patted her on the back as her sobs dissolved into slow snuffles and hiccups.

She took a deep, shaky breath, finally calming.

"So we're to my house, yeah?"

"Fine."

The rain began to let up as Finn pulled into his drive fifteen minutes later. During the trip he tried to conjure a mental picture of the interior of his own house. Not pristine, but the mess was bearable. After the rental cottage, his would shine in comparison.

Gran would have gone round the bend if her cottage was untidy for a guest.

While Bridget gathered her grocery bags, he headed inside with her suitcases.

"It's a bit cold inside," he called over his shoulder. "While you clean up, I'll put the kettle on and get a fire going. And I'll get you something for that cut."

She followed him into the cottage then stood motionless in the doorway as he hung his coat, keeping all the muddy, drippy parts contained on the braided rug. Finn scooped up the scattered takeaway containers and shuffled them into the bin, then gathered the post into a pile. He hoped Bridget didn't see him nudge the stray socks and towel under the sofa.

He watched Bridget out of the corner of his eye as he bustled about. Crying women weren't foreign to him; he'd grown up with three older sisters, after all. All prone to loud outbursts of tears and wails. But quiet ones–those were different. He knew enough to not make sudden movements.

After a moment, she set down her grocery bags, turning her head to take in the cozy cottage. Wordlessly, she took off her dirty shoes, setting them on the rug.

"You have anything that needs the fridge?" Finn gestured toward her grocery bags.

Her voice sounded raspy when she spoke. "Milk, yogurt, cheese. Juice too."

Finn scooped up the bags. "I'll get them sorted. Can't have them spoil while you're cleaning up." She stood still on the center of the tiny rug, an island in a storm. "The plumbing's a bit finicky. I'll get the water started now. It can take a minute for the hot to pipe in."

He dropped the bags on the kitchen counter, putting away her cold items. With a glance behind him, he slipped to the bathroom and gave a cursory swipe of the sink and faucets with his washcloth. The bath wasn't perfectly clean, but it would do. Leaning over the ancient tub, he turned on both spigots, waiting for the water to find a compromise between freezing and scalding.

While the tub filled, he searched under the sink and came up with a bandage and bottle of surgical spirit. In the wooden linen cabinet, he found a spare towel and face cloth. She was still standing on the rug when he returned. "Water's good now, you won't catch your death. I've got a bandage for your chin here."

She demurred, moving the mound of napkins away from the wound. "It's stopped bleeding, I don't think I..."

"Hush. Let me clean it with the spirits at least. God knows what was in that muck."

She wavered for a moment, then nodded, tipping her head back to give him access. Finn dabbed the spirit on the washcloth and gently began to clean the cut on her chin. She winced as he touched the cloth. He pulled back slightly, his stomach twisting with the idea of hurting her. "Sorry, it stings."

"It's ok." He noticed tears welling in her eyes. They were an unusual color–mostly gray, with flecks of gold and green. A few more swipes of the cloth, and the cut was clean.

"Thanks," she murmured.

"Don't worry about it. I need to look after some things out back, but I can make some calls to hotels while you clean up."

She nodded and moved past him to the bathroom door.

"A bath?" she asked.

"Yeah, sorry. Have to take a bath. No shower at the moment. Which suitcase has something you can change into?"

"Why?"

For the love. "Because I'll put it outside the bathroom for you. Last thing I need is those muddy wheels tracking along the floor."

"The big one. With the pink luggage tag." She stepped into the bathroom and shut the door, clicking the lock.

Finn heaved the suitcase up by the side handle. "What, did you pack rocks in here?"

Her voice was slightly muffled. "Just so you know, I dropped a pin so my roommate knows where I am."

He wasn't the big bad wolf, for God's sake. "Your bigger concern should be looking presentable. No self-respecting hotel will let you in their lobby looking like you've been swimming in a pigsty."

He dropped the suitcase with a thud outside the bathroom door. "I'll be in the kitchen making tea if you need anything." He paused as he heard a splash.

"Wait, could you plug my phone in for me? It just died." The phone skittered from under the door out to the hallway, a few drips of water on its face. "Charger is in my laptop bag, not sure where I put the adaptor."

"Sure."

Somehow, the idea of a naked American woman using his bathtub seemed less intimate than sifting through her laptop bag for her charging cord, even with her permission. The cord was nestled against a bright white binder, with "Ireland Trip" labeled on its spine. Finn paused, running his fingers across the colorful, hand-labeled section dividers at the top: Itinerary/Insurance/Project Requirements/Cottage Info/Story Starters.

Finn glanced toward the hallway, then pulled out the binder and flipped to Cottage Info. The pages were slippery in their plastic sheet protectors, but he thumbed through printouts of the listing from HouseHijack ("a lovely cottage in the middle of everything"), a map of the area, and finally the copy of the rental agreement.

His suspicion was confirmed in black and white: Hosted by Bernard Coughlin.

"Bastard," he muttered. All the chaos of the day could be laid at one person's doorstep. A cretin only out to make money off unsuspecting travelers. Now that he'd seen the callous disrepair and haphazard upkeep of Bernie's cottages, he'd sooner starve before letting that scrubby man cross his threshold again with contracts to sell Gran's cottage.

Taking a breath to calm his anger, he slid the binder back into her bag. Finn brought Bridget's phone and charger with its American plugs and adaptor into the kitchen. As soon as he plugged it in, it began to ping with missed calls and texts.

Tea. He needed tea. He clattered the kettle onto the hob and lit the burner. Rifling through the cupboard, he found two cups that weren't chipped. He muttered, "I hope you take your tea without sugar because I'm out. If you need milk, we'll need to crack yours open."

What the hell is wrong with you? She was making him fuss

like an old woman. She was lucky to have a safe, dry place without mice or leaks to figure out her plans.

After about 15 minutes he tapped on the bathroom door. "Oi, not sleeping in there are you? You're getting texts from people."

Splashing. "Hang on. I'll be out in a minute."

He didn't mean to create a mental picture of her getting out of the tub, water streaming down her body as she stepped onto the mat. It was never his intention to picture her warm and pink from the bath, wrapped in his towel. But it was hard to ignore the idea that an attractive woman was wet and naked in your home, just on the other side of a door.

Stop it then. You're acting just as she feared.

A few moments later, Bridget padded out of the bathroom barefoot, her brown wavy hair heavy against her head. She was wearing clean sweatpants and a pale blue jumper looking calm but tired.

She smiled up at him, her gray eyes covered with heavy lids. "Thanks. I hung my towel on the back of the door. I hope that's ok?" she asked, running her fingers through her damp curls.

"Sure. What about your clothes? I can do a quick cycle on them." *What are you doing?* The sooner he got her out of his hair, the sooner he could reach out to Claire and get that job. He was hours late, dinner was long over. "Or something to eat?" He cringed at the thought of his mostly bare cupboard, but he could scrounge up some crackers or beans.

She shook her head. "I'll take care of my clothes at the new place. Hopefully it will have a washer. A roof that works would be a plus," she added. "Besides, I can't put you out any longer."

"No bother. Phone's in the kitchen. I put a cup of tea out for you as well." She found her phone and began scrolling through her texts, tethered to the wall to keep the charge going.

While she was occupied, he busied himself sorting through the mail, sneaking covert glances every few minutes. When she finished her messages, she stood in the doorway of the front room, her expression soft as she cradled her mug with both hands.

"It's funny...this is more what I pictured," she said, looking around the room.

"What do you mean?"

She walked to the piecrust table covered with Gran's nice linen placemat and picture frames of family. "When I heard 'quaint Irish cottage' this is what I had in my mind. The stone walls, the stove with a fire. It's cozy. Homey."

A warm bubble of pride swelled within him. He hadn't realized her good opinion of the cottage would matter so much. "My Gran lived here for 67 years, and it was her father's before her. She left it to me when she died last year. I lived here too, helping her out when I moved out of my ma's place."

Bridget wandered toward the hearth, taking in all the knickknacks and photos on the mantel. Finn felt compelled to explain. "I kept most of her things in their place. Bit fussy, but it didn't seem right to move them."

"It's definitely got cottagecore vibes," she mused, sitting down in the wooden rocker.

Not there. He tamped down the urge to have her move from Gran's rocker.

"Thank you," she said quietly. "I know you didn't have to do all this for me."

"No bother, like I said," he added, clearing his throat. This was starting to get personal. He pulled out his phone. "What's your budget for a place to stay tonight?" No point in looking at 200 euro hotels if she had a scant bankroll.

She took a moment to answer. "They gave me a stipend for expenses, so the client doesn't have to deal with receipts. But I don't want to spend much. Maybe 100 euro? Or a little less if you add in taxes."

"They don't give you much to go on, do they?" Finn scrolled slowly over the listings, most well outside her budget. "I can probably find a place for you to stay tonight, but it might be more than that. A basic room back in Killathay is about 120 euro."

Bridget looked discouraged. "They told us in our onboarding meeting that any hotel outside the rental agreement would be on us, for weekend trips and such. I don't want to be on the hook for it if they're not going to reimburse me." She gave a tired smile. "Especially with your hourly rate."

Was she teasing him? "A decent roof over your head isn't too much to ask," said Finn tightly. "What kind of company sends a woman out to a foreign country with nothing to go on but a picture and a listing? And you out here, at loose ends." He'd harbored no ill will toward HouseHijack until he saw Bernie's name on the paperwork. Now they were complicit, in his mind.

Bridget stiffened. "I'm capable of handling things on my own, as I told you."

Prickly, this one. But he felt an ember of kinship; he didn't want to be managed either.

"You're sure they're not taking advantage?" *Don't borrow her trouble.* He had enough of his own to worry about.

She gave a huge yawn and tucked her feet underneath her on the sofa. "I don't know when I'm going to hear back from Mary. Would you mind if I lay down a minute here on the couch?"

"Make yourself comfortable." He scrolled through the hotel listings, looking for something that was available within her budget. Someplace he'd be comfortable having his sisters stay.

Within moments, he heard a low rumble: Bridget was out

like a light. Poor thing was shattered and it was only half seven. He paused for a moment listening to her low snores, debating whether to let her sleep. A light sigh interrupted her snoring, and he couldn't help but smile. One of Gran's quilts stretched across the back of the sofa, so he slid it down to cover her.

Let her sleep a few minutes, clear her mind, and the rest should be easy. He had to deal with the animals anyway.

Finn slid into his coat, then left the house through the back door. He gave a loud whistle as he walked behind the barn to the pasture gate. "C'mon boys!"

The two old donkeys lumbered to the gate, full from their day in the fields. They were placid beasts for the most part. They were Gran's animals and they merely tolerated Finn, but only if their meals weren't late.

He ushered them into their stalls in the barn, adding a bit of fresh hay and giving each a pat before heading back into the house. In the far side of the barn across from the stalls sat his workbench, tools, and woodworking projects, sadly neglected yet another day. The donkeys gently whuffled as he closed the front barn door behind him, disappointed they couldn't escape.

Now to the kitchen. It wasn't in terrible shape, but Gran would be shamed if guests were in her house and it wasn't spic and span. As quietly as he could, he binned the papers and trash, swept the floor, and wiped down the counters.

A growl in his stomach prompted him to peer into the refrigerator. Avoiding Bridget's fresh groceries, he found a mealy apple and some leftover spaghetti. He looked out toward the front room to see if his cleaning had disturbed his guest.

The low snores confirmed he was good to keep going. Spaghetti it was.

His phone vibrated with a call. Claire.

Decline.

Immediately, he received a series of texts in quick succession.

I hope you're ok.

Call me and I can reschedule that meeting with my father.

Or come by tomorrow for supper?

He'd deal with that problem tomorrow. Putting the phone in his pocket, he hunted for his laptop. He found it gathering dust on the bookcase. In between bites of reheated spaghetti, he booted it up and opened a browser as it whirred.

He typed in 'HouseHijack.com.' "Let's see what sort of racket this is," he murmured.

The listings of houses and apartments, spare bedrooms and converted lofts around the world were staggering. He located the search button, plugged in "Ireland", and got more than 700 listings. He narrowed the field to "Southwest Ireland" and clicked "search" again. This time, it was a more manageable 34. Adding "whole property" yielded only 13 locations. The first one was Bernie's horrible cottage.

Clicking on the listing, he read the description. "Charming two-bedroom cottage on a two-acre property with animals and natural views. Enjoy a full-service kitchen, open air terrace and charming, old-world appointments. Set in the middle of everything.' Not surprisingly, there were no reviews yet.

"Charming, he says," Finn muttered. "I should leave a damn review with the truth of it." The gall of this man to charge 110 euros a night for that hovel. Even if HouseHijack took a cut of his fees, it was highway robbery to take money for that pit. It galled him to think ow much Bernie stood to make on his scheme.

He skimmed the other listings nearby, but paused when a button on the corner of the page caught his eye: *List Your Property.*

If he made a listing, it would tell him what Bernie would make on letting his rundown cottage after the fees were deducted, wouldn't it? His cursor hovered over the *List Your Property* button for several seconds. *Click.*

A few more boxes filled in, and ten minutes later, Finn got up to take photos of his bedroom. And of the bath. And his bedroom.

The living room was more difficult. He hovered over the sleeping form of Bridget to shoot the left side of the room, then moved around her to the right. Another snap.

It was too dark to get a good photo of the outside of the house, but Finn skimmed through his phone to find something that worked. A few quick edits and it was ready to go.

He uploaded the photos, added a price of 150 euro and a 300 euro cleaning fee. And voila, Red Door Cottage was listed on HouseHijack.

Pretty simple, really.

He looked over at the sleeping Bridget on the sofa. Wonder if she knew how easy it was to get listed on the page, no vetting, no checks. He probably could've uploaded photos of Buckingham Palace and been approved.

When she woke up, he'd show her the listing he created. He'd make the point about stupid scammy operations like HouseHijack, have a laugh and take it down. Hopefully he'd have a place for her to stay by then, and the longest workday of his year would be over.

He looked up the numbers for a few of the hotels in Killathay. Even if they were booked, he might be able to ring them up and see if being local would help. As he searched, an email came through.

RE:New Email-HouseHijack Inquiry
Dates: 02/12 - 22/12
Guests: 1
Total Charges: EUR3300
Message: I saw your rental come online and wanted to see if it was immediately available. I have a stranded passenger who needs accommodation through December 22. Please reply immediately to confirm. - Mary

Surely this was Bridget's boss trying to book her to stay at his place. He started to call out to her and have a laugh but stopped himself as an idea formed in his head. Wild idea. Crazy even.

He stared at the email for a hot minute, his eyes focused intently on the 3300 euro total. *He'd have to be mad.*

His cursor hovered over the buttons that read *Accept* and *Decline.*

She'd likely be furious.

Then he just hovered over *Accept.*

Click.

Chapter 5

Boundary Issues

Bridget woke, sleep-drunk and confused in the darkness. Several panicked moments passed before she remembered she was in Ireland, in her driver's cottage, and somehow covered with a soft quilt. On the plus side, not murdered. *Yet.*

Trying to be silent in the unfamiliar house, she crept toward the kitchen where a nightlight glowed from the same outlet as her phone. *Surprisingly thoughtful.* The screen read 6:22 a.m. with a whopping thirty-two text messages.

Eleven hours? How did she sleep almost eleven hours? Her brain was muffled and fuzzy, but she was pretty sure the math was right. Did Finn not wake her up last night? Or was she sleeping so soundly he couldn't rouse her? *Did he put something in her tea?* She tamped down the alarm and clawed her way back to sense. Nothing that indicated anything untoward had happened, other than he let her get some much-needed rest.

Using the phone's flashlight, she navigated from the kitchen back to the parlor and into the hallway. She paused at the closed door to her left; her skin prickling at the thought that Finn was likely sleeping there. *Don't wake him.*

She eased the bathroom door open, flinching at the slight whine of the hinges.

Her trip to the bathroom complete, she pulled the chain, splashed her face with water and braced herself to catch up with her phone. Her text messages jolted her back into clarity.

About half of the texts were from Tran, unsatisfied with her single text the night before saying she was safe and fine.

> Got your pin - but send me his name
>
> Tell me you're safe
>
> WHERE ARE YOU?!?!?!?
>
> IF YOU DON'T ANSWER I AM COMING TO IRELAND TO IDENTIFY YOUR BODY

Bridget picked up her phone to reply.

> Not dead, just exhausted. First cottage was a disaster. Mary is trying to find me a new place. Will text you when I get there. You would be so proud of me, world traveler

Then she worked through the barrage of texts from Mary:

> Ok, I've been looking for hours, and there's a place near Rois, but you have to take a train 3 hours north.

Doesn't look like there's much around there
to do

Do you like sheepdogs? It has a sheepdog

HOLD ON - new listing came online

It's adorable and super close to where
you are

Let me know asap

Bridge? I need to know

HELLO?!?

I'm guessing you're asleep at a hotel, so I'm
going to book it

CONFIRMED—I will send you the details in
email

And your post from yesterday is approved

Relief flooded through her. A new place, the video was approved–things were looking up. She pulled her laptop out in the dark room, tucking the quilt around her to stave off the chill.

While her emails downloaded, she posted the approved video to her channels. *Check.* In the glow of the laptop screen, she felt her way toward the kitchen, patting down the wall to find a light switch. The room filled the room with light and she blinked to adjust.

Aside from a few dishes in the sink and an ancient refrigerator, the cottage looked clean but cluttered. She gingerly pulled open a drawer to find silverware, takeout menus, candlesticks and napkins—a haphazard mess. She moved to start putting them in order, but drew back. *You're here for travel, not to organize Irish kitchen cabinets.*

Could she do both, and improve her chances with Container Corner?

Tucking that thought away, she peeped through the floral curtains of the kitchen window. There was no sign of sunrise, only the dark gray lumps of shadowy outbuildings and the mountains in the distance.

Then she heard the noises.

Three of them, in quick succession. High-pitched and wild, clearly painful. As though someone was murdering animals right outside the back door. She froze in her tracks, terrified.

She counted the seconds of silence. Ten. Eleven. Twelve.

It came again. A blood-curdling bray, cut off quickly. Bridget whipped open the kitchen drawers and scrambled through them until she came up with the biggest weapon she could find—a rounded butcher knife that wobbled in its wooden handle.

She flew to the closed door in the hallway, her heart pounding. She rapid-fire knocked at the door. "Finn!" she hissed. "Someone hurting an animal outside! *Finn!*"

No answer, nor any sign of life.

Screw it. Tucking the knife under her arm, she switched on her phone's flashlight then wrenched open the door. The thin line of light showed Finn asleep on his stomach in a wild tumble of blankets and sheets, one hairy leg hanging off the bed. His smooth, untroubled face looked more boyish in sleep, with his dark hair rumpled and wild. He was clad only in a skimpy pair of crimson boxer briefs that hugged his tight, round behind, with the hint of a dimple at the small of his back.

"Finn!" She hissed again. He murmured something unintelligible. "*Finn!*"

He slowly came to consciousness, then all at once scrambled to the far corner of the room, knocking his bedside lamp over and his alarm clock to the ground as he crouched against the wall. Despite her panic, she noted his boxer briefs left little to the imagination.

"What the hell! What're you doing in my bedroom with a butcher knife! Are you mad?" His eyes darted around the room as he balanced on the balls of his feet.

Bridget hid the knife behind her back, like that was any better. "Sorry! Someone's outside hurting animals, killing them! We have to call the police!"

Finn eased himself up to full height, keeping his eyes trained on her. He righted the lamp and turned it on, blinking in the bright light. "Get the fucking knife out of here first!" After a moment's hesitation, he scooped up the blanket from the floor and covered his crotch.

"Fine." She laid the knife on the floor and slid it out to the hallway. Two bloodcurdling animal screeches echoed in quick succession, followed by low groaning. Bridget pointed to the back of the cottage. "There! Did you hear that? We need to call the police!"

Finn cocked his head toward the noise from outside. "That? Oh aye. We definitely need the Garda out for this." He mimed speaking into a cell phone. "Hello, Garda? Yes, I'm needing you out to deal with my Gran's *goddamn donkeys* that need feeding." He dramatically hung up his invisible phone. "Hungry *donkeys*, you daft woman! You turned the kitchen light on, didn't you?"

"I...yeah...what?" Bridget could not wrap her head around the idea that the cacophony came from impatient livestock wanting breakfast. "You have *donkeys*?"

Finn waved his arms about. "It's the countryside, everyone has donkeys or goats or sheep! If they think you're eating before they're fed, they can wail like a banshee, a right pain in the arse." He bent over to pick up the alarm clock, groaning as he read the time. "For waking me, you'll come help me with them at this godforsaken hour. Put on your boots and let me get dressed if you don't mind. And maybe put my damn knife back in the drawer."

She felt her face flood with the heat of embarrassment. Bridget fumbled for a defense, and settled on anger. "How was I supposed to know? And you never woke me up last night!"

"You never asked me to wake you." Finn's voice wasn't quite a shout, but it was certainly bordering on that territory. "You asked me to let you sleep. And I did."

"You knew I planned to get a hotel room."

"I tried a couple of places, most were booked or out of your price range," he snapped. He closed his eyes for a moment, drawing in a deep breath. In a more measured tone he added, "As a kindness, I let you sleep here."

"That wasn't your decision!"

His jaw tightened. "I'll remember that the next time you need help. Now, unless you're looking for a show, I need to put some trousers on."

He cocked an eyebrow as he started to lower the blanket.

Bridget spun on her heel, not sure whether to rage or cry. Probably both. Holding it together, she sat down at her laptop. After that debacle, the sooner she could get out of this house, the better. Hopefully Mary found her a nice, quiet cottage she'd have all to herself, where she could decompress, get her head straight and focus on the task at hand. A surge of longing for her own cozy apartment flowed through her. Somewhere she could be completely at ease, not on edge, always worried about the next move. It was stressful enough managing the demands of travel and content creation. Add the emotional toll of dealing with the uncertainty and it might just—*ding!* She looked down to see her emails had downloaded. She opened the first from Mary.

> Saw the pics, I'm so sorry. Those must have been AI pictures. I think the client is getting them kicked out of the system. Let's just say HH is having some challenges. Yikes. But OMG, you do NOT know how hard it was to find something else for you. I was on the computer for almost 2 hours, but just as I was about to give up, this cottage came online. In the same area, so you don't need to do more research. Move in at noon! Xoxo Mary

Bridget clicked the link. The first photo loaded: an Irish cottage with charming red doors and windows.

A cute little parlor, full of knickknacks and family pictures.

And a kitchen with an ancient refrigerator.

"Oh no," she whispered.

Finn came out of his bedroom a moment later, tucking a white t-shirt into his jeans as he walked to the kitchen. "You're welcome, by the way. Not only for all the time I spent transporting you—missing out on an actual real, long-term job, mind you! But putting you up in my own home, free of charge—"

Bridget spun up from her chair, "What the hell, Finn?"

He stopped short, freezing in place with one hand still trapped inside his waistband. His eyes flickered to the photos on her screen in the HouseHijack app. He took a second too long to reply. "What do you mean?"

He couldn't meet her eyes.

The steam of her anger propelled her forward. "I just got an email from my client, telling me I'm now booked in a new cottage." Her hands were shaking. "You...you put this house on HouseHijack without telling me. Without asking me?"

He jutted his chin out and crossed his arms. "What now, am I supposed to tell you everything I do then?" He turned away and headed to the kitchen.

Oh no you didn't.

She stormed after him, slamming her hand on the countertop. "I don't care if you put your house online. Do what you want. But you wouldn't have even heard of HouseHijack if I didn't tell you. You couldn't do me the courtesy of letting me know you were putting this place online? I was literally ten feet from you."

He grabbed the kettle from the stove and whipped open the tap to fill it. "And dead asleep." He paused as another round of braying from the donkeys interrupted him. "You snore, by the way."

Her eyes narrowed. "I am going to ask you one question. When you took this booking... did you know it was for me?" She stepped close enough to him to breathe the same air. The scent of sleep was still on him.

"I...had a fair idea," he replied grudgingly.

"And you agreed to the listing."

Finn turned away from her without a word, putting the kettle on the stove and lighting the burner. *Unbelievable.*

"You don't think that was taking advantage of the situation?" she pressed, her outrage giving her mounting anxiety a coat of armor.

"I looked up that disaster of a place from yesterday, and you know who put up that listing? Bernie Coughlin. The dosser has been trying to buy up homes all around the county, including this one, all to fleece rich tourists. Who's to say your next place wouldn't be Bernie's as well, banjaxed like the last one? At least this way, you know the house is sound. And a bargain at that."

"But you don't get to—"

"Not all of us have expenses-paid trips as influencers, Bridget. Some of us need money and have to work for a living." For a split-second, the raw emotion of his words hung in the air. His eyes darted away from her gaze and he cleared his throat. On cue, the donkeys screamed again, providing him an escape hatch from the conversation.

Bridget fumed. "Oh yeah, I have a ridiculously glamorous life. I'm an office manager for a tax accountant, living in a tiny apartment with a roommate."

His brow furrowed as he ran a hand through his hair. "Could be a very posh accountant?" In the light of the kitchen, his eyes twinkled as he grinned.

You're not going to charm your way out of this! "Definitely not."

"Think of it this way: you're already an amazing influencer," he said, deftly changing tactics. "You influenced me to put my cottage on HouseHijack."

"Please." She rolled her eyes at the transparent flattery.

Finn pulled out two cups from the cabinet next to the sink. "Tea?"

A growl in her stomach made her pause. "Actually, I need food. I didn't really have anything to eat last night. I'm starving. But this isn't finished!" She shuffled past him to open the refrigerator, finding her yogurt in the refrigerator among some questionable leftovers. "Want some?"

"No, I'll make some porridge in a bit. As my penance for not waking you or telling you about the rental, I'll go turn out the beasts myself. Pour me a cup when the kettle goes, would you? Oh, and don't mistake the whistle for a woman screaming." He grabbed a jacket hanging near the back door and walked out, leaving Bridget to simmer in her embarrassment.

She pulled the yellowed lace curtain back from the kitchen

window and watched Finn trudge to the barn in the earliest glow of sunrise. When the kettle whistled, Bridget poured the boiling water into the two cups, added a Barry's tea bag to each, then sat at the tiny kitchen table.

Finn walked in the kitchen door, windblown with two bright spots of color on his cheeks. "Bit of a chill today."

Now that her stomach had something in it, Bridget's mood had decidedly improved. She took a sip of her tea. *Needs sugar.* "Everything good with the donkeys?"

"As good as it can be, spoiled eejits." He hung his jacket up and sat down across from her, took a gulp of his tea, and sighed contentedly.

"So, where will you be going?"

"What, today? No great plans in my diary."

Huh? "But at noon? When my rental begins. Where are you staying?"

He looked at her as if she had three heads. "I'm not going anywhere."

"You're staying...here?" She put down her cup.

"On-premises management," he said, sketching an exaggerated bow. "Welcome to Red Door Cottage."

She felt her anger return like a tsunami. "You have *boundary issues.* I don't know you. This isn't a rental, this is your house!"

"Which makes it better than a rental because it's fully stocked. Point in my favor, surely."

"It's not a rental because you *live* here. And fully stocked? I saw the inside of your fridge. I am not going to be your roommate."

He crossed his arms defensively. "You don't think that managers live in hotels? Or owners of bed and breakfasts live on premises?"

"I need to *work* here."

"So work then," he shrugged.

She stared at him, narrowing her eyes. "Do you even have Wi-Fi?"

"Broadband."

"Transportation?"

"Can you drive manual?"

"You mean stick? Not since Driver's Ed."

He grinned again. "Then hire me as your driver for your stay."

Charming had now crossed into presumptuous. "So you can make even more money off of this situation?" *The nerve!*

"Listen, I know plenty of people who drive tourists around. My brother Cillian makes a small fortune doing it. He charges Americans more than 400 euro a day to trot them out all over the Ring of Kerry. But if you hire me, five days a week, mind you, I'll do it for 1,750 euros a week."

Her eyes narrowed slightly. She had a reservation to rent a car for a fraction of that price that she was scheduled to pick up at noon. But after her experience last night, the idea of driving on the wrong side of the winding, narrow roads was daunting. While it did solve her problem of hiring transportation, this was too convenient for him.

"Frankly, I'm not sure all this...togetherness is a good idea." She pushed away from the table and walked toward Finn's bedroom door. Peeking in, she noted that his room was decorated more sparsely than the rest of the house, without any of the quaint cottage décor. Several of the dresser drawers were slightly ajar, and Bridget itched to push them in. Pushing away a mental image of Finn's red-clad bottom from the morning, she noted the bed was hastily made with a simple quilt and two pillows. "I'm not sleeping on the couch again. Is there even a lock on this door?"

"That's my room, madam. But maybe I need a lock since you're in the habit of waking me up with a knife in your hand."

This was the last straw. "Are you kidding me? So where am I supposed to sleep? The couch?"

"Calm yourself, there's two bedrooms here. If it makes you happy, I'll put a lock on the other room today."

She stared him down as she weighed her options. He did help her yesterday, more than anyone else might have. But with this scheme, she'd be completely at his mercy.

"Let me see it."

Finn walked her past the bath to the closed door at the other end of the narrow hallway, something that she didn't even notice yesterday. He seemed reluctant to show her the room, so her warning level was high by the time she stepped inside.

It was clearly his grandmother's bedroom. She walked in tentatively, looking for faults that would take the heat off her saying no. But the room was cozy and full of antique furniture—a lovely carved headboard and matching vanity with a stool and mirror. A sturdy armoire stood in the corner. She walked up and pulled a drawer open. It was empty, save for a few extra linens, and the closet only had a few boxes on the upper shelf. The bed was covered in a sweet, cornflower blue hand-stitched quilt.

"Your grandmother's room?"

He nodded. Finn's expression was inscrutable, but he answered in a gruff voice. "The dressing table and chair, those were a wedding present from my grandfather." The emotion in his voice chipped away at her anger. *Don't get soft, Bridget. He's still taking advantage.*

She sat down on the bed and the frame gave a soft groan. It was more comfortable than she'd expected.

Finn stepped forward. "I'll put fresh linens on this morning and air out the quilt. Give it a good dusting too." His voice cracked slightly as he spoke, and any residual anger swept away.

But she couldn't avoid one fact: it defied logic to put her entire assignment, even her life, in the hands of a man she barely knew.

"I appreciate the effort, but I don't see how this is going to work. I need someplace I can be alone. To concentrate on work without having to worry about...people."

"I can give you space. That's not an issue."

Bridget ran her hand along the comforter. "I've known you for less than 24 hours, and I just can't agree to living in the same house with you for the next few weeks."

His blue eyes opened wide and innocent. "You have a roommate at home, yes? And I was nothing but a gentleman last night, wasn't I?"

She raised an eyebrow. "When you created your house listing without waking me?"

Finn let his head drop in a hangdog expression. "Perhaps I may have overstepped a bit. I saw a solution to the problem, and I should have checked with you first." He looked up at her, the picture of repentance. It was a start, at least.

And his eyes are such a gorgeous blue.

He continued. "I know you have work to do, and I would absolutely give you space and time to do it. It will be easier on you if you stay here and hire me as your driver. Let you focus on making your videos."

She shook her head. *This was a bad idea.* "I just don't think—"

He cut her off. "I'll do it for 5000 euros total, and I'll be available every day if you need me. And I'll take you to the airport in Dublin on your last day, so you won't have to take the train. Any driver would charge you way more than that, and this is far safer than you renting a car yourself when you're not used to the correct side of the road."

That argument got her. Last night's journey through narrow, winding roads cemented that her city-girl driving skills would be woefully inadequate, even if she could drive on the wrong side of the road. He was right; she'd have to hire a driver and there was no way she'd be able to cover as much ground as she planned if she had to pay a daily rate.

Maybe she could stay somewhere else and use him as a driver? But then she'd need to tell Mary that the cottage wouldn't work, which would put her whole assignment in jeopardy.

If she was going to be an influencer, she'd have to do it. No other option.

"Fine. But my rules, my itinerary, and no grief about having to make stops." She thrust forth a hand for him to shake. "And it includes yesterday's fees."

"That's probably 400 euros alone, and it goes to my brother."

She raised an eyebrow again.

He thrust out his hand. "Fine. It's a deal."

She nodded and shook his hand once, firmly. "Our first stop today is a hardware store."

He inclined his head quizzically.

"My lock."

Chapter 6

Bound to the Binder

With the negotiations settled, Finn resolved to be the perfect host. He turned the donkeys out to pasture, then returned to find Bridget hunched over her computer in the front room. *All business this one.*

He stripped Gran's bed, steeling himself against any thought that Gran was the last one who'd slept in her room. The faintest scent of Gran's beloved Estée Lauder dusting powder still lingered in the room.

Focus on the washing. Heaving up the sheets and pillowcases and quilt, he carried them back to the kitchen and made a grand show of starting the linens in the laundry, setting the quilt on the counter by the back door. "I'll set the quilt out to air in a bit," he called. Bridget looked up but said nothing, training her eyes again on the screen in front of her.

Now for the rest of the room. The last thing he wanted was a complaint about the accommodations, or a legitimate concern with the property and his hosting. Nothing that would negate the contract. With the driving and the rental fees, he'd clear almost 8000 euro easy—even with the outrageous cut that

HouseHijack took. By Christmas, he'd knock down his tax debt by more than half.

His excitement at this windfall was tempered by a creeping sense of shame. After all, Bridget had merely asked to sleep a little while. By accepting a rental request, he gave her no choice but to stay with him.

He took a dust cloth to Gran's bedroom with the can of furniture spray from under the cupboard, clearing away dust as he tried to talk himself out of his nagging guilt. This situation was good for both of them. She had comfortable lodging with a roof over her head, a newly fixed roof at that! Sure, it helped him as well, but that was just an extra benefit. She was lucky he was looking out for her best interests, instead of being stuck with some chancer who'd take advantage.

He paused, glancing at the doorway. *Bleedin' hell.* No use trying to put a shine on it. It was a dirty trick to force her into staying at the house. If someone had managed his own plans like that, he'd be out the door in a heartbeat.

He'd managed Bridget the same way his family always tried to manage him.

Damn.

He'd make it up to her. Somehow.

The sunrise cast a warm glow on the hills as Finn took Gran's quilt out to hang on the line. The air was damp, but no rain. Not ideal for an airing, but it would have to do. He heard the kitchen door open behind him.

"It's wild—it feels like April in Chicago," Bridget came out of the house dressed in a smart jumper and jeans with her hair pulled up in a clip. She picked her way through the soft grass to join him by the line. "Do you ever get snow here?"

"Every once in a while. Not often."

Bridget inhaled deeply. "It smells like spring too. Strange to think that Chicago has a ton of snow right now."

"Have you always lived there, then?" Finn stepped back from the line, raising his arms over his head in a long stretch before heading to the small woodpile next to the barn. He gathered a few sticks of firewood, stacking the small bundle in his arms.

"My whole life. Grew up in a neighborhood called Beverly, which is a big Irish part of the city even today. Let me get that." She swooped ahead of him as he moved toward the door, pulling it open for him.

Finn dropped the wood on the hearth at the parlor stove, then bent to stack it as Bridget continued. "My mom's Irish but my dad was Polish. My parents divorced when I was 2, so my mom and I moved back in with her parents. My dad took a job in Thailand right after. I only saw him a handful of times growing up. Every few years he'd come back and visit me and my Polish grandparents, at least until he passed away six years ago. Those grandparents made sure I could pronounce my name correctly."

"About that..."

She smiled. "Ko. Lo. Jay."

"How you get "Ko-lo-jay" from a name with d and z? Makes no sense." Finn brushed the dirt off his hands from the firewood.

Bridget gave him a look of amused disbelief as she leaned against the counter. "The Irish have no room to talk with names. "S-a-o-r-i-s-e? Pronounced 'ser-sha?'"

"Fair enough." He grinned, glancing toward the back window. "I can't leave the quilt out long in this damp, but let's give it an hour to freshen up."

"So we'll head out around nine, good." Bridget pulled her

binder from the bag, sat down and opened it on the table. "I thought we'd start with a few of the highlights of Killathay," she said, thumbing through pages of printouts from Internet searches. "I outlined a few places I'd like to go this week, like the ruins and the park. Is there anything in the gardens this time of year?"

"So just tourist stuff?"

She rolled her eyes. "Yes, my assignment is to post touristy things. It's literally in the job description."

"So you just need to go around Ireland and show people what it's like here? Why here and not Dublin or Galway or the Ring of Kerry?"

Bridget shrugged. "House Hijack is pretty new in Ireland, so there weren't a lot of options, I guess. But I'm sure there's plenty to see around here, right?"

"Let me see those." Finn reached for her binder. Bridget flinched to pull it back reflexively, then reluctantly slid it across the table. Finn settled into the chair and flipped through the pages. Printouts of county websites, 'best of' articles and travel guides were interspersed with tourist reviews from multiple sites. Old ruins, churches, scenic overlooks. "Sure you're not missing the Blarney Stone?" he asked drily.

"I would have, but it's too far for a day trip," said Bridget, irritation creeping into her voice. "I have done hours of research and I've organized the destinations by day. You said this wouldn't be a problem for you."

"Calm down, I'll take you where you want. I'd just have thought you'd want to see more of the real Ireland."

"And what's the real Ireland then?" She crossed her arms and sat back. "Brian Boru driving out the Vikings? St. Patrick and the snakes? The Easter Rising? Music by Kneecap?"

He felt his own temper stirring. "Americans think a few paragraphs make history. Half the people who live in these mountains, their people have been here for centuries. That's what history is. My Gran was a Stack, and Stacks go back more than a thousand years in these parts. They lost their holdings as forfeit in the 1600s under Cromwell, the price of rebellion. Gave everything to a poser English lord. And of course, everyone scattered in the 1800s, mostly to America."

The hell, Finn. Calm down. He realized he'd raised his voice and took a shaky breath to quiet down. "Real Ireland is those of us too stubborn or stupid to leave, I guess."

She digested his words for a moment and offered, "I'm sorry. I didn't mean to make light."

Finn shrugged. He had to get things back to an even keel. "You said your mother was Irish?"

She nodded. "Maiden name McCarthy."

"You're not going to be dragging me around looking for your great-grandad's gravestone, are you?"

"I'm supposed to make my followers want to travel, not bore them to tears," she said, her slight smile dissolving much of the tension.

"Then we should get on with it."

The quilt safely back indoors on Gran's bed, they departed in relative silence, in tight quarters in the confines of the compact car. A heavy cover of gray clouds blurred the mountains in the distance, turning them into dark green shadows looming over the valleys. The hills were crisscrossed with low stone fences, like pencil lines written with a shaky hand.

"It's amazing how such a tiny country can be so hilly," Bridget mused. "Where I live, everything is so flat. Except for the buildings, I suppose."

"No hills or mountains in Chicago?"

She smiled. "Nope. Not until you drive four hours west to the Mississippi River, for the most part."

The road back to Killathay was not well-traveled, making it seem like they were alone with the sheep that dotted the hills. At one point, Bridget leaned forward to peer out the window.

"Those sheep, are they polka-dotted?" she asked.

"What now?" Finn craned around to look out the passenger window.

"Is that...paint?" She wiped her sleeve against the window to clear the fog and get a better look. "Can you stop the car?"

"What, now?"

"I want to get video."

Channeling saintly patience, Finn parked the car on a small shoulder along the narrow road. "Sure, those spots are how they mark the flock. The blue sheep belong to one farmer, and the ones that are orange or yellow or red will belong to another. But they can hire one shepherd and use the same sheepdog teams to move them back and forth."

"Doesn't it permanently color the wool?" Bridget pivoted in her seat to dig into her bag. Fishing out her phone, she opened her camera app.

Finn tried to suppress a smile. "Their coats are filthy by the time they're sheared. When they cut it in the spring, they wash and bleach the wool so it's not an issue. I'm sure I can find a sheepdog show somewhere in the county if that would satisfy your tourist curiosity."

A bloom of heat rose on her cheeks. "I'm going to get some footage." She slipped out of her seat and wandered a few feet from the car. He watched her strike comical angles to try and film the sheep: crouching low, holding her phone high above her head, a selfie angle. She reviewed the video on her phone as she walked back to the car, her brows furrowed.

"Couldn't get a good shot," she muttered. "I'm not used to

wide-open spaces like this. I'm going to try using my other equipment." Bridget tugged the large tote bag out of the back seat as the wind whipped her hair around. She unpacked a giant circle light, a tripod, and other pieces of equipment, still in their boxes. She stopped abruptly, holding up the end of a cord with a look of frustration, then stuffed it back in the bag.

"Not a lot of places to plug in out here."

"I meant to charge them last night," she said archly. "But for *some reason*, I didn't have time." Bridget bumped the passenger door closed with her hip. He watched her set up the camera with the selfie stick first, but the wind began to kick up, driving many of the sheep farther away from their location. Improvising, she put her phone on the tripod, zooming in on her touchscreen to catch the stragglers of the flock, constantly adjusting the tripod as sheep sauntered out of her shot.

It was against his nature to let her struggle, but she made it clear this was her show. He wasn't getting out of the car to help unless she asked. He, after all, was not in charge. After 15 minutes she grabbed her equipment and returned to the car, pink-cheeked and breathless from the wind.

"Get what you need?" he worked to keep his voice neutral.

"I don't know. I'm going to have to get back and see what I can do with this," she frowned, reviewing the footage. "The ring light would have helped. Without it I couldn't get anything with me in the shot. Maybe I can piece together something from the b-roll." She put her hand to her mouth, worrying her thumbnail as she thought.

He should have helped her. Or offered. *Stop feeling guilty about this.* "On to Killathay then?" He didn't wait for an answer before starting the car up. "What kind of videos do you need for your posts? This wind is shite for sound, no?"

She turned her head. "Are you on social media?"

Finn snickered. "I'm not exactly the kind of person who has hours to scroll on TikTok."

"Most people our age use social media."

"Never interested in it. Always seemed like a huge waste of time to me."

"You think I'm wasting my time doing this job." Bridget's tone was flat.

Well, if she's asking. "I think it's ridiculous that a company will pay you to fly around the world with no regard for your well-being, booking you at a terrible place like that cottage."

"Social media is more popular now than regular media. It's more influential, it drives more purchasing decisions—it shapes public opinion," she added.

"I don't doubt it. But social media isn't exactly like the news, is it? Not a balanced story."

She thought for a moment. "Not news reporting, but I tell people how long something takes, what it costs, the mistakes I make. I try to be transparent about all that."

He stifled a laugh.

She rounded on him, the seatbelt pulling tight across her. "What?"

Finn glanced at her. "You going to tell your social people the truth about the first house? All of its attractive features? Or keep your thoughts to yourself, just letting them book that cottage without a word of warning?"

Bridget opened and closed her mouth a few times, then replied, selecting each word with care. "Since it's not the house I'm staying at, no. I won't be featuring that cottage."

"But you will tell people that they might get a house like that?"

"Don't be ridiculous." She turned away from him to look at the scenery. *Fine with me.*

The area around them showed evidence of being more

populated, with a smattering of traffic and houses clustering on either side of the road. Soon the lush hills gave way to the town of Killathay. At quarter of 10, there weren't many people milling about, merely a handful of folks at the grocery store, some walking to the bank or the shops.

Finn slowed as he neared a wide intersection. "The hardware store is right in town. If I'm lucky, I can get a shower curtain there as well and rig up a shower for you. Won't take me more than a moment, so where to after that, Boss Lady?"

Bridget looked down at her binder again. "There's an Irish shop first, Wilson's Irish Treasures?"

"Tourist trap. Full of leprechauns and shamrocks and overpriced nonsense for your people back home."

Bridget frowned, the plastic pages of her binder snapping as she flipped through. "How about Sugrue Proprietors?"

"More of the same. Did your Mary give you this list? You should tell her it's shite."

She closed the binder with an air of frustration. "No, she booked my accommodations, I put together the itinerary."

"And you said you researched this?"

She huffed. "I had to pull all this together last-minute."

"Last minute?"

"I only found out I was coming to Ireland a little over a week ago, filling in for someone else. I didn't have a lot of time to research every single place because I was a last-minute addition. I downloaded area guides and trip reports." Bridget pinched the top of her nose and closed her eyes. "I need to get an interesting Irish destination to feature. It's what I have on the schedule for today."

"I'm sure we can't mess with your schedule," Finn murmured, trying to keep the sarcasm to a minimum. "Do you want me to make a recommendation?"

"That depends," she said. "It has to be something we can do

in the next two hours. I have to get an edited video off to Mary before she gets in at 9 a.m. Chicago time."

"Then I'll take you to the quintessential Irish destination. Give me two shakes to grab the lock for your door."

As the cashier rung up the slide lock and the clear plastic shower liner (best he could find), Finn pulled his beat-up leather wallet from his back pocket. His fingers hesitated as he pulled out his last two twenties to cover the purchase. Yesterday he was staring down the reality of coming up short on the tax bill. Today was a whole new financial reality, thanks to the American. He felt lighter than he had since Gran's passing.

A spring in his step, Finn returned to the car, tossed the bag in the boot, and spun around to the passenger door, where Bridget sat scrolling. With a flourish, he swung the door open and offered his hand to Bridget. "Madame? I shall now escort you to the pinnacle of Irish culture," he said, exaggerating the affectation of a genteel aristocrat.

Bridget's eyebrows raised as she took his hand. "We're walking?"

"A short stretch of the legs." They walked side by side around the corner, Bridget listening with a bemused smile as Finn waxed rhapsodic. "No other place in Ireland has done more to advance the culture, the music, the arts, the family structure than this destination. The crossroads of an Irish community, the barometer of its custom and tradition, the seat of our philosophy and the solace in our grief."

At the corner, he stopped to allow her passage in front of him. "And here it is, in all its glory."

Bridget eyed him with skepticism. "A bar."

"Blasphemy! It's a pub...an Irish pub. Nothing like it in the world. C'mon." He pulled open the door to Malone's and ushered her in. "Two birds with one stone—you need a place to film and we need to eat."

He'd walked into Tommy Malone's hundreds of times, but as Bridget took it all in, he imagined seeing it through her eyes. The building was long and narrow, with the bar anchoring the left side of the room. The shelves behind the bar were filled with a wide variety of liquors, including an impressive selection of Irish whiskies. The bar was dotted with sets of branded paper coasters, and above, glassware hung like stalactites in a cave. An eclectic assortment of Guinness advertisements, football regalia and old photographs dotted the walls. The maroon-and-white checkerboard floor tiles led to a room at the back of the building. Some tables had stools; others had a random collection of chairs. The room smelled of beer mixed with the faint memory of pipe smoke, long banished from indoor establishments.

"Okay to sit at the bar?"

"Sure." She slid onto the stool closest to the door. "What's good here? I'm starving."

Finn leaned forward on one arm, bringing his head closer to hers to convey his inside information. "Normally at a pub, I'd recommend the stew or shepherd's pie. But here, at Tommy Malone's...you need to get a toastie."

"A toastie?"

He closed his eyes in rapture. "Picture this: a lovely cheese on toast, hot and melty."

She side-eyed him. "So, grilled cheese."

Finn dismissed her with a shake. "Totally different. I've seen your grilled cheeses. Basic. Plain. These...these are *elevated.*"

He had to give her credit -- she was game to try his recommendation, even going with his advice on a cider with her luncheon and adding vinegar to her chips. She filmed both their meals, slicing down the middle of her toastie and engaging Finn to pull the two halves apart to capture the stretch of gooey cheese. After they finished (and she paid the tab) Bridget wandered around filming the bar décor.

"I think I'm all set." She slid back into her seat across from him and placed her phone on the table to snatch up one of the last chips from her plate. "Just need to figure out how to convince people that a toastie and chips is *not* the same as grilled cheese and fries."

"So we're to the cottage then?" Seemed like a waste of petrol to come all the way into town for not even two hours, but this was her show.

She flipped her phone back over again and appeared to do time zone math in her head. "It's 6 am Chicago time, so by the time we're back at the cottage, that gives me about two hours to edit."

"As you wish."

Chapter 7

Cottage Industry

At the cottage, Bridget plugged in all her equipment to charge and downloaded all the footage to her laptop. Sure, she could edit on her phone if she had to, but the laptop version of her video editing software was her default mode, the larger screen giving her more precision and control.

With every file she opened, her heart dropped. The footage from their roadside sheep stop was practically useless, a mess of jiggling shots and random sheep in the distance. The pub footage was great...until it dawned on her that her HouseHijack contract guidelines prohibited the promotion of alcohol.

Not a great start.

With a low moan, Bridget let her forehead fall to the tabletop with a soft thud. She thumped it again for good measure.

"You all good in there?" Finn called out from the hallway to her bedroom. The lock he was installing wouldn't provide Fort Knox-style security, but it would do.

"Fine," she called out, then muttered to herself, "just watching my career go down in flames before it even started."

A tool clattered to the floor. "Lock's done. I'm going to take a quick kip unless you need me. Someone woke me up with a knife this morning and I'm knackered."

Bridget didn't have enough headspace to devote to his teasing. With only eighteen useable seconds of sheep footage, and a very tight shot of a cheese toasty, there wasn't much she could do to salvage the assignment. She fought the urge to add gifs, captions or graphics to jazz things up. Over the next hour, she struggled to cobble together something halfway decent. With her first video due by 3 p.m. local time, there wasn't time to go out to shoot additional footage.

She was out of options. She closed her eyes and hoped for the best as she clicked *Send*. In moments, her phone was ringing.

"Bridge, what the hell. I can't send this to the client."

"I know, it's rough, but—"

"It's too short, you're not even in it, and it's not that interesting. "

Bridget swallowed hard around the lump forming in her throat. "I got some really great footage of a pub but—"

"No alcohol."

"I know. That's why I didn't send it to you. But Mare, I don't know if I can go out and get anything else today."

Mary went silent for a moment. "Where are you now?"

"At the rental cottage. I'm home for the night."

"Bridget. Are you kidding me?"

Idiot. "Shoot a video showing off the cottage, of course. I'll talk about the features, showcase how cozy it is."

"Now you're getting it. That's perfect. Use the hashtags. Put the rental link in the caption. I can give you until noon, so three hours? Can you get something that looks like you're a professional content creator by then?"

Bridget took a breath. "Yes, I'll get it done right now."

Relief mixed with chagrin that she didn't think of this obvious solution herself before she sent that video to Mary. Her sleep hangover was still muddying her thoughts.

A quick text from Mary buzzed as soon as she hung up.

> Make sure to add the link to the rental and use the hashtags #ad #househijack and #yolosolo. My first recap report for the client is due by end-of-day tomorrow. Make it look amazing xo

Bridget walked to the hallway and put her ear to Finn's door. Still asleep.

It was now or never. She plugged in her ring light, set up her selfie stick and began to record.

"Hey guys, it's Bridget. This is the adorable cottage I'm staying at in Ireland—link in caption! Can you believe how cute this is? I mean, this entire house is about the size of my apartment in Chicago. Look at these exposed stone walls, the wood beams, and the colors—"

She hit *Stop*.

Recording the cottage felt wrong. This was Finn's home and she was a guest. She was intruding on his privacy and—

Stop that. She wasn't a guest in someone's home, she was a paying client for a rental property. A client whose job it was to film and promote the destination...and that included everything within the four walls. Meeting her deadline wasn't going to happen unless she shot something right now. Bridget straightened her shoulders, lifted her chin and hit record again.

"If you follow me for tips on how to make the most of

compact spaces, this cottage is a perfect "before" project. Let's start over here by the mantel..."

Within the hour, Bridget had the video filmed, edited and sent to Mary, who forwarded it to the client without any edits and a compliment that fueled her good mood. "Exactly the kind of content I want to see."

Finn shuffled out into the living room looking a bit rumpled with an air of sleep about him. "All good?" he asked, rubbing the corner of his eye.

For a split second, she flashed to her memory of him asleep in his tight red boxer briefs. "Everything's great! I'm just waiting on client approval for my video." She stopped short, but he was distracted by the buzz of his phone.

He paused to check his phone, then sighed and rolled his eyes heavenward. "I have to run over to my ma's house in Tilleen. She's having trouble getting a box of Christmas decorations down from the attic. For some reason, that's my job. I'll be back in an hour or two, but she'll probably stuff me with food before I leave. Want me to pick up something for you on the way back for supper?"

"No—I'll just make some soup and a sandwich." Bridget's eyes flickered toward the kitchen window. "Are the donkeys still out?"

Finn nodded. "I'll put them up when I get back. They're happy in the field." He glanced at the hearth, where the fire he'd set before his nap was burning down to embers. "I'll put some more wood by the back door. There's a remote for the TV, and help yourself to anything you need."

"Thanks."

A few minutes after Finn left, her computer gave a small "ding."

From: Mary D'Esposito
To: Bridget Kolodziej
RE: Re: Content

Client loved the house vid–post asap!

A flood of relief washed over her. She posted in quick succession to all her accounts, then sat back to watch for comments and likes. This was the true test, the other part of the equation. Would fans of her organizing videos like her travel content?

An email notification broke her out of her reverie.

From: Tran Ho
To: Bridget Kolodziej
RE: Abandonment Issues

Girl, you cannot run off to a foreign country and then text me in the middle of the night that you are stranded and homeless. I was getting ready to scrub in on a massive fistula and all I could think about was you being strangled by a rando. TELL ME YOU ARE FINE.

I need more than just a scrawny little text. Otherwise I'm sending out James Bond. And shut up, I know he's from England, but 007 is resourceful enough to get to Ireland. I will not be able to enjoy my vacation if I'm worried about you. Save Fiji. I NEED PROOF OF LIFE!

Your Ho

She read every word of that email in Tran's voice. Immediately, Bridget began typing out a reply.

> My favorite Ho—
> Not dead, not dying, and safe. Call off MI-5. Unless you count me falling on my ass into a muddy mess. But as you know, me falling down is a daily occurrence. Thank God I live with a doctor.
> So –one big update. My cab driver from the train station is letting me rent his house. I'm sending you the link to the listing below, and his name is Finn Malloy. He's also going to drive me around the area five days a week, so you don't have to worry about me falling off the wrong side of the road.
> I already have a million things to tell you about, like near-murdered donkeys, waving knives at men in under-wear, and of course, falling on my ass.
> Your girl is doing ok.
> Love you, nerd.
> B

A wave of homesickness washed over her as she sent the email. She felt a deep yearning for the mental comfort of Tran, curled up on the couch and giving her a running analysis of Bridget's life choices.

What would Tran think about Finn?

More to the point...what did *Bridget* think about Finn? It was fair to say she wasn't a fan of how he boxed her into staying with him and serving as her driver. Or how he dismissed her job. Or made her sound high maintenance.

But he did offer to get dinner for her. And he helped his mom. That counted for something.

She flinched as a key turned in the lock. *That was quick.* Bridget smoothed her hair and turned toward the door, which swung wide open with the wind.

The man on the threshold wasn't Finn.

He stopped short, his mouth dropping open. "Who the hell are you? Sorry, that was rude. I didn't expect to see... Sorry, where's Finn?"

"He's...out," she stammered, then mentally cursed herself. *Great, now he knows I'm alone. At least I know where the knives are.* "But he's going to be back very soon!" she added hastily. She calculated the steps it would take to get to the back door.

The confusion on his face quickly turned to a sheepish, handsome grin. "I'm sorry, it looks like I scared the piss out of you. I'm Cillian. Finn's brother." He closed the door behind him, carefully staying on the rug as he peeled off his gloves.

Heavy exhale. "Not a murderer then?"

He grinned and Bridget could see the family resemblance. His smile was disarming. Not that she'd seen Finn smile much.

"Not today. Sorry for my manners, I'm not used to encountering strange women at Finn's place. Or any women for that matter. And you are?"

"Bridget." She rose from the table, extending her hand. *No women, eh?*

"Bridget," he repeated. The spark of humor in his eyes faded. "You're the American my brother picked up from the train station Sunday?"

Uh-oh. "Yes. There was an issue with the cottage I rented. The listing completely misrepresented it." She felt like she was tattling.

"Let me guess, Bernie Coughlin." Cillian's irritation plain

on his face. "I'm sorry, miss. When I hired my brother to pick you up, I didn't expect him to bring you to back to his place. Let me take you to a nice hotel while we sort this out. On me." He pulled out his phone and began texting.

"No, it's fine. I'm renting here instead. Finn's going to be my driver." This was all coming out wrong.

"Is he now?" Cillian tone walked the line between shock and skepticism.

"Yes, he's offered to be my driver for the next few weeks. He took me into Killathay today and I've got a full schedule of places to see. He should be back home within the hour if you want to wait. He had to run to his—your—mother's house. Something about Christmas boxes?"

Cillian looked up from his phone. "Wait, he's staying here? With you?"

"Yes." Doubling down on the tattling.

"And that's fine by you?" Did she detect a hint of judgment in that question?

Had Cillian been here yesterday while negotiations with Finn were underway, she would have jumped at the chance to go to a hotel. But now...as much as Finn had been a literal pain in her ass, she felt the urge to keep it all settled this way.

"He's been helpful," she said, measuring each word.

Cillian looked around the room, running a hand through his hair as he considered her words. He was taller than Finn, with similar features –same dark curls, same blue eyes. Really quite good looking. When he turned back to face her, the twinkle in his eyes and dimple in his cheek were on full display. His charm turned on like a light switch.

"Well, I hope he represents Malloy Tours well, Bridget. You have my number if you need someone to replace him. My brother's a good man, but he can be rough around the edges. If you get sick of him, give me a call." Cillian smiled wide. "I want to make sure you're *completely* satisfied with your stay."

Damn. He was attractive and he knew it. Sadly, that didn't make his appeal any less potent.

"Thanks Cillian. I appreciate the offer."

He smiled again. "At your service." He tapped the back of the chair with his gloves. "Tell Finn I stopped by, eh?"

After Cillian left, Bridget made a quick meal. She juggled a sandwich plate and hot bowl of soup back to the table, bottle of lemonade under her arm. She'd stoked the fire with the fresh wood Finn had stacked, and she settled into the couch under the soft glow of the lamps around the room. It was really quite pleasant. She blew gently on her spoonful of soup as she contemplated the peaceful country life of Ireland. *I could get used to this place.*

She looked up as the door swung open.

"What did you do?" Finn stormed through the door waving his phone. "Why the hell is my phone blowing up with reservations? I've four emails for this place in the last hour!"

She drew back in confusion. "What are you talking about?"

"Bleedin' HouseHijack," he huffed, turning the screen back toward himself. "Am I reading this right? I can't tell them no because I didn't block out those dates? Or I'll pay a penalty to cancel these reservations--twenty percent of the fee? This is mad!"

The wilder Finn's outburst became, the more Bridget composed herself into a tight, governed posture.

Finn wrestled his jacket off and flung it to the ground. "Was this you?" he demanded.

Bridget set down her spoon and answered primly, "I

feature this cottage in a video. Which I posted"—she checked her watch—"about an hour ago."

"You had no right!" he paced around the room. "You invaded my privacy. This is my house."

Bridget got to her feet, matching his volume with her own raised voice. "And HouseHijack is paying you for it. The company that requires me to make videos about it."

"You didn't have my permission to make the video. Take it down."

"No." She folded her arms across her chest.

"No?" Finn's voice scaled up as his mouth dropped open in surprise.

"I said no. If you weren't so preoccupied trying to maneuver me into being your renter for my stay, you would've read the fine print about the fees. Not to mention that the rental agreement says HouseHijack has the rights to use images of your property in their marketing. *Which is what I did.*" She glared right back at him.

Ding. He glanced at his phone and gave a cry. "Another one! Who's going to pay for these fees?" he sputtered.

"That sounds like a *you* problem. You might want to mark your unavailable dates as soon as you can." Putting her lemonade under her arm, she picked up the sandwich and soup and headed for her bedroom. "I'm an amazing influencer, so your phone may blow up with requests all night. Oh, and your brother stopped by."

She didn't slam the door—that would be childish. But she turned the new lock with relish. She could hear Finn cursing as he typed away on his laptop. Setting down her dinner, she grabbed her phone from her pocket and texted Finn.

Please be ready to leave tomorrow by 9 a.m.

Laura Ridgefield

[Message Read]

84

Chapter 8

Olive Branch

After Bridget retreated to her room, Finn spent a good two hours trying to navigate the HouseHijack website, set all his dates to unavailable and calculate his financial risk. He had four reservations for the cottage: a weekend in March, two full weeks in May and June and a four-night reservation in July. If he kept the reservations, he had the potential to make another 5000 euro, the only silver lining to this whole debacle. If he declined them, he'd be out close to 600 euro.

He stewed the rest of the evening but didn't respond to the inquiries. He had 48 hours to accept or reject the requests. No point to making a hasty decision. Worst case, he'd bunk with Cillian those days.

But the thought of perfect strangers in his bed and Gran's bed made his skin crawl. Sure, Bridget was staying there, but that was different.

The next morning, he stared at the cracks on the ceiling as he was forced to confront his previous night's behavior in the clear light of day. Not the filter he wanted to use. He'd lost his temper, and he needed to make it right with Bridget.

An idea. "Two birds, one stone," he murmured, reaching for his phone.

"Ollie, it's Finn." His voice was still rough from sleep.

"Finn! Tell me you're done with those platters and bowls—I need them this week!" He was obviously on speakerphone as he could hear his cousin Olive rustling and stapling papers. "You're behind on two orders I promised by mid-month."

"Not done yet, sorry. But I need a favor. I've got one of Cillian's Americans I want to bring by. You opening the shop today?"

"I need a favors too, Finn. Those pieces. They're Christmas presents." The threat in her voice was clear.

"Trust me, I'll get them to you. But my guest?"

Olive paused for a moment. "When?"

"Half nine? Ten?"

He heard her sigh. "I was going to open at 10:30, but if you're tight you can come round at 10. American, yes? Do I have to break out my ghillies and dance a reel for her?"

"Unfortunately, I think you'll like her. We'll see you at 10. Thanks Ollie."

"I need those pieces!" she hollered as he hung up.

He was offering Bridget a literal olive branch.

In the front room, Bridget was showered, dressed and ready for the day. "Good morning," she said stiffly.

"Can I make you a cup of tea?"

"No, thank you."

Time to fall on his sword. "I was an arse last night. I'm sorry."

Her expression flickered. "I appreciate your saying that. We have the Eirhann Waterfall on the schedule this morning." All business, this one. She wasn't going to make it easy for him, was she?

"If it makes you feel better, I got a call from Cill last night, who lectured me up one side and down the other after you went to bed."

She arched her eyebrow, remaining silent.

He plowed on. "You mentioned that you wanted to visit a shop, so I called in a favor this morning. Olive's my cousin, and she has a gallery here in town with artists from all over the region. She said we can come by after 10." He paused. "That is, if that works with your agenda. Or I can ring her back and tell her we're doing the waterfall instead."

The impassive facade cracked a tiny bit. "No, that sounds good. We can do the waterfall in the afternoon."

Bridget bit her lip, as if weighing whether to say something. She continued, "I made a couple of calls last night to Mary and the HouseHijack team. Since you came in clutch with a last-minute booking for me, we talked HouseHijack into waiving the fees if you want to cancel those reservations."

He sat back, a bit stunned. Even as furious as she was the night before, she called in a favor to help him out, saving him hundreds of euro. An unexpected kindness.

"Thanks. Really." He grinned at her. "Who knows—maybe I should keep the reservations. I'm getting the hang of being a host, right?"

She huffed a laugh of disbelief. "With your people skills, I'd worry about your reviews. C'mon, let's eat and then head out."

After breakfast, Bridget softened back up. She peered out the window as they drove into Killathay, and the faint glow of sunshine was seeping through the clouds.

"Do you have a lot of family around here?"

"You could say that," he smiled. "My sisters are older and married with their families nearby. My brother—who you met last night—runs the driving service you hired and he lives in a flat about half a mile from here. My mum has a place in Tilleen, which isn't far at all."

He zipped into a street-side parking spot in Killathay, pulling up the handbrake. "A quick walk from here."

They fell into a steady cadence with their steps. The town was sleepy as promised this morning. In the distance, a steeple loomed large over the smaller buildings. "That's St. Brendan's," he said. "My family's been in this parish for hundreds of years."

Almost on cue, a Fiat pulled up next to them, bumping a wheel up on the kerb. Finn stepped in front of Bridget as a reflex, stretching his arm across her body to hold her back.

The window rolled down. "Finn Malloy, is that you now?" With an inward groan, Finn pasted on a smile. Father Tim was not the diversion they needed today.

"Careful there, Father. The kerb's there for a reason, you know."

The priest looked slightly embarrassed. "I'm overdue for my glasses, it's true. But your young lady is safe from me."

"Father, this is Bridget Kolodziej. I'm showing her around town. She's a professional tourist, making videos for Americans." The last thing he needed is word getting round that he was squiring a woman around Killathay. But Father Tim was notorious for making sure news was spread far and wide.

"A social media influencer, actually," piped in Bridget.

"Oh, an influencer!" the priest said, clapping his hands together. "Showcasing our fine city, are you? Come by the rectory –I can give you some local flavor and the inside story on this one." Father Tim winked and nodded his head toward Finn. Great. Now every infraction from his school days would find its way onto the Internet.

Father Tim's broad smile seemed to disarm Bridget. "Sure, we'll swing by," she said. With a cheery wave, the priest bumped back off the kerb and buzzed down the street.

Finn groaned. "Now you've done it. We're in for hours now. Father Tim is not known for being brief."

"Well, maybe we can skip it—tell him we got busy," she shrugged.

Finn laughed. "You can't lie to a priest!"

"Fine. We can tell him we've got a reservation for lunch, so we'll have to leave on time."

"Sure, that's going to work." There was more than a note of sarcasm in Finn's voice. "We'll be lucky to get out by supper. And don't tell him anything that you don't want the whole county to know—the man is a huge gossip."

"I thought priests were supposed to keep secrets?"

"Are you planning to go to confession? If you tell him there, you're safe." Finn shoved his hands in his pockets. "All else is open season. Word of you being in town is going to reach every little old lady he sees."

Including Ma. Finn sighed. He knew Cillian could keep his secret, but once his mother knew about a woman staying at the cottage, he'd be subject to an inquisition. Especially if she thought the news would get around the parish.

"Olive Branch is this way." Finn turned right, heading down a quiet lane. The good news (if there was any) was that Olive could be counted on to take his side.

"What kind of shop is it?"

"You'll like it. It's different than the touristy knick-knack places. She works with local artists all throughout the county. Handcrafts and such."

Bridget's face lit up. "That's perfect—exactly what I need. Do you think she'd do an interview?"

"Who, Olive? You'll be lucky to get her to stop talking."

When they reached the Olive Branch, Bridget gave a gasp of delight. "This is perfect!" Three square tables in the center of the shop displayed pottery, jewelry, dyed silks, and knitwear, while the walls were covered in landscapes and portraits done in watercolors, mixed media, mosaics, and acrylics.

"Finn!" Olive sprung from the back room, and Finn gave a sideways glance to see how Bridget would react to his cousin's jet-black hair streaked with blue, nose ring and smattering of tattoos. Olive rocked him back and forth with a forceful hug. Turning to Bridget, Ollie grabbed her hand warmly, making the silver bangles on her arms jingle. "I'm Olive, and welcome to the Olive Branch!"

"Bridget," she answered with a smile. "Love your hair!" She gestured toward the nubby wool sweaters and shawls that covered the tables nearby. "Your store is beautiful—thank you for opening early for me. I hope I didn't put you out."

Olive shook her head. "Don't think on it—happy to have you here, even if it means putting up with the sour mood of this grump." She elbowed Finn in the ribs harder than necessary.

He picked up a pair of deep blue hand-knit mittens, tossing them Bridget's direction. "You know those sheep with the blue mark we saw earlier? They made these from the blue wool." It wasn't a great joke, but it deserved a laugh, right?

"Oh, shut it, Finn," said Olive. "Has he been teasing you all day? He's a wretch, but I love him." Olive linked arms with Bridget and steered her to the back wall. "Just to punish him though, I'm going to show you—"

"Ollie...don't." The last thing he needed was his private

work a subject of discussion. Like always, Olive ignored him, leading Bridget to a display of his wooden bowls, platters, pillars, and candlesticks. "See these? Made by that idiot. Spalted beech wood, which he finds and cuts himself then finishes into these gorgeous pieces."

It wasn't that he didn't want to show Bridget his woodworking, he just hated seeing this display. It felt like thievery to ask such an inflated price when he could see every uneven cut, every flaw, every mistake he made. Olive praised his pieces to such degree that it was embarrassing. He gave a grunt of disgust and began walking toward the front of the store.

In a stage whisper, Olive said, "Finn hates the fact that I think he's terribly talented, so he's a monster to me. I put up with him because he makes these gorgeous works of art. Americans go crazy for them. They're solid wood, and not much to look at until he polishes them up. They're so damn heavy I usually ship them to the States for people. So they're Finn in a nutshell—not much to look at initially, but something of value if you put in the effort. And always making extra work for me."

Thanks Olive. Always dressing up compliments in the clothing of criticism.

Bridget picked up the largest of the four bowls to look closer, running her hand over the smooth edges and tracing the markings. She turned to Finn, "You made these?"

He didn't respond, but instead crossed his arms and looked mutinously out the front windows. Taking Bridget here was his penance, but this was beyond the pale.

"He did, but he's just being a baby now." Olive smirked. "I have some other things you might be interested in as well. A group of nuns that have a community over the hills are doing some gorgeous things in fiber arts—look at these book covers."

"Hang on," Bridget said, digging in her bag. "Olive, would you mind if I filmed you showing me some of your favorite pieces in the shop? I'm a content creator on social media, and everything here is so beautiful. I know I won't do it justice myself."

"Give me a minute…I'll run into the back and be ready in two shakes." To Finn she added, "If you're going to sulk, there's three boxes by the back entrance that can be carried up front. Put them behind the counter."

Without a word, Finn followed Olive to the back room. When they were out of earshot of Bridget, he said, "Leave off on my pieces, Olive. Her posts have already caused me a world of headaches."

Olive dug through her bag for her lipstick, which she applied in the reflection of the window. "So they get attention, do they? The boxes are over there."

The boxes were heavy and awkward, and when he finished carrying in the last one, he saw Bridget had set up her ring light and tripod in the far corner, away from the door with his wood-working in plain sight. With a thud, he dropped the box to the ground. "You're not going to put my things in your video." He had to make it clear, right from the start.

"I hope that box wasn't ceramics, the way you just dropped it."

"I mean it. I don't give permission to be held up to the masses for consumption."

"I guess that's up to Olive, isn't it?" Irritation crept into her voice. "It's her shop, after all." As an afterthought she added, "Stinks when people make decisions for you, doesn't it?"

While he geared up for a retort, Olive returned in full makeup—dark red lipstick, pink eyeshadow, and thick black eyeliner. She pasted on a bright smile and called out to Bridget, "Ready when you are."

Bridget transformed into her producer mode, brisk and professional. "Great—so I'm going to try to make it look like we're having a conversation, so pause before you answer my questions. I want to give myself enough space so I can edit it together. Don't worry if you mess up, we can start over. I'll probably have to do several takes myself. Ready?"

For the first time he could remember, Olive looked a bit intimidated, but nodded.

"Good. I'll start. Ok...three...two...one." Bridget's wide, bright smile appeared again.

"Hey guys! It's Bridget! We are continuing our series of the amazing things that can be found in and around the southwestern coastal area of Ireland, thanks to our friends at House-Hijack.com." Bridget paused a moment to point to an invisible spot in the air in front of her. "One of the most amazing things I get to do is discover hidden treasures, something this woman knows a lot about! This is Olive, the proprietor of The Olive Branch in Killathay. Olive, tell me a little about what we can find here in your shop."

Finn was impressed by how easily Bridget coaxed Olive into a comfortable dialogue about the textiles, jewelry, and the local art she curated in her shop. Sure, Bridget had to restart a few times as she stumbled over her words, but in no time, the two of them were chatting animatedly about the history of the building and town, sharing stories and anecdotes about the kinds of people who stopped in over the years.

Feeling a bit useless, he wandered around the store, careful to stay out of the shot.

Olive continued, "...so it was just after filming began on a big-budget superhero movie—you'd know it, huge box-office hit —and everyone in town was buzzing. I was wrapping up a beautiful mosaic for the lead actress that was made by a dairy farmer in Conneen. She buys artwork in all the towns she visits on location, because spending here had a much larger impact than in Manhattan or L.A.," Olive said.

"You're not going to tell us who?"

"No, but if you pop in, I'll tell you in person." Olive winked.

Finn snickered slightly. Olive was savvy when it came to her shop. His chuckle made Olive glance his way. "But I did want to tell you about one of our artists—a particular favorite of mine. He makes amazing bowls made from Irish spalted beech wood..."

Sonofabitch. "That's it, stop." Finn lurched from the corner with his hand extended to block the shot, knocking over the ring lamp in his effort to derail Olive's next comment.

Bridget lunged to catch the lamp but couldn't get to it in time. It hit the ground and the light snapped off its stand, decapitated.

"Finn, you beast! What are you doing!" Olive cried out.

"Why did you do that! I could have just edited that out. Now it's broken!" Bridget was picking up the pieces of cracked plastic that had fallen from the frame. "I barely used it and now it's broken. My roommate gave it to me."

She sounded crestfallen. And he felt like a first-class heel. He stood uselessly as Olive punched him in the arm. Hard.

She bent down to help Bridget collect the broken pieces. "I'm so, so sorry Bridget. I only meant to tease him. I paused and everything so you could edit it."

"It's not your fault." Bridget glanced pointedly at Finn.

"Here, let's try to tape it back in." Olive slipped behind the counter and began rustling in a desk drawer. Tape in hand, they pieced together the fractured plastic enclosure around the light, but the tripod was shattered and useless.

How did she upset him so much? Finn reached out his hand. "Give it here. I'll hold the light so you can get this done." More penance for his sins.

Olive arched an eyebrow. "Sure that won't be too much trouble for you, Finn?" The sarcasm in her voice was thick.

Bridget handed him the light, her face tight and controlled. "Keep it steady."

He held it in front of his chest like a bleedin' human lighthouse.

Olive sniffed. "As stubborn and rigid as you are, that should be no problem."

Chapter 9

The Irish Inquisition

Watching Finn serve as a human tripod *almost* made up for the loss of her ring light.

"Olive, your gorgeous store is amazing. I've linked her website in the comments. Until then, thanks to HouseHijack.com, and thank you, Olive!"

Bridget froze, smiling tight at the camera for a few beats, then hit stop on her phone. Without looking at Finn she added, "Turn off the light."

Finn laid the precariously patched light on the counter, then gave a curt goodbye to Olive. Turning to Bridget he added in a quieter voice, "I'll wait outside while you finish up."

"I need my bowls!" Olive called after him.

"They'll be there, quit your carping," he snapped.

As soon as the door closed, Olive leaned toward Bridget. "He's feeling like an arse right now, so you have the upper hand if you need him to cave on anything. Make your move."

Bridget grinned. "Good to know. He can be a bit—"

"Stubborn? Mule-headed? Bossy?"

"Something like that." She reconsidered a moment. "All of that."

"Don't let him get away with it. He's a miserable wretch because he should be woodworking full-time, but my aunt and cousins are bent on him having a settled job. So he feels these pieces are just a side job, a nixer." Olive popped behind her computer while Bridget folded up the cords and gathered the broken pieces of her tripod. "He's wrong, though."

Olive pulled up a shopping site on her computer. "I'm ordering you a new ring light right now, but I'm having it sent here to the shop for two reasons...one, it will get here a lot faster than out in Kildunne, and two, I want to make sure you come back to see me."

"Count on it," Bridget smiled. Olive was one of those 'instant friend' people.

After a quick hug, Olive shot a look at Finn, pacing outside the window and sighed. "Bridget...as much as he can be a grumpy bugger, he's a good man, give you the clothes off his back. His personality just gets in the way."

"I can see that." Bridget tried to give a convincing smile.

"Here, I want you to have these." Olive whisked to the counter and picked up a pair of dangling blue glass earrings. "They'll look so pretty against your curls."

"I couldn't —"

"Wear them in your next video and give me credit." Olive winked. "Now get on with you, big day! And welcome to Ireland!"

Outside, Finn leaned against the wall, pouting.

"Your cousin was nice enough to buy a new ring lamp for me," Bridget said, making her voice as neutral as possible.

"I'll pay her back for it, of course." He kicked at a stone with the tip of his shoe.

"I'll take it off your overtime bill." She peered down the street. "Is the car that way? I want to make sure we get to the waterfall while we still have good light."

"Not so fast there. We'll stop in at the rectory first—that's on you." He craned his head around Olive's awning to squint at the sky. "Besides, it's about to pour down." As if he conjured it, the first few fat raindrops began to spatter on the sidewalk.

Bridget sighed audibly. "We can't stay long."

The rain stayed mostly a sprinkle as they hustled up the block. The St. Brendan rectory was a tidy stone building surrounded by a short wrought-iron fence and a knot garden leading up to the front door. At the doorway, a narrow archway clustered with vines gave a bit of cover from the rain. Bridget pushed her hood back.The exertion of their quick walk had her breathing heavy. She was not in trek-all-over-Ireland shape. Finn gave the bell a quick buzz.

A birdlike woman in a turtleneck and thick cardigan opened the door. Finn smiled. "Good morning, Mrs. Plover. We're here to see Father Tim."

"Could you not have come without bringing the weather with you?" she said reprovingly. "Come in, come in." She moved ahead of them as they walked down the dark hallway that smelled of pipe smoke and lemon oil. "He'll be in his office now, won't he. I suppose you'll want some tea."

"No, we—" Bridget started to decline. The last thing she wanted was to put this poor woman out for a cup of tea.

Finn shook his head slightly as he whispered, "She loves it. She'll dine on this for weeks." Louder he added, "If it's not too much trouble, Mrs. Plover."

"Thinks he should get an old woman out of her chair to make him tea. Probably biscuits too." She paused at the end of the hallway. "You'll know where the office is, Finn. Mrs. Keating sent you over enough when you were small."

She turned the corner toward the kitchen and Finn had a faint look of dread on his face. "Was Mrs. Keating your principal?"

Finn shrugged. "Sunday school teacher."

"You were a frequent guest here, then?"

"I might have questioned some things that Mrs. Keating considered infallible," he muttered.

Bridget grinned. "That sounds about right."

They reached the door at the north end of the hallway and Finn tapped it with the back of his knuckles. "Father Tim?"

"Ah, Finn! Come in with your lady friend."

The rectory office was wall-to-wall dark wood, which seemed to swallow the lights Father Tim had burning all over the room, including a fire in the hearth. "I asked William to set a fire for us so we could be cozy with the drizzle. Sit, sit!"

Bridget looked to Finn questioningly, and he inclined his head toward the sofa. Father Tim moved toward the worn leather armchair positioned at a right angle to the fire.

The older man sat down heavily, his impressive belly straining against his cardigan. "Now, usually when I entertain young couples in here they have a date in mind," he said with a wink. "When did you two meet?"

Finn jumped in. "Nothing like that, Father. Like I said, Bridget here just arrived to the county yesterday, bit of a mix-up too. Got stuck on the train and had to go all the way to Tralee and back."

Father Tim gasped dramatically, placing a hand to his chest. "No! That must have been so unsettling, my dear. I'm so sorry that happened."

Bridget smiled. "It wasn't that bad. My suitcase was stuck, but Finn boarded the train to help me get it loose."

"Saved the day, did he? You got off safely, that's what matters. Are you staying in town?"

"Uh..." Bridget looked at Finn, his eyes wide with alarm. Still, Finn's dire warnings about lying to a priest echoed in her ears. She had no better response than the truth. "I've rented out Finn's grandmother's cottage."

"Really?" Father Tim leaned forward, Finn straight in his crosshairs. "And where will you be staying while you rent out Rose's cottage to this young lady?"

"I spoke to Cillian about that yesterday." Bridget gave him a sideways look. *What was that about lying to a priest?* Finn continued, "As I said, Bridget is here to do social media featuring the area."

Father sat back again, slapping his palms to his thighs. "Well now, that is something, isn't it? I've got plenty of stories to share about the area. Are you on the TikToks then?"

Bridget grinned. "Are you a big fan of TikTok, Father?"

He waved away her question. "I know the boys and girls from the school tend to get in trouble for the TikTok and Instagram and whatnot. I've had plenty in here for a stern talking to, just like Mr. Malloy used to get back in the day."

"So I've heard," said Bridget. "I usually make content about cleaning and organizing things around the house, but I had the opportunity to come visit here in Ireland for a few weeks, so I jumped at it."

"You do well with this career?" The priest arched an eyebrow. "Good money, is it?"

A bit personal. "It's not my full-time job. Well, not yet. Hopefully someday. For now, I work in an accounting office."

"Excellent. Do us proud, young lady." Father turned toward the doorway, calling out, "Mrs. Plover, do you need a hand with tea?"

The rest of the visit was full of mildly salacious gossip

(always introduced with a "we must pray for her" or "we hope to turn his heart, but...") and a recounting of the history of the nearby villages.

Bridget noticed that Finn began to plant the seeds for their departure a good twenty minutes before they finally extracted themselves from the rectory. Before leaving, Father Tim asked her to write down her social media handles. "I'll have to keep tabs on your adventures, young lady!"

Stepping outside the rectory, Bridget pulled her jacket tight around her neck. "If I add two dozen grannies to my followers in the next 24 hours, I'll know who's behind it. But he was sweet. That was fun."

"Fun, was it?" Finn groaned. "It'll be a world of trouble for me. Cillian and Olive can be discreet, but Father Tim is probably on the phone as we speak to everyone in the county. Why did you tell him you were renting the cottage?"

"I thought I wasn't supposed to lie to a priest?" she retorted.

"If I don't have at least two of my sisters checking up on me in the next 24 hours to find out why there's a woman in Gran's house, I'll drop dead from shock." He shoved his hands in his jacket pocket again and began striding ahead of her in the direction of the car.

Bridget stared after him for a few seconds, her mouth hanging open in disbelief. All at once, she nearly broke out into a run to catch up with him, her tote bag banging against her side in her haste. "Well, well...if it isn't the consequences of your actions!" she called after him.

He stopped short and turned to face her, his face a near-comical combination of shock and anger.

Bridget caught up to him, a tad out of breath. "Don't blame me for getting cornered by the priest about the cottage. That's on you."

"You shouldn't have mentioned the cottage."

"You're the one who trapped me into staying there!"

"All because you're too posh to stay in Bernie's run-down rental..."

Bridget picked up her tote bag with both hands and shook it at him. "You were such a bully that you broke my ring lamp!" Her voice scaled up to a shout, but she caught herself. *Stop.*

Finn opened his mouth to make an angry response, but he, too, seemed to catch himself. "You're right. I insisted we go to town. Lunch first, then I'll take you to the waterfall. No later than 1 p.m., so we can honor your mighty schedule." Bridget was primed to take offense, but the small curve at the edge of his mouth clued her in that he was teasing.

Bridget glanced at her watch. Despite only being 11:30, her stomach was already growling. "Lunch then. But I'm getting dessert as your penance."

He grinned. "Penance, eh? That's amateur-level. Father Tim never let me off so easy."

Instead of eating at Tommy Malone's in Killathay, Finn drove outside the city to a pub called McCann's. The stack of chairs and outdoor tables piled near the door hinted at a bustling establishment during warmer months, but on this cool, rainy December day, McCann's barely looked open.

Finn opened the door wide for her, and Bridget blinked to let her eyes adjust to the dark room. The windows were thick and leaded, letting in very little light from the outside. A series of tables dotted the floor and heavy wooden benches lined the walls. In the corner, a makeshift stage stood only about four or five inches above the floor. The long wooden bar ran almost the full length of the room, and voices and clatter could be heard coming from the kitchen in the back.

Finn bumped his fist on the bar twice to signal their presence. "Good if we sit?"

A forty-ish woman with a cropped blonde haircut popped her head out of the kitchen. "Anywhere, loves. Out in two with menus."

They chose a spot near the windows and settled in. While they waited, Bridget replayed the video she'd taken at Olive's shop. She made a great show of editing out Finn's interruption, making her edits with the sound on for his benefit.

She could feel a wiggle in the table -- Finn's knee bounced in agitation as he seemed fixated on the window. "Everything ok?"

"Sure." His body was perched on the edge of the bench.

Three men walked in the pub, taking up all the oxygen in the room as the . The group made a beeline for them, their voices echoing in a jarringly loud volume. "Finny boy! Finn! Malloy, what are you doing here? Sneaking about so no one sees you at Tommy's?"

The tallest of the three—heart-stoppingly good looking, with chiseled jawline and cheekbones for days—reached out his hand. "Who do we have here?" This man knew the power of his charm, and Bridget could feel herself getting flustered. "You sneaking out with this lovely girl, Finny?"

"Bridget," she said, trusting herself only to manage a brief reply. The man took her hand and made a great show of covering it with his own.

"An American beauty, no less. I'm Jerry, this is Mickey and Brian." The men appeared to be in their early thirties, all clad in jeans and t-shirts. Their mud-crusted boots suggested it was a workday for all of them.

Finn was not amused. "She's a client, Jerry." His tone implied a warning.

Jerry winked at him. "Nice work if you can get it, eh?" The

other two men laughed, and Bridget felt herself shrink into her seat. Instead of moving on, Jerry stood closer to her, crossing the border of personal space.

"I'm her tour guide for the area," Finn said in a clipped voice. "But we're just catching a quick bite and we'll be on our way."

Jerry placed his heavy palm on Bridget's back, his thumb sliding ever so slightly along her shoulder. "We'll let you two enjoy your lunch, then. A pleasure, Miss Bridget." He winked at her as they went toward the bar.

She gave Jerry a weak smile, and watched as Finn slid back in his seat. His eyes didn't leave the three until they were safely ensconced on their stools at the bar.

"How do you know them?"

Finn blinked, breaking his steady gaze on the trio. "They were my brother's year in school, and made his life miserable for a while. Which is a hard thing to do, because pretty much everyone likes Cill. But those three, mostly Jerry, didn't like anyone being a bigger man about town, so when they were about 14 or 15, they made things rough for a time. They all outgrew it, but I remember so badly wanting to fight those boys."

Bridget looked over toward the bar again. "How old were you?"

He smiled. "I was about 10 or 11, thin as a piece of paper. They'd have knocked me silly, but it didn't stop me dreaming of it."

The woman from the kitchen emerged from behind the bar and pulled three pints for Jerry and his friends before coming to their table with two dogeared paper menus. "What can I get started for you both?"

In moments, two bowls of lamb stew were on the table, and Bridget was in heaven. "This is amazing," she said, digging in with gusto. "I thought I hated stew. My mom's was a catch-all for all the leftovers, a cheap cut of beef and canned vegetables. All of it went in the crockpot and it would come out a gloppy, stringy mess. This is delicious."

"Was your ma not much of a cook then?"

Bridget made an effort to not wolf down her portion. "She and my stepdad run a travel agency, so they were busy most of the day. I would stay after at school, and they would pick me up when they left work around 5:30. If mom didn't have something going in the crockpot, it was a lot of sandwiches, cereal and fast food."

Finn nodded. "I'm the youngest in my family. By the time I came along, my oldest sister was 17. Everyone had jobs and were running all over town with friends and meetings and such. She always insisted that we be home for supper on Sundays, but after my dad passed, that became harder."

"How old were you?"

"Right around the same time that lot started going after Cillian. I was 10."

Bridget had a twist of pain for that little boy, trying to defend his older brother because his dad wasn't around to protect them both. Her heart melted the tiniest bit. "I'm so sorry."

Finn waved his hand. "Long time ago. Now let's focus on the bigger issue: what you're having for dessert."

Chapter 10

Don't Go Chasing Waterfalls

Bridget's mood was markedly improved after lunch, and Finn made a mental note not to delay meals in the future, for both her comfort and his. And a stash of snacks at the ready.

In the car, she pulled out her white binder again, slipping the pages out of their sleeves to jot notes in the margins. She studied a set of notes with highlighter markings, glancing at her watch several times. Finn waited as she worked her system.

His capacity for patience tapped out at 90 seconds. "To Eirhann Falls then?"

"No...hang on. How long will it take to get to Eirhann and then back to the cottage?"

"I'd say we'd be back around half three, maybe four."

She bit the corner of her thumb, deep in thought. "That's tight. I need this video edited and turned in by six tonight. I can do some of it on my phone, but I prefer to do it on my laptop."

"Did you bring your laptop?"

"No. I thought we'd be back earlier."

Finn sighed. "If we go back, we're done for the day. It's not

"

worth coming all the way back out. I'd need a few liters of petrol."

"Fine, let's head back."

He cocked his head. "You sure? I promised you the waterfall today."

"It's more important that I don't miss this deadline. Mary will hire a hitman. With my luck, you'd answer the ad and get the job."

At the cottage, Finn made a great show of giving Bridget time alone. She was hunched over her computer, fervently editing, so he slipped out back to the shed. Might as well get the damn bowls finished up for Olive. The last thing he needed was more grief from his cousin when Bridget's ring light came in.

He shook his head at his own stupidity there. Had to be a bull in a china shop, knocking over her equipment. At this rate, he'd owe *her* money by Christmas.

Woodworking was his relief, his distraction. As he sanded and shaped the wood beneath his hands, he felt his stress and frustration dissipate, washing away with the hum of the lathe. The rough cuts of wood—pieces he discovered and cut down himself—took on forms that could not be planned, only realized. The piece of wood in his hands had a smattering of faint bluish specks along one side. He'd originally intended to make this piece into a bowl, but as he cut and shaped it, the wood became a shallow platter that showcased the natural beauty of the speckling. Now that its shape was defined, he began to sand it in long strokes, the rough edges becoming smoothing under his attention.

When his back started to ache (and his stomach began to growl), Finn glanced at his watch. Nearly 8 p.m.—he was shocked at how long he'd been caught up in the process. He gave the worktable a quick tidy-up, then he settled the donkeys for the night.

A note was propped on the kitchen table:

>Didn't want to disturb you.
>I'm heading to bed.
>I'll be ready to go at 9 tomorrow.
>—B

Bridget's laptop was closed and quiet, and a bowl and plate were in the drying rack by the sink. He felt a bit put out that she ate without him. He stretched his back again, pressing his fist against the knot at the base of his spine. Nothing left for him to do but go to bed himself.

The next morning, a clatter woke him with a start. Grabbing at a pair of pajama pants, he wobbled into them and came out of his room to discover Bridget sitting on the kitchen floor sitting among a pile of metal bakeware.

"The hell are you doing down there?"

She turned with a start, putting a hand to her chest. "Don't sneak up on people like that! You nearly gave me a heart attack."

"What's all this?"

"I'm still getting up too early. I figured I would make banana muffins. I was looking for a muffin tin."

"In there?"

"My thing is organizing, right? So..." she shrugged. "I couldn't help myself."

"You thought you'd bang pots and pans around at what, six in the morning." He squinted blearily at the clock. "Sorry, 5:45 a.m."

"I was being very quiet until your Jenga tower of metal pans decided to fall out. I didn't turn on the light, though." She gestured to a small jar candle she'd lit, sitting beside her on the floor. "Go back to bed—I'll wake you when the muffins are done."

Finn rubbed his hand over his stubbly face, weighing the question of sleep or shower. He rubbed his eyes with the heel of his hand. "Don't wake me before seven," he grunted.

His second attempt at consciousness was more successful. An extra hour in bed improved his mood, and the scent of banana muffins wafted through the house. He trudged toward the kitchen, passing the dining table where Bridget was scrolling on the internet, still in relative darkness.

"Morning...again." She turned a bright smile toward him, and he grimaced in return. It was still a bit early for cheerfulness. "Muffins are on the stove."

He had to admit, waking up to a warm muffin improved a cold Wednesday morning. Three muffins did even better. He joined Bridget in the dark parlor as she scrolled social media. "Did you make your deadline yesterday?"

"With an hour to spare. Mary approved it last night, so I posted before I went to bed. I'm finally starting to get some decent engagement. Everybody loved Olive." She leaned back from her laptop. "I did pretty well with the interview. My roommate was shocked to see me talking to strangers like this. Look." She pointed at a message on her phone.

"That's your roommate?"

Bridget smirked. "She's stalks me online, but almost never posts. "

Finn nodded absently, not fully processing the information. "What's the plan for today?"

"The waterfall, and maybe that sheepdog demonstration in Conneen if it's nice enough and we have time."

Finn sighed, Tourist nonsense again, but he wouldn't rock the boat. What Bridget wanted, Bridget would get.

The trip to Eirhann Waterfall was an hour's drive away, then a short hike up a moderately easy trail. Bridget's bright yellow Hunter wellies made him raise an eyebrow. "Are those the best shoes you have for hiking?" he asked.

'They're waterproof," she said, a bit defensively. "I figured that was the priority."

"We'll see."

After parking the car at the base of the trail, they crossed a wooden bridge to the signpost. He waited as Bridget picked her way through the sodden leaves on the path. "In summer, this is well-traveled with tourists, you can barely park. But in the winter, it's rough terrain. Slippery. You want me to go first, or should I follow you?"

Bridget looked around. "Let me get a little establishing video first. I want to get myself in the shot with the sign." She dug around in the tote bag for a moment. "Shoot, I think I left the selfie stick in the car."

Finn rolled his eyes and extended his hand. "Give it over."

"Really?"

"How hard can it be to shoot a video?"

She seemed to weigh the options, but handed him the phone. He opened up the camera app and said, "Go."

"Absolutely not." She plucked the phone out of his hand, turned it vertical, showed him where to stand and framed up the shot for him. "Hold the camera up a little higher. Always shoot down. Fewer chins."

He held the camera steady as she walked toward the signpost. Her curls were damp and wild, and she ran through them with her fingers to try and tame the strays.

"Do I look ok?" She smiled up at him.

"Deadly." He meant it. The damp had made her auburn hair wild and windblown, and the crisp air and exertion made her cheeks pink and gave a sparkle to her gray eyes.

"Is that good?"

He promptly ruined the moment with the most awkward thumbs-up gesture known to man. *Idiot.*

He hit *Record* and gave Bridget a nod.

"Here I am at Eirhann Waterfall, outside of Killathay, where legend has it that a sip from the stream will give you dreams of your one true love. It sounds better than our American version, which involves sleeping on a piece of wedding cake. If you've ever tried it, you know it leads to frosting in your hair and worse, wasted cake."

She moved toward the camera. "I've been warned by my guide that the trek up to the waterfall can be slippery, so hopefully you will see me in one piece when we're done." The frozen smile came out again, and Finn waited until she composed her face more naturally before hitting the stop button on the phone.

"Got it," he said. She wordlessly took the phone from his hand and replayed the video, a furrow on her brow as she watched.

"Pretty good, but you should try to keep the camera as steady as possible next time. It makes it tough to edit if it's jumpy."

Bridget looked up at his silence. "I mean, thank you. I know it's not in the job description."

"Ok, Boss Lady."

Finn had climbed to the top of the waterfall dozens of times in his life. The path ran up the side of the mountain in a zigzag pattern, littered with fallen branches from recent storms. Decaying leaves and moss made the path slick in the damp air, and in a few spaces, he grabbed a branch to steady himself.

Behind him, he could hear Bridget breathing heavy from the climb. At one point, she jerked back with a cry, as a thorny branch caught in her hair.

He circled back. "Hang on, let me." He held her hair firmly at her scalp, so he could work her curls free without hurting her. His reward? A long scratch on the back of his hand from the thorns.

"Thanks." She smiled, then inclined her head. "I think I hear water."

"Just a bit farther." When they came to the clearing, he stood toward the side, allowing her the full view of the waterfall.

It wasn't a large waterfall, but the stream skipped over the smooth rocks and outcroppings, rippling and bubbling along. Lush plants sprung forth around its edges and in the cold morning air, a miasma of mist gave the whole scene an other-worldly feel.

He watched Bridget's face as she took it all in, absorbing the full beauty of the sight.

"It's so pretty," she murmured. "You can almost imagine fairies—"

"Stop with that," he said, cutting her off. Not that he held stock in fae folk, but no point in borrowing trouble.

"You're superstitious?" Bridget gave a half-laugh. "I would never have guessed!"

"Not superstitious...cautious." The two of them stood together, watching the water cascading down the smooth rocks, the sound of rippling creating an ethereal rhythm.

"You going to take a sip?" he asked.

"Got to find out my one true love, right?" she said lightly. "Would you film me again?"

While Finn set up, Bridget dug into her tote bag for her water bottle. She emptied it at the base of a tree, then turned to the camera. "We made it! Look at the gorgeous Eirhann Waterfall—it starts a good 200 feet above us, and the water is so bubbly here it looks carbonated. Rest assured there no chance I'm taking a sip from a waterfall without a filter. Not a fan of cryptosporidium. Instead, I'm going to take this water home and after a hearty boil, I'll report back if I see the man of my dreams."

Finn started to lower the phone but she called out, "One more shot, keep going."

He hit *Record* again. Bridget leaned over the edge of the waterfall and placed the bottle into the stream catch a small rivulet of water. As she straightened, her foot slipped on a patch of moss. With a cry, she pitched sideways, landing on her backside as her water bottle bounced off a tree trunk.

"You hurt?" he called out.

"No. I'm fine." She flinched as she tried to get up. "You've seen I'm a klutz. I do this all the time."

"Stay put." Finn slipped the phone into his back pocket. In two strides, he was braced and offering his hands to help her up. Her foot slipped again, forcing her off-balance into his chest. Her hands gripped his forearms as she struggled to find her footing, and he maneuvered her from the slick stones to the more traction-giving trail. He held her for a few extra moments, not wanting to release her until he was sure she was steady on her feet.

"Take a minute," he murmured. She turned toward him, those dove gray eyes intent on his. For a moment, they were frozen together.

"Sorry," she said, pulling away.

"Sorry," he echoed. "Stay there." Stepping across the slick stones, he retrieved her bottle, refilled it in the stream and capped it. Wordlessly, he handed it to her.

"Thanks." She didn't meet his eyes, and instead, turned to make her way back down.

"Wait." Sliding on the mossy stones had left a green smear on the back of her trousers. "You've got a big stain there."

She twisted, trying to see for herself. "Oh no!"

He watched as she swatted at the stain. "Don't worry, we'll head back so you can change."

The frustration rang clear in her voice. "No, it'll be fine. We're done here. Just keep the camera off my butt for the rest of the day."

She meant it as a joke. She couldn't have intended to make him start thinking of the curves of her backside. *Right?*

He reached out his hand again, but with a shake of her head, she headed down the trail on her own. Finn gave himself a moment to appreciate the view.

Now keep your eyes off her backside!

Chapter 11

Milky Ways & Photographs

*W*hat. *Was. That?*

Bridget picked her way down the trail, chiding herself. *What were you doing, leaning in like that? Don't be stupid! He's your driver.* It's not like she could avoid him. They were joined at the hip for the next three weeks.

Bridget shook her head, trying to clear her thoughts. Somehow she ended up in the arms of her employee, who was also her landlord? Smart women don't behave like this. Logic. Reason. *Boundaries.* Her mind drifted into dangerous territory, like what it would have felt like to go in for a deep, intense kiss while pressed up against Finn's chest.

Fuck.

No. Definitely not that. *Boundaries.*

Back at the car, Finn barked, "Turn around." She gave him a questioning look but obliged. He swiped at her backside, running his hand from the small of her back down the curve of her behind in three brusque motions. "Little sore, are you?"

Bridget's face flamed as he opened the door for her. His

touch felt intimate; too personal for the time they'd spent together. On the heels of that moment at the falls, she felt a rising panic. *Time to reassert boundaries.* She took a breath. "While I appreciate your help, I think it's best that we don't get..." She struggled for the right words. "Overly familiar."

Finn's face closed tight to a stony, emotionless expression. "You got it, Boss Lady. Just trying to make sure you don't get muck on my upholstery."

Great. He's offended. "I didn't mean..."

"Don't need to say another word. Completely understand." His tone was cool.

Stop thinking of yourself as the bad guy. "We just need to keep things professional, since we're going to be in such close quarters." Straightforward. Clear.

"Sure then." He patted his back pockets, pulling out her phone. "Here you go," he said, laying it on her outstretched hand. He walked back around to his side of the car and got in. "Some lunch? Strictly business, of course." He paused. "I know I'm not an influencer like you, but you might want to edit out that fall."

Her face grew hot again as he served up her own words, with a sour chaser of embarrassment at her own clumsiness. *Well done, Bridget.* "Of course."

He stopped at a gas station in town to pick up a sack of sausage rolls and two Fantas for lunch. A small picnic bench was set outside, ostensibly for tour buses in high season. Finn's mood didn't encourage conversation, so she spent lunch scrolling through comments and replying to posts on her phone.

Finn continued his stony silence on the way to the sheepdog demonstration in Conneen, even opting to wait in the car while she joined a small group of tourists from New Jersey and Virginia along the wood-and-wire fence. Bridget watched enthralled as three black and white border collies snuck up on the reluctant sheep with laser-focused purpose, circling them and maneuvering them back to shelter.

Despite her best intentions, Bridget caught herself glancing back toward the car. Finn's dark mood cast a pall on her enjoyment, but she filmed the exhibition until the final exercise, even lingering in the small gift shop to buy a postcard to send to Tran.

Finn was reclined in the driver's seat with his eyes closed when she returned. As Bridget knocked at the window, he cranked up the seat, unlocked the doors and started the car.

"Thanks for waiting."

"That's the job."

They returned to the cottage in near silence as the sun slipped down toward the hills. Instead of coming around to open her car door, Finn didn't give her a backward glance as he walked toward the cottage. He peeled off his jacket and tossed his keys on the table, then went to his bedroom and closed the door without a word.

Nothing like an atmosphere of awkwardness. Her discomfort at the silence made her want to knock on his door and apologize. She took one step toward the hallway, then stopped short. *I did nothing wrong,* she thought, slamming a mental door on her inner voice. She sat down at the kitchen table and threw herself into edits.

Half an hour later, Finn emerged from his room, passed by her and grabbed his jacket. "Need anything?"

"You're going out?" Bridget asked, surprised.

"I'll bring the donkeys out of the rain, and then I have some things to do in town," Finn said, his tone businesslike. "You need time alone to work. I can bring you back a late supper if you don't have anything left from your grocery run. If you know how to make a fire, there's wood by the back door."

"Thanks, I'm fine."

With a curt nod, Finn was out the door. Bridget pinched the bridge of her nose. He would have to be a problem for later.

She returned to her edits, fingers flying over her keyboard as she cut, enhanced, and edited the videos. Her cursor hovered over the section showing her fall. Delete completely or save it? Maybe she would need an outtakes video when inspiration dried up. Her video last July of a kitchen drawer slipping off its casters and dumping everything on the floor got more hits than her original organizing video. Failure was funny, and good for engagement.

She clicked *Save*.

With the video off to Mary for approval, she pulled three highlighters, two colored pens, the binder, and her travel notebook out of her tote bag. She'd been in Ireland three full days and barely scratched the surface on her itinerary or her assignments. Time seemed to go more slowly in Ireland, and everything was taking longer to complete than planned.

The clock on the fireplace mantle chimed on the hour, and Bridget dug a fist into her back to stretch. Three hours she'd been at it, finishing the videos, taking notes, and doing research for her next destinations.

Finn still had not returned.

A loud and petulant growl in her stomach drove Bridget to the kitchen. Her grocery rations were meager, but she boiled a pot of spaghetti and added a bit of butter and salt. A regular Julia Child.

After she washed her dishes and put away her computer and paperwork, she caught herself glancing at the door. *Do you have to keep looking for him every two minutes?* She sat on the couch with a huff, deliberately picking up a novel to keep her thoughts off Finn. Sure, having him as her tour guide made her feel much more comfortable in a strange country. In any other circumstance, she might indulge in the idea of a dalliance with someone like him. The way he gently untangled her hair from that branch. Why was that man bothering her so much that—*oh shoot!*

The water!

She foraged in her bag for the bottle. She dumped the whole bottle into the clean spaghetti pot and set it to boil for a good 20 minutes.

While she waited, she picked up her book and tried to read again. Ten times she read the same paragraph, without a single word comprehended. Her mind was too scattered to concentrate. She picked up her phone and shuffled to the kitchen.

She filmed the pot for a few seconds as it bubbled and roiled. *Can't have people thinking I just drank it right from the stream.* Like Chekhov's gun, she couldn't tell her followers about magic romance water and not show them she drank it. Bridget poured a bit of the water into a mug and sat on the sofa. She recorded for a few seconds to test, but the footage felt off on the heels of the cottage tour video. She needed something new.

She opened the front door to an icy blast of damp air swirling around her. Bridget moved forward, the gravel crunching beneath her feet as she blinked up at the night sky. The clouds had parted to reveal a sky brilliant with stars. The glow of the Milky Way, visible and dazzling, took her breath away.

In the city, she was lucky to see the occasional Big Dipper, or maybe Jupiter or Mars low in the morning sky over the lake. But this? This was unreal. The mountains loomed almost purple in the shadows, highlighting the vivid show of stars above them: glitter above a pool of ink. At once, she felt both insignificant and interconnected—part of something complex and magnificent, immense, and intensely personal. Mystical. Even holy.

She wasn't sure how long she'd stayed outside, enthralled by the expanse before her.

When she finally remembered her phone, she filmed the sky as best she could. She recorded a quick standup, drinking the waterfall water as the cold seeped into her bones, pulling her out of her reverie with shivers.

She slipped from the chill of the night into the embrace of the cozy cottage. While the images she captured of the night sky couldn't possibly capture what she experienced, they were beautiful. She snipped and pasted her outdoor clips into her previous video. As she sent the updated version to Mary, she got a text.

> Waterfall video approved. Nice job!

> Just sent an update with an addition at the end. Check email.

> Love it— don't even have to send to the client. Approved!

Sitting back, a wave of relief washed over her and a lump rose in her throat. *Maybe she could do this thing. Make content. Be an influencer.* With a sniffle, Bridget uploaded the post for all her channels. Immediately, comments began to post.

> @mcallen9280: Gorgeous! Not what I expect from you. <3

@glassbeegle: Like something out of a movie.

@kmcowSING: So cool! On my to-do
list! LYSM

For the next half hour, she posted replies to her commenters. *Keep that engagement up.* A few of the social handles were familiar, as they'd posted on her content before. She clicked on @mcallen9280's account. A mixture of cat reels and crochet videos. She zoomed in on user's profile photo, a young woman with a purple bob and thick cat's-eye glasses with a geotag of Sandpoint, Idaho.

Bridget felt a pang in her chest. @mcallen9280 followed her for organizing content and now she was getting Irish tourism videos. She closed her eyes and silently beseeched, *keep sticking with me, @mcallen9280.*

She shifted in the wooden chair, her backside still achy and sore from her fall. Maybe a bath would ease the ache.

Finn had put up the clear shower curtain liner for her that morning, finally making a shower possible. It took a while that morning for Bridget to master the Tinkertoy-like structure of pipes for the shower head. But right now, a deep, hot soak was calling to her. She fiddled with the spigots until a stream of hot water sprung forth. Steam rose from the surface as she peeled off her clothes and eased herself into the water, her tender bottom getting some relief.

After an indulgent soak, she rose from the tub pink from the heat. The lip of the enamel tub was generous enough for her to perch on the edge as she shaved her legs.

The tub could be styled with a little tray, maybe a book, a glass of wine...even some fresh flowers. Olive mentioned that

Finn's bowls and platters were food safe, so maybe he could make one for her.

As she toweled off, her mind continued to work on styling the tiny vanity sink with the calico curtain around its base. Curtain off, for sure. Maybe a discreet basket for toilet paper, a floating shelf with those cute ceramics that Finn's grandmother had in the front room. Or bud vases with fresh wildflowers.

In her mind's eye, the cottage could be the perfect combination of trendy and traditional. This was her sweet spot, making content that was second nature to her. The kind of content @mcallen9280 wanted.

She brought her towel back to the room, hanging it on the back of her door while she slipped into leggings and a t-shirt for bed. She tackled the living room first, arranging things in an inviting manner, balancing the aesthetic for the entire room. She moved on to the kitchen. Then the bath. She avoided Finn's room—that was off-limits.

But her room...she could make it amazing. She picked up an old silver hairbrush and mirror set from the vanity and searched for something to style it on. Bridget pulled open one of the vanity drawers, in searching vintage items. The left side drawer held a few half-squeezed tubes of arthritis creams, Q-tips and hotel samples of lotion. The right drawer stuck a bit, so she tugged and wiggled it loose. Inside was a jumble of photographs—square black-and-white snapshots from the 1950s and '60s, faded color prints from the 1970s, and a mish-mash of letters, postcards, school programs, and ticket stubs.

She started to close the drawer, but one photograph caught her eye. A little boy, maybe eight years old, cuddled in the lap of an older woman sitting in the old wooden rocker from the parlor. The boy had a shock of black curls, and his eyes were closed tight as his arms wrapped around her neck, the older woman kissing the top of his head.

It had to be Finn.

Well, that wrecked her. She traced her finger along the edge of the photo, remembering what he'd said about his father dying when he was ten. She wanted to pick up that little boy and hug him. Bridget stared at the photo for several moments, then slipped it back into the drawer.

She began to collect items from the room, carefully placing them on the window ledge. Bridget diffused the light from the table lamp with a few tissues across the shade, then arranged the hairbrush set and a figurine of a dancing girl. She surveyed the bookshelf to find something to set the mood. Her fingers stopped on an old red-leather chapbook of Irish poems. When she flipped through it, a pressed flower fell to the rug.

She picked it up carefully, but the tiny blue petals were so fragile they began to disintegrate around the edges. Bridget laid it back into place in its book, the pages naturally falling open to the flower. It was nearly perfect.

She hesitated, then opened the drawer again, taking out the photo of Finn and his grandmother. She propped it up against the book and snapped a photo.

This wasn't part of her HouseHijack assignment, so she didn't need to run it past Mary. Bridget added a caption to the group of photos: "Past and present, traditional and modern. A window to the past, with a bright day on the horizon. #Kildunne #Ireland"

At the last moment, she hesitated. Instead of *Post*, she hit *Save* and sent it to her Drafts folder.

She slipped the photo back into the drawer, placed the trinkets back where they belonged and took the tissues off the lights. As beautiful as that photo was, she couldn't shake the feeling that it crossed a line.

Crossing more lines was the last thing she needed with Finn.

Chapter 12

Penance with Noreen

Keep things professional. Overly familiar. Those words played over in Finn's mind as he shoved the key in the ignition and spun up a handful of gravel to reverse out of the driveway. Carelessness, that's what it was. Her for slipping on the rocks, him for helping her up. Should have left her on the ground with those ridiculous boots. She made it perfectly clear that she didn't need him to help, so that's what he was going to do. Next time, she could figure it out on her own.

Without thought, the car began to head toward Tilleen. In his current mood of self-flagellation, it was what he deserved. The drive wasn't long, but it did require attention. The rat-a-tat of raindrops began again, and the comforting metronome of the wipers took the edge off his thoughts.

A few more turns and he found himself in the heart of Tilleen. The tiny hamlet boasted a compact town square, with a church, three pubs, a handful of shops and several lanes of row homes that seemed to lead from the square like the spokes of a wheel. He eased the car into a spot on Listow Street and turned up his collar against the rain as he ran to the door of number 34.

He gave two sharp raps on the door before turning the knob. "I told you to keep the door locked, Ma!"

A woman's voice from the kitchen called out. "How would you be getting in then? Don't track in the rain. Give a good stomp before you sit, you great rascal."

Noreen Malloy walked out of the kitchen wiping her hands on a tea towel. She hung the towel over the back of the kitchen chair before offering her cheek for a kiss at the front rug.

"Rain's stopped, anyway."

Noreen sniffed. "To what do I owe the pleasure? Something to eat? I have a chicken curry I can get you. Or leftovers from my lunch with Mrs. McIlvaine. Or boxty?" Without waiting for an answer, his mother moved toward the kitchen again.

He tried to protest to no avail. No force in nature was stronger than an Irish mother who was certain you were wasting away to nothing, particularly if she had a crumb of leftovers to pawn off.

In moments, Finn was seated in front of a microwaved feast, comprised of small portions of leftovers and a large bowl of curry. Easier to eat than argue. If there was more than a single bite left on her plate, Noreen routinely boxed it up for later. Surely the bane of every waiter in the county.

She pulled out the chair next to him. "I hear there's a young woman staying at Gran's cottage with you."

Finn put down his fork. The straightforward nature of the inquiry wasn't innocent enough to disguise the trap that was being set. "That didn't take long."

"Had four calls about it yesterday." Father Tim was efficient, no question. "Shame I had to hear from Molly Hannigan and not my own son that he's got a lady friend." She got up again and went back to the kitchen.

"Definitely not a lady friend, ma. She's renting the cottage from me."

"After you put up such a fuss about Bernie's offer? Now you want to rent your house out?" Somehow another dinner roll and small side of green beans appeared on the table.

"We saw one of Bernie's houses. That's where Bridget was supposed to stay for nearly a month. It was an old cottage on the thruway, near the O'Mahoney place. Would you believe there were buckets to catch the roof leaks and paper peeling off the walls?"

His mother sniffed. "I suppose you couldn't let her stay in such a place. But I'm sure Fiona or Maggie could put you up. Even Cillian has that nice sofa. Or I can put a cot in my sewing room."

"And risk being smothered by bolts of fabric?" Finn dodged a swat. "I'm not going anywhere, Ma. Lots of guest houses have on-site hosts. Besides, she's hired me to take her about. Like Cillian does for his Americans."

Her eyebrows raised. "Driving around an American girl. I'd pay a pretty penny to see that." She sniffed as she put her teacup to her lips.

"The perfect gentleman host." Finn brought his mother's hand up to his mouth for an exaggerated kiss.

Noreen responded with a weak slap at his hand. "I'll not have you up there making us the talk of the parish, Finn."

"Strictly professional, Ma." Those words carried a sting. "I even bought a lock for Gran's bedroom door."

Noreen pursed her lips, registering her disapproval without saying a word. That stare had caused Finn to confess to many a sin over the years. But he held steady, meeting her gaze with an earnest expression. The verdict returned: "Bring her to dinner here on Friday, then."

Finn groaned, "No, Ma..."

"I want to meet this girl myself and feed her a decent meal." She raised one hand to stop his protestations. "After all, I've seen your refrigerator."

"Just the three of us, Ma?" Perhaps he could get away with not having the whole of the family together on an off night.

"Would you be having me turn away your sisters and my grandchildren?" He stifled a groan.

Noreen's expression grew serious. "Finny, what about this job Cillian mentioned? Claire McKibbon's family is it?"

"Ma...don't get all excited."

"This fuss with the American girl, is it making you put off a good living? If Claire gets wind of you living with this young woman—"

"Ma, she's renting a room. If the McKibbon job depends on whether I have someone in my house, then it's not worth having." He shoveled the last bite from the plate in his mouth and pushed away from the table with his plate, conditioned from a young age to immediately wash and dry his dishes.

Noreen swiveled in her chair to track him as he left the room. "Claire's a nice girl, Finn. Good family."

"Not happening, Ma."

His mother changed tactics. "While I've got you here...I have just a few little tasks that need doing."

Finn returned that evening just shy of 11 p.m. The cottage was dark and quiet; the curtains in the front room were closed tight but the banked red embers had a soft glow, giving off a bit of heat. Bridget's computer was on the kitchen table, closed.

He hung his coat on the back of a chair and looked around the room.

Something was different.

At the mantel, he saw his first clue. Gran's Irish pottery was clustered into groups, not spaced out evenly along the mantelpiece. The doilies had been swept away from the tabletops, and there was a vase with greenery and a bit of red ribbon. Who knows where she found it.

Walking to the kitchen, he clicked on the light switch and stood in awe. All the washing up was done, even the things that had been lying in the sink for a few days. Every surface was scrubbed clean. Without even meaning to, he opened the cabinet next to the sink. The glasses and bowls were spaced and turned so every pattern was the same direction. A wooden cutting board was set on the countertop with an orange, a paring knife and again, some greenery.

Nothing looked bad, and he couldn't complain that she tidied up the place, but it still felt off.

He pulled out his keys, tossing them onto the counter. They skittered into the sink, creating a louder noise than he anticipated. He froze for a moment, waiting to hear a sound that would indicate Bridget was awake. Instead, he heard the gentle rumble of snoring through the wall. Unbidden, an image of her sleeping form rose in his mind's eye.

"Guess she could sleep well enough after her fall," he murmured, fishing the keys out of the clean sink. He saw her water bottle washed and drying on a tea towel and wondered if she'd drunk the water from Eirhann. He didn't let himself speculate on who she'd dream about.

If she could remember not to turn on the kitchen light and wake the damn donkeys, or decide to wallpaper the place at 4 a.m., he might get a full night's sleep.

"Cabinets and whatnots," he muttered. Could there be

anything more ridiculous in the world than someone making a living organizing cupboards?

Other than a brief flirtation with Facebook when he was eleven, Finn had sworn off social media. Bunch of cranks, show-offs and fakers, cherry-picking the best of their sorry lives to make others feel worse. He never had a reason to engage with social media. Until now.

Finn picked up his phone. A couple of swipes and he created an account on one of the social media apps. Bridget said she was on most of the apps, cross-posting content. With the tiny magnifying glass, he attempted to plug in "cabinets and countertops and closets." A whopping 12 million videos returned.

"Ridiculous," he muttered, tossing the phone to the side. How could a person even watch 12 million videos? Who had the time to make that many videos?

He picked up the phone again, scrolling through the videos to try and catch a glimpse. Nothing. He changed the search bar to "cabinets countertops closets and waterfall."

Voila! Bridget's face appeared as the cover photo for the first video on the screen under the title, "Putting the 'Fall' in Waterfall at Eirhann." He hit *Play*.

Immediately, he understood why Bridget had him shoot the directions and angles she did. The falls looked glorious and mystical, and the small screen transformed Bridget into a wild, enchanting persona. From the flash of her gray eyes to her wet and wispy curls, she looked like she was born to be in Ireland. She even included a tiny bit of her fall, referencing a sore behind in the caption.

At the end of the video, the scene changed. She was outside in the dark, right in front of the cottage. He leaned in to listen closely, not wanting to raise the volume.

"Before I take my drink from the falls, I had to show you

the sky. I know my camera can't do it justice, but look." She flipped the screen of the phone and the star-filled expanse twinkled dimly on the screen for several seconds. Bridget's face returned, looking enraptured, her eyes sparkling in the glow of the screen.

"All I can tell you is that living my whole life in Chicago, in a big city...I've never seen the stars like this. I'm going to take a drink of the water from Eirhann Waterfall, well-boiled and hopefully safe. I don't know that I'll dream of my true love, but after tonight, I do believe there's magic in Ireland. Now, off to bed, so I can dream of my one true love. Sweet dreams!"

He played the video two more times, then walked outside. The clouds had once again filled the sky, hiding the stars and galaxies from view. Disappointed, he closed the door and picked up the phone again. He noticed more than 50 comments already on the video.

He switched to the comment view. It was like reading in a different language.

"OMG that waterfall is giving fairytales!"

"#GOALS"

Finn froze when he scrolled to:

"Who's holding the camera? Hope he's the one in your dreams!"

He scanned the video once again, looking for some sign that he was in the shot. Nothing.

Wait.

A snippet of his voice came through in the video of her fall. *Great.*

Finn began to scroll through Bridget's other content. Wild to think that people cared this much about organizing their sock drawers. It struck him that most of the videos were from her own home, the apartment she shared with her roommate. It was well-appointed and modern, with sleek appliances and minimalist furniture. Couldn't be more in contrast to his little cottage.

That apartment reflected who she was. And it was the polar opposite of him.

If he was smart, he'd remember that.

Chapter 13

Donkeys and Hauntings

The house was dark when Bridget woke the next morning, at a near-normal 6:30 a.m. She sipped her tea by the light of her phone screen then double-checked the plan for the day. If she was going to be in charge, it was up to her to stay on the schedule.

When she heard Finn enter the bathroom, she slipped back to her bedroom to make sure she was ready to go at a moment's notice. She was mid-mascara at the vanity when a sharp rap on her bedroom door made her jump.

"Come in."

Finn, still damp from his shower, leaned in the doorway wearing jeans and an unbuttoned flannel shirt over a dark tee. His face was freshly shaved, and the faint scent of soap hung about him. He rubbed the back of his neck. "Morning. Sleep well?"

So we're back on speaking terms, then? "Yes, thanks."

"Come out to the barn then. I want you to see what needs doing in case you want to turn the kitchen lights on some morning. You escaped this the other day."

"Five minutes?"

He nodded. "I'll be out back."

She took a moment to compose herself. All her talk about keeping things professional and he shows up at her bedroom door looking damp and hot.

"And Bridget?" he called out. "Wear the rubber boots—you'll likely get shite on them."

Just like that, the vibe was gone.

It was bright enough in the pre-dawn glow to walk to the barn behind the cottage without a light. As they neared, Bridget could hear the animals rustling inside.

With a practiced move, Finn threw the bolt to open the door and switched on a set of lights hanging from the rafters. The barn smelled of animals and fresh hay, oddly pleasant to her city sensibilities. Hay covered the clean and well-kept floors near the animal stalls along the side.

"I didn't expect it to have lights," Bridget remarked.

"It's my workshop as well. I ran electric out here when I moved in with Gran." Finn gestured to the long table to the right, covered with bits of wood, vises, and other equipment she didn't recognize. Bridget wandered toward the table, running her finger over its fine layer of sawdust, noting woodworking projects in various states of completion while Finn walked to the back wall of the barn.

Two brown donkeys stood in stalls on the far side of the barn, one with a thatch of black hair on his head, the other with a large white spot on his side. Finn called out to her, "These are Tim and Tom. Tim's got the spot, like the dot on the 'I' in his name. Tom's got the long whiskers and is the devil's own."

He knocked off the top of a large bin with his elbow as he

picked up a pail to scoop a load of pellets. "One bucket in each of their troughs should do it, and if they look like their water is low, there's a hose round the corner. That will buy you enough time to have your breakfast in peace. But be sure to cover the feed again—mice go mad for the grain."

Despite her shudder at the thought of mice, Bridget stepped in front of Tim's stall, and he looked at her with baleful eyes. "Is it ok if I pet them?"

Finn stepped up next to her, reaching out to give Tim a pat on his nose and got appreciative nickering in response. He vaguely moved toward Tom and the donkey lunged forward as if to bite.

"Try petting Tim. As you see, Tom is a grumpy old wretch and likes to bite."

Bridget eyed Tom warily, giving him a wide berth as she moved closer to Tim's stall. She touched the donkey's snout cautiously, surprised by the feel of his rough, wiry hair. He raised and lowered his head several times under her palm.

"He's looking for a scratch, that one. Behind his ears is his favorite." Bridget dutifully scratched as Finn took the empty bucket from the feed troughs and hung it on a peg.

"I'm going to turn them out to graze, stand clear." Finn opened the door of Tom's stall and led him to the back door. "You don't need to do this in the mornings, I'll take care of it. But always double check that the front door is closed and latched. Tom's been known to escape by running at me full force, and I've a scar on my forearm courtesy of his teeth."

Bridget moved to the door, pulling the handle secure. Finn patted the cantankerous donkey, leading it out into the grassy area behind the yard. It bucked and pulled at him as they walked together, Finn alternating between patting its back and tugging his lead. He returned to fetch Tim.

"Can I come?" she asked.

Finn nodded, and the two walked to the back of the barn together. Bridget reached out to gently pat the side of the donkey and was rewarded with a nuzzle. "He likes you," Finn said.

"He's very sweet," she replied, running her hand down his broad back. "I never had animals when I was a kid. My mother is allergic to cats, and my stepdad said our apartment was too small for a dog."

A roof-like structure jutted off the back of the barn, which Bridget surmised was for sheltering the donkeys during rough weather. A short fence led them to the pasture gate, and the donkeys ambled through as the bright glow of sunrise came over the field. The pasture behind the cottage was thick with scrabbly grasses and shrubs punctuating the large expanse. Once Tim was through the pasture gate, Tom turned as if to weigh his options, then took off at a half-hearted pace to join his friend.

"They won't run away?"

Finn shook his head. "As long as they're in the field, they're fine. It's been years since they've gotten into mischief from there. But give Tom an opportunity to leave out the other door, and there's hell to pay. The last time, we found him almost 30 kilometers away and stealing food from someone's pony barn."

"They were your grandmother's animals?"

Finn nodded. "She had goats and sheep and chickens at one time, but as she got older, she either gave those away or didn't replace them. Tim and Tom were her 'good boys' as she called them, so I didn't have the heart to give them up. I've never seen Tom behave as well as when she was around. She had this thing where Tom would come straightaway when she'd whistle, and trot alongside her like he was a hunting dog. Besides, it was part of the package—getting her house meant getting her donkeys."

He brushed off a bit of hay from his jacket. "What's the plan today, Boss Lady?"

"Olive has the ring light in, so let's do one of the farther-out places and pick it up on our way."

Ballymourn Castle was a two-and-a-half-hour drive from the cottage. Their quick stop at The Olive Branch stretched to almost an hour-long visit. By the time they arrived at the castle, the temperature had dropped and the winds kicked up. Bridget's stomach was growling and a migraine threatened. Not a promising start.

"Have you ever been here?" she asked, doing a quick re-read of her binder entry. "The main structure dates back to the 1300s."

"Does it now?" Finn looked decidedly unimpressed. "All that history polished up and roped off for tourists now. All I can say is, at 24 quid for entry—plus parking!—they better let you take a nap in the beds."

"Don't worry, I've got it."

"How much spending money do they give you, anyway?"

She frowned. "My contract gives me a stipend of $10,000 for expenses—in American dollars, of course—and then hiring you took up more than $5,000 with the conversion rates. I had to use it for my expensive last-minute flight, too. About $1,000 a week for food, tickets, everything."

"So about $150 a day, then? Give or take?" He sounded upset. "And you want to spend half of it to tour this old ruin?" He shook his head.

"You don't have to come," she said, irritation threading through her voice. Bold of Finn to criticize her spending when his services took up most of her budget. "Stay in the car if you're going to be a grump about it."

"You're not paying me for a cheery mood," he retorted. "Fine. I'll stay here."

"Fine." Picking up her binder and her tote bag, she double-checked to make sure she had her equipment and new ring light ready.

The dustup with Finn didn't dampen Bridget's excitement to tour the castle. The larger hall was appointed with faded flags and banners, identifying the families that had ownership of the castle, before and after the English invaded under Oliver Cromwell in the 1600s. Some furniture was in the rooms—a long trestle table, a few heavy carved chairs—but in general, the rooms were sparse. Most of the rooms were cordoned off with ropes, but Bridget leaned in to get a better look.

"Not exactly Buckingham Palace, is it."

Bridget spun to see Finn standing with his hands in his pockets, nodding toward the room. "Drafty old place. The electric lights are a sight better than smoky tallow candles would have been. Or peat in the fireplace."

"You made it." She couldn't help but smile up at him.

"Had to make sure the ghosts didn't get you," he said gruffly.

"Ghosts?"

He quirked his lips. "They didn't tell you about the ghosts? Lady Slane lived here in about 1350 or so. While her husband was off fighting, she brought a young man named Maurice to her bed. Her husband came home and found them in his bedroom. She thought quick, and claimed he was an intruder. The husband stabbed poor Maury through the heart and he died on the bedroom floor. They say he haunts this place even today."

"That's grim. Poor Maury."

He grinned. "That's nothing for Irish history."

They moved through the great hall to a wooden staircase

that took them to the second floor. The stairs were sturdy and built safely with a handrail, but Bridget still pressed her hand against the cool stone wall for balance, the selfie stick bobbling in her hand.

"Here, put that away. I'll be your camera person," he said.

At the top of tower staircase was a large gothic door, which Finn pushed open for her. As their eyes adjusted to the darkness, they saw two rooms, one with a straw-stuffed mattress on a wooden frame bed, the other with pallets on the floor. Both had thin, narrow windows cut into the walls, floor to ceiling. "The scene of the murder," Finn whispered.

Bridget shivered as he spoke. Ireland seemed to have a thinner veil between natural and supernatural. "That's completely creepy. It's freezing in here."

Finn shrugged. "Poor Maurice was probably happy to have a bed and a warm body to curl up with, especially on a day like today. Those windows are angled so arrows couldn't get you. But they probably had heavy drapes to keep the cold out in winter. Here, you want me to film?"

"What was the woman's name again?"

"Lady Slane." Bridget nodded and signaled to begin recording.

"Hello, my friends! Today, thanks to HouseHijack we're at Ballymourn Castle. Did you know that the Irish were the people who basically invented Halloween? And do I have a ghost story for you. This castle dates back to about 1250, and I have it on good authority—" her gaze flickered toward Finn – "that this was the site of a gruesome murder. Lady Slane's husband had gone off to battle, and while he was gone, she took a man named Maurice to her bed. When her husband came home early, he stabbed poor Maurice in the heart. They say his ghost still walks the castle walls today."

Before she could finish talking, the gothic door behind

them creaked and moved a good six inches toward closing, then stopped.

Bridget froze. Finn grabbed her hand and she gripped him tight. Every hair on her arms stood straight up.

"What the fuck was that?" he whispered, his eyes wide.

"I think we're done here, ok?" Bridget's voice squeaked.

"Yeah, ok," Finn said, steering her with purpose towards the staircase. "Sorry, Maury," he called over his shoulder. "Happy hauntings, mate!"

There was no argument as they both headed directly to the exit. The modern gift shop attached to the castle offered a sparse assortment of sandwiches and pastries in the off-season, but the girl behind the counter offered a complimentary cup of tea to make up for lack of options. Finn began to chat her up.

"So, there's ghosts here?"

"Oh, aye. You know the legend of the young lover?"

"Maurice, is it?"

"That's the one," she said, handing over cheese sandwiches and two cups of tea in Styrofoam cups. "He's been known to fuss with the lights and slam doors."

"I think we just saw him," Bridget said, pulling out her phone. "The door started to close as we were recording!"

She advanced to the end of the video. "...they say his ghost still walks the castle walls today." Instead of the door creaking, the audio began to make a loud humming noise. Bridget swiveled to look at Finn, eyes wide as her own. "That...that wasn't what happened. The door creaked and almost closed!"

The girl behind the counter made a subtle sign of the cross. "Must be angry today."

Bridget saw Finn's hand twitch to cross himself as well, but he restrained himself. "I think we'll take our tea and eat on the way out."

She wasn't about to argue.

Chapter 14

Beech Bowls

Over the next few days, they settled into a comfortable pattern. Bridget would wake up, consult the binder, then Finn would grumble as they headed off to whatever destination was on the agenda. But he never refused or remained in the car. He was the holder of the ring light, the car attendant and the lunch planner, but it was always Bridget's direction they followed.

He was the help.

In truth, the work wasn't hard. He finagled their travel agenda to return late on Friday–the perfect excuse to beg off dinner at his mother's. And if he was honest, he enjoyed exploring without a worry about cost or schedule. This independence was one of the few perks of not having a steady job.

Their normal fare consisted of old houses, bleak gardens and every shop that sold Irish linens, woolens, pottery, or jewelry. Bridget became a different person when she was on camera, chipper and bright, chatty and effusive. She complimented every display, every artist's piece, and gushed about the charms of every shop and owner.

140

Old men, teens, children—they all got a starring role in her little videos. Most of them pulled out their phones to follow her on the spot. Luckily Bridget was a sucker for a pub, and he was happy to eat and drink on her dime.

The line between business colleagues and roommates was trickier, especially sharing a 700-square-foot cottage. In the evenings, they'd share a quick meal, alternating cooking responsibilities. When the weekend came around, Bridget insisted that Saturday and Sunday were his days off from being her porter, even though he'd offered to work every day.

But the cottage was small, and the urge to make himself scarce to give her space was always in the back of his mind.

Late Saturday afternoon, Bridget was hunched over her computer, sending ad codes and links to her client and pulling reports on her reach and impressions. Finn took the opportunity to slip out to the barn.

Olive was clamoring for another bowl or plate, but he'd been saving a piece of wood to shape. Sometimes the wood revealed itself to him in the rough cut, giving clues to what would best show the intricate lacy patterns of the spalting. A few hours of shaping and sanding, and a long, narrow platter was revealed. A few more passes with fine sandpaper would make it baby-smooth. Sanding he did in the barn, but oiling and buffing required the less dusty house.

"What's that?" Bridget looked up from the table, binder and paperwork spread around her, speckled with her multi-colored highlighters.

"Olive was looking for some larger pieces, and I've almost finished this one," said Finn.

She craned her neck over her laptop. "What is it?"

"A serving plate."

"Can I see?"

"I'll bring it over." Finn carefully laid the platter on a few sheets of newspaper on the table, clearing a large space.

Bridget closed her laptop and stood next to him, running her fingers delicately over the fact of the platter, tracing the grain lines of the wood. "What wood is this again?"

"Spalted beech."

"What does spalted mean?"

Finn leaned over her pointing out the deep discolorations that made patterns in the wood. "See these lines? A fungus crept along a sick or dead tree. It makes this pattern, and if you get the right cut of wood, you can show it off."

"It's beautiful. Do you cut the wood yourself?"

"Sometimes. There's beech trees on the back of Gran's property, and while I've done it, it's a big job. Lately, I buy from a man I know near Tipperary."

Bridget traced her fingers along the spalting lines, brushing up against his own fingers. "What do you do next?"

She was making him lose his concentration, being this close.

"I oil it—tung oil. It's strong, stinks to high heaven, but it brings out the color."

"Can I watch?"

A little flicker of pride and a desire to show off his skills kindled inside him. "Sure." He went under the sink in the kitchen and brought out a cotton rag and the container of tung oil. He poured a tiny circle of oil in the center of the platter and began to rub it into the wood in a steady, circular motion. Bridget remained at his elbow, watching as the patterns in the wood became more vivid and pronounced.

"You want to try?" He was rewarded with an eager smile. "Take it like this." He handed her the cloth, and put his hand over hers, guiding it in concentric circles. "If you feel the cloth snag or catch, let me know. But it should be well-sanded."

He stood behind her as Bridget eased the cloth over the wood, turning it to thoroughly coat each curved edge. The top of her head was almost at his cheek, so close that he could detect the citrus scent of her shampoo even through the pungent smell of tung oil. Bridget's elbow brushed against his stomach as she rubbed the oil in. After a few minutes, she looked back at him. "Is this enough?"

He cleared his throat. "Bang on. Let it sit for a while, then we'll wipe it down, flip it over and do the backside," he said. He silently berated himself. *Could that have sounded any more sexual?*

She turned toward him, their hands connecting on the cloth. For a few heartbeats, neither moved.

Her lips parted as if she was preparing to speak, but no sound came out. If he leaned in just a little more, he could kiss her. And if he did that, there would be no turning back. The thoughts bounced around his brain:

She's your customer. You're the help.

You have to live with her for two more weeks.

Get hold of yourself.

Finn broke the tension by grabbing the cloth from her hands. "Now we let it sit for half an hour." Bridget's mouth snapped shut, and she moved around the table back to her computer. "Good. I have about that much more work to do. Then I think I'll go to bed early."

Finn gave her a quick nod. "I'll just clean up then."

"Finn?"

He turned toward her, tamping down the little flicker of hope that sparked in him.

"Would you like a day off tomorrow? Except for driving me to the train station?"

A flash of hurt at the thought of her traveling without him. "Where will you be going, then?"

She walked over to her tote bag, pulling out the binder. "There's a day cruise to one of the coastal islands—North Dun? —from Condalk. It's a knitter's tour."

"You knit?"

"Not really. Not well at least. My grandmother taught me when I was in middle school, but I've made the odd scarf. And I mean odd." Bridget smiled.

The idea of a knitting holiday held absolutely no appeal to Finn, but still he wavered. "You sure you don't want me to take you?"

"It's got to be hard to share your house. You haven't had a moment to yourself since I arrived."

"You've leased it—fair's fair."

"I know. But this is easy enough by train, and it will give you a bit of a break from me." Her eyes flickered up to meet his gaze.

"Are you back the same day?"

She flipped through her flyer. "I have to take the 7:18 out in the morning, and if all goes well, I'll be home tomorrow night around 8:30."

"I'll pick you up then." It was on the tip of his tongue to offer again to join her, but he squelched that urge. She was right—they negotiated a few days off from escorting her.

Maybe she wanted time away from him.

Maybe he needed time away from her.

His alarm clock woke him at 5:30 the next morning. He could hear Bridget already in the shower, so he dragged on his pants and boots to head out to the barn. Opening the back door, he was hit with a blast of cold wind, enough to make him wince as he trudged through the grass.

Finn made quick work of turning out the donkeys, then came back inside to see Bridget dressed and eating breakfast. "It's pretty grim outside, you sure you want to go today?"

Bridget paused. "Unless you think it's going to be a rotten day?"

"It's going to be windy, for sure. Especially out on the islands."

"Should I go?"

There was a weight to this question, a level of trust. Was she really going to defer to him? After all her talk about doing things herself?

But then, the nagging doubt. *She wants a day without you. She just doesn't want to say it.*

His voice was gruff. "Dress warm, you'll be fine."

They were out the door in short order and made the trip to the train station in near silence. The wind swelled as they drove, to the point where Finn kept both hands on the wheel to steady the car in the gusts. As he pulled into the carpark for the train station, he couldn't help himself.

"You sure you're good for this cold? You've got warm things?" *I sound like a granny.*

Bridget chuckled. "You know I'm from a place nicknamed 'The Windy City,' right? I've had wind gusts nearly blow me over while walking to work. It's not even freezing right now."

"It's close," he grumbled. Why was he making such a fool of himself this morning?

"I'll be fine." She patted his arm, then reached behind him to grab her backpack. "I'll see you tonight at 8:30, ok?" She pulled the hood of her coat up, grabbing the collar around her neck tighter as she sprinted toward the station.

Finn kept the car in park, tapping his thumbs against the wheel.

I'll just stay in the lot until she gets her ticket.

I'll just stay to make sure the train's on time.

I'll just stay and watch to make sure she doesn't miss it.

When the train finally pulled out of the station, he started the car and headed home. There was nothing else to stay for.

Finn filled the day with chores around the house, replacing light bulbs in the bathroom, fixing the wonky drawer in the kitchen, and patching up a few chips in the floorboards. What he didn't have to do was straighten up. Bridget's orderly influence was everywhere. Not a paper out of place, all Gran's knickknacks at the mantle grouped together and somehow made more appealing. Those little touches that had felt like a violation on her first days somehow put a breath of fresh air into the place.

He got out the mop, bucket, and dust cloths to make sure everything was spic-and-span for his guest. Kitchen, parlor, his room, the bathroom...all were neat as a pin in no time. There was just one more room to do.

Finn paused outside Bridget's bedroom. Was it intruding, going in her room to clean when she wasn't home? It wasn't as though he'd disturb anything, but it still seemed like a violation of privacy.

"For the love of Pete, hotels have room service, don't they?" he muttered. Irritated at his own reluctance, Finn pushed the door wide and went in.

The gut punch he expected from walking into Gran's room didn't come. Somehow, the room was both Gran's, yet unmistakably Bridget's. The little dressing table with Gran's silver-backed hairbrushes had a burnished glow on them, like someone had taken a cloth to rub the tarnish clear. The windows and corners were free of cobwebs, and every surface was clean to the touch. On the wooden chair in the corner,

Bridget had her suitcases stacked. The top one was open, with sensible packing cubes. Across the back of the chair was hung a cloth he recognized from the linen closet. It was slightly damp, as though she'd washed it and wrung it dry after using it to clean the room.

He was a little guilty at how dusty this room must have been that first night. After Gran's funeral, he and his siblings had deep-cleaned the house after the undertakers had left. But since then, it was rare he'd gone in.

She'd done it all, not saying a word.

He picked up his mop and scrubbed the floors with vigor. The least he could do.

By late afternoon, the house was too quiet. The silence was making him stir crazy.

Jotting down a quick list, he drove back into the village to pick up a few things—washing-up liquid, and maybe pick up a new bathmat and shower curtain to go over the liner. While Bridget hadn't objected to the plastic liner, it would make the bath nicer.

He wandered for an hour or two, idly browsing through a few shops and trying to kill time. On Sundays, the stores in Killathay closed early. By five o'clock., he found himself at Tommy's, his hands curled around a pint.

"This seat taken?"

Claire McKibbon's smile was genuine, but a little tired. As Finn started to speak, she raised her hand. "Look, I wanted to apologize."

The surprise must have been so evident on Finn's face that she laughed. "I'm not trying to chase you down, I promise. I'm here with my friends. But when I saw you...I want to talk to you." She gestured toward a group of two other women in their early twenties, making no effort to hide their staring.

He gestured for her to sit on the stool next to his.

"Can I get another pint, Joe?" she called over to the bartender. Turning back to Finn, she added, "If you've been getting half the grief I've gotten after the factory scene, you must be near sick of me."

"No, I mean..."

"Half of Killathay has us standing up together at St. Brendan's by New Year's, thanks to my mum, no matter how much I try to tell her that's not the case. I'm truly sorry that it's caused you such grief. This whole situation's been blown way out of proportion."

Finn breathed an exaggerated sigh and smiled. "I've gotten it from every end, it's true."

The bartender brought over Claire's pint and she took a healthy swallow. "I appreciate what you did to Roddy. I do feel terrible that you got the boot for it."

Finn shrugged. "I'm sorry I left you hanging for supper last weekend. It's just that—"

She cut him off. "The American woman you're driving. Something about a train, then?"

He nodded. "Got her bag stuck and couldn't get loose. By the time I wrenched it free, we were halfway to Tralee."

Claire laughed. "You sounded so angry in your voicemail, I can just imagine that poor American not knowing what to make of you." She skimmed the rim of her pint with her finger. "Where's she today?"

"Believe it or not, she took another train, this time to North Dun."

"With her luck she might end up in Belfast." Claire laughed again. "Poor thing. You were kind to rent a room to her." She took another sip of Guinness.

"You heard that." Finn squirmed. "She was in a tight spot, so I offered her my Gran's old room.

"You're driving her around, seeing the sights?" As casual as Claire's tone was, Finn was fully aware that every word must be well-considered. "She's here until the 23rd, and offered me more than my skinflint brother does to drive her. I take her around to her destinations."

Claire turned around on the stool, resting her elbows on the bar behind her as she nodded. "Good of you to give up your whole December for her."

"Pays well."

"What will you be doing when she goes back to the States?"

Here it was. "I suppose I'll be asking you to set up a meeting again with your dad."

Claire gave a bright smile, spinning back around toward the bar. "I know he'd help you, Finn. I'll tell him that you'll reach out after you're done being a tour guide." She slipped off her stool, leaning over the bar to put a fiver near the tap as she picked up her glass.

She put a hand on his shoulder. "Thanks for understanding."

Finn nodded as she slipped off to her mates. Not as bad as he feared. In a town as small as Killathay, it was inevitable that he'd need to face her to make amends.

Still, he was glad Bridget wasn't around to see it.

Over the next two hours, Finn glanced at his phone every few minutes, keeping tabs on the time and checking for a call or text from Bridget saying she was safely on the train.

At 7:30 p.m., he left the pub and waited in the car at the station.

At 8:00 p.m., he waited on the platform, shivering in the wind.

At 8:30 p.m., the train rolled in, and Finn felt his heart

speed up. He scanned the train cars, trying to make out Bridget among the shadowy figures disembarking. The late Sunday train wasn't very full, but a few dozen people disembarked from the train.

None of them were Bridget.

Chapter 15

Seal of Disapproval

Bridget collected her gear well before her stop in Condalk, happy to see the sun peeking through the clouds. First to the door, she peered through the train windows at a man with a donkey cart set up just past the station who was braiding St. Brigid's crosses on a folding stool, an obvious bait for tourists to get a photo for a tip.

Sure enough, a guided tour exited from another train car, making a beeline for the man. Bridget smiled at the thought of Finn rolling his eyes at such touristy behavior. Hanging around with Finn was turning her into a travel snob.

The ferry dock was about a mile and half from the train station. Bridget paused a moment, weighing her options. A shuttle bus was loading folks for a few pounds each to cover the short jaunt, but one of Finn's favorite (and more annoying) refrains echoed in her mind: "Just a stretch of the legs, Boss Lady."

The gift shops in Condalk were clustered along the well-traveled route from station to dock, and Bridget noted the windows were full of the same trinkets and souvenirs as in Killathay. As much as she groused about Finn's strong opinions, he did steer her toward quality shops, like Olive's.

The wind picked up as she drew closer to the seashore, and Bridget ducked into a yarn shop to get out of the wind and put on her hat. The door blew wide as she opened it, leaving her to struggle to shut it all the way.

"Good morning! Bringing the wind in with you today?" A young woman with jet-black hair and pink cats-eye glasses waved at her from behind the register.

"Sorry, yes. I needed to pop in and get my hat on. Had to cover my ears." She dug her knit cap out of her bag then looked up, taking in the displays around the shop. The walls and tables were covered with scarves, hats, blankets, sweaters, vests, and all sorts of knitwear, no two pieces alike. "Are these all hand-made?" Bridget asked, fingering the stitching on one of the scarves.

The shopgirl grinned, lifting up her hands to show needles, yarn and about six inches of what looked to be a sleeve. "By yours truly, for the most part."

"You made them, all of them?" Bridget looked around the room, at the dozens of pieces.

"I knit when I'm anxious...so I knit a lot." She laid down her needles and yarn and came around the counter. "They're based on traditional patterns and stitches, but I do my own dyeing, so the colors are definitely not the traditional bleached-off-the-sheep cream color. I'm Aoife."

"Bridget." She reached into her bag again, this time for her tripod. "Listen, I'm doing a bunch of social media videos on my trip, would you mind if I filmed you and your shop?"

"Like for Instagram?"

"Instagram, TikTok...I've been documenting my stay."

"Do you have a load of followers then?" Aoife leaned on the counter, her chandelier earrings swinging forward.

"Just hit to 100,000 on Instagram."

A wide smile spread across Aoife's face. "Fuck yeah, let's do this."

While Bridget set up the tripod and ring light, Aoife looked up @CabinetsCountertopsClosets on her phone. "Why do you have that name if you do travel content?" she asked, swiping through Bridget's videos.

"I mostly do organizing videos." Bridget could feel her coolness cred slipping away. "What's your shop's name?"

"Aoife's Nook," she replied, still scanning the videos. "Who's the guy? Is that your—" Aoife snuck a glance at her left hand "—partner?"

"No, I mean...what guy?"

Aoife gave her a level look. "There's obviously someone filming you, and you can hear him when you slip on that waterfall."

"I hired a driver for the trip." She felt her cheeks get warm. *Does every emotion have to show on my face?* "I'll get started in this corner. Anything you want to highlight?"

Aoife thought for a moment, then pulled a few things from the front window. "These bags are kind of popular now. I sold two last week." She set out three crossbody bags, knit with bright orange and yellow yarn. "Do you need me to say anything?"

Bridget fiddled with her phone, getting the right brightness settings, and extending the tripod a bit higher. "I'll introduce you and if you want to give out the address and the website at the end, that's great."

She nodded, wringing her hands a bit. "Do it quick before I become a coward."

Bridget hit record and stepped into the shot. "I'm here at Aoife's Nook in Condalk, where I've discovered some truly original hand-knit treasures. You'll see knitwear in traditional colors all over Ireland, mostly cream and gray and the occasional blue or green. But owner Aoife Wilson dyes her own yarn, and the colors are gorgeous."

Bridget stopped short, saying nothing for a second or two.

"Do I talk now?" asked Aoife.

"Sorry, I'm just getting some dead space so I can edit in footage of the bags. I'll come to you in just a second."

Another beat went by. Bridget picked up one of the crossbody bags. "Super cute and functional. Aoife, tell us a little about your shop."

Aoife stared straight into the camera. "Fuck, I completely forgot what I am supposed to say."

Bridget grinned. "No worries. I can edit like a pro. Just tell me the name of the shop, the address, website if you have it and I'll do the rest."

With a wide-eyed nod, Aoife swallowed hard.

"I'll start again. Aoife, tell us a little about your shop."

"Aoife's Nook, on Ryson Street in Condalk. Follow us on Instagram at @AoifesNookCondalk."

Aoife looked over at Bridget. "Fuck, that was too fast, wasn't it."

"You want to try it again?"

By the time she left the shop, Aoife's piece of the video was smooth and natural, and she sent Bridget off with her gratitude, a hug, and a knit headband in a rich indigo color —as long as Bridget promised to wear it for a future video.

One piece of content down. A few more videos in the can

and maybe she could relax a bit. The demands of social posting starting to wear on her. In the back of her mind, she was brainstorming what she could post, how to make it look different, how to connect with her followers. If she could get ahead, maybe she could spend a day relaxing with Finn.

At the thought of Finn, she felt her heart thrum in her chest. Yesterday, standing together as she oiled the platter, did he feel the same tension between them? When he covered her hand with his, did he feel the same pull?

Is that why I ran away to Condalk for the day?

Bridget shook her head to clear her thoughts. A quick glance at her watch prompted her to set off at a brisk pace. If she missed the ferry out to the island, it would be two hours to the next one. The bells on the boat chimed that departure was imminent, and she boarded with a few minutes to spare before the gangway was rolled away.

Despite the choppy water and high winds, she was determined to stay on the deck of the boat to get footage of Condalk from the sea. But after a few minutes, her hands became too stiff and cold to hold the phone safely. She retreated to the somewhat-warmer seating area, with long wooden benches, contained within thick plastic sheeting.

At the island dock, the metal gangway was slick from the spray as the wind drove the water against the rocks, spraying a fine mist around the boat. Bridget pulled her hat down tight around her ears and made her way to the top of the pier. A tiny older man with tufts of white hair sticking out around his ears was waving madly, holding a sign that read, "Knitter's Tour."

Hitching her bag on her shoulder, Bridget made a beeline for him. Several of the ladies from the boat joined her, but Bridget was the youngest by far.

"I'm Michael, your tour guide for the day." The man spoke

with a tinny voice and thick brogue that carried over the crowd. "You might be asking, what would an old man know about knitting. Shame on you, I've been knitting my whole life. But my true calling is escorting the lovely ladies of the world around my home." He winked at one of the older women in the group, making her giggle like a schoolgirl. He pulled a battered notebook out of his jacket pocket, unwinding the rubber band that held the thing together. "Now, we'll be off in a heartbeat, let me collect all my chickadees."

Michael led them to a microbus parked on the side of the road. He heaved himself up into the driver's seat as the group settled in. "Drinks and such up here, but the first toilet isn't for an hour. You've been warned."

North Dun was home to more sheep than humans. Low stone fences criss-crossed the island, and twice in the first hour, the bus had to wait for sheep to cross the road. Their first stop was a farm with a workshop attached, where artisans carded wool and spun it into yarn. Other shops demonstrated dyeing the pale cream-colored yarn into vibrant colorways, using powdered dyes and plants. Like Aoife, each of the artisans were savvy to the benefits of social media, eager to showcase their skills.

After filming a few times, the other ladies on the tour began to treat Bridget as a minor celebrity:

"You should stand over here, Bridget."

"Oh, get this little sheep, she's darling."

"I'll tell my granddaughter that I'm famous now."

The rest of the shops offered similar things—uncarded wool, patterns, buttons, and buckles, finished goods and more traditional souvenirs. When the tour paused for a late lunch, Bridget found herself carrying three large bags of her purchases.

Wilson's Knit Shop was the last stop of the tour—quite popular and a bit longer on the schedule, as restroom facilities were more modern and could accommodate a larger group. Bridget wandered the displays of sweaters and caps. In the back of the shop, she discovered a large binder on an old dictionary stand. She imagined Finn's teasing comments: *Always with the binder.* Flipping through, she discovered it was a selection of knitting patterns for purchase, all tied to Irish family names.

"Are you looking for a particular name? A few are out of stock, but I can make a copy if you need." The shop clerk looked up from her computer, a pair of readers perched at the end of her nose. Her computer looked completely out of place in the building that easily dated back more than a hundred years. But in her cozy sweater and bias-cut wool skirt, the clerk looked timeless.

"Are these really patterns used by various families? Or are they just named for them?"

"A little of this, a little of that," she said with a wink. "They're all traditional Irish designs and a good number were family patterns." The woman joined her at the display. "This one here, Mullen, that's my family name and my Gran taught me this stitch when I was a wee thing."

"Is there a Malloy pattern?"

"Are you a Malloy, then?"

Bridget blushed. "No, my friend is."

The shopkeeper nodded, a twinkle in her eye. "Ah, a special friend."

"No, not like that."

"Sure and it's a lovely pattern too." The clerk flipped several of the pages back from Mullen. "Have to get through all the 'Micks' first."

She landed on Malloy, tapping her finger on the page. "Legend says that fisherman families created these patterns for a reason. When their menfolk would go off to sea, they wore these patterns in their sweaters. If there was a shipwreck or a drowning, they'd know their sons and husbands by their patterns, you see."

Bridget turned, horrified. "That's awful."

The shopkeeper gave a shrug and a soft smile. "It brought them home to their family."

Despite the macabre story, Bridget bought the Malloy pattern for five quid. As she turned to leave the register line, her eyes lit on the most gorgeous sweater. It was a deep green, with tiny flecks of blue and gold in the wool. Glancing at the tag, she hesitated. It was ridiculously expensive, but it would look so good on Finn.

"Sorry, add this too." She handed her credit card over again.

The sun began to cast long shadows in the sleepy town, so the group boarded the bus to return to the pier, 20 minutes before boarding for the next ferry back to Condalk.

Waiting passengers wandered along on the rocky beach area by the pier. While Bridget sat on a low stone wall, a flurry of shouts and exclamations rose from the beach. A pair of seals, one gray, the other a mottled brown and cream, had flopped onto an outcropping of rocks, sunning themselves in the relative warmth of the late afternoon. They were enormous, easily five feet long and hundreds of pounds. Several people gathered at a safe distance around the sleek, imposing creatures.

How could she resist? Bridget picked her way down the dark gray rocks to the beach. She wound her way around to the tourists snapping photos of the seals, who seemed generally unfazed by the scene they were causing.

Pulling out her phone, Bridget started recording. As she approached the wide circle, a child threw a stick toward the seal pair, earning him a quick tug away from his mother. In response, the larger seal began barking and making lunging movements toward the group, moving off the rock and to the sand.

One man put his arm in front of his children, saying loudly, "I think we better give them a little more space."

With murmurs of agreement, the group began to retreat, but the larger seal still looked agitated. Bridget paused a moment to zoom in on the smaller seal, rolling languidly on the rock, hoping to get a few moments of footage.

"Look out, miss!"

While she was focused on the rock, the larger seal had begun to lope toward her, propelling itself on the ground faster than she would have thought possible. With a squeak, Bridget began backing up to the safety of the rest of the group. The seal paused in its pursuit, watching as the group continued to move backwards.

Not wanting to take her eye off the larger seal again, Bridget continued to walk backwards, and caught her foot on a tangle of seaweed. With a cry, she stumbled backwards, but managed to keep herself from falling. But in her efforts to keep herself upright, her phone flew out of her hands, landing almost six feet away, near the edge of the water.

No!

She scrambled to her feet and began to move toward the phone, but as she did, the seal moved toward the phone as well.

It was a classic standoff. Each move Bridget made toward the phone was matched by the seal. For several minutes, they edged toward each other, getting dangerously close.

"Just leave it!" called one of the other tourists. "They bite!"

All her video. All her notes. All her content! What if her backup didn't work? Not to mention how long she would need to wait for a replacement phone.

She stared into the inky black eyes of the seal. *I need that phone.*

Behind her, she heard the horn of the ferry approached the dock. Bridget crouched in a defensive position. Her phone was only inches from the encroaching waves.

"Come away, there!"

"Leave it!"

The crowd had retreating to the pier, calling down from their safe perch above. But she couldn't leave her phone. For several minutes, she waited, heart racing as the boat docked nearby.

She broke her gaze with the seal for a moment, glancing toward her phone. She gave a cry as the next wave washed up to the front edge of the phone. Her phone case would only keep the water away from the edges, not the charging port.

With a grunt, she made a move to the phone. The seal barked once, loudly. Bridget froze again. Out of the corner of her eye, she saw the wave crest and crash, covering about half her phone.

The ferry began to lower the ropes, allowing the waiting passengers to board.

Ohmigod ohmigod ohmigod.

The next wave picked it up and carried it a few inches away.

She was running out of time. Bridget straightened to full height. In what she hoped was an authoritative voice she said, "I am getting my phone, seal."

The seal cocked its head, as if it was trying to understand her. *It's just a sea puppy.*

"Be a good boy, don't kill me. I'm going to get my phone, because if I don't, I will not be able to do my job." As she spoke, she gently took a step toward the phone. This time, the seal didn't move forward to meet her advance.

Another wave lifted her phone, carrying it about a foot down the beach.

She was ten steps away. With each advancement, she kept her calm litany for the benefit of the seal (and herself). "That's a good boy. Do not murder the nice phone lady. Stay right there and let me get this phone."

The seal cocked its head to one side, not moving. Clearly it thought she'd lost her mind.

Just as soon as her phone was within reach, another wave came up, lifting the phone with enough momentum to take it out to sea. Bridget lunged. The seal lowered its head and barked at her. Bridget grabbed the phone, turned tail and began to run for the rocks. A cry of cheers rose from the spectators by the pier.

Finally at the rocks and out of breath, Bridget panted as she clutched her phone, willing it to be ok.

"It got wet. I've got to let it dry out," she muttered. "Rice. I need rice." She knew that much, but could it wait until she was back at the cottage or would it be too late? Bridget gave a cry of distress. How was she supposed to know how to save this phone if she couldn't turn it on and Google the answer?

Three short blasts sounded from the ferry horn, and Bridget looked up to see it pulling away from the dock.

She missed the boat. Which meant she'd miss the train.

She'd have to call Finn and tell him she'd be late. Her finger hovered over the power button of her phone, a force of habit. *Don't turn it on!*

Her mind flashed to Finn, sitting at the train station, waiting for her. She tore open her bag to pull out the binder. Damn. In all her planning and attention to detail, she never wrote down Finn's number on paper, only saving it in her phone. All she had was Cillian's business number.

Because she and Finn were never apart.

She closed the binder, putting her hand to her forehead to shade it from the setting sun. The tiny grocer she'd passed would have rice. Once her phone was restored, then she'd call Cillian, and hopefully he'd let Finn know.

She just needed to stop worrying about Finn for the next two hours while she waited for the next ferry.

Chapter 16

Blanket Absolution

here is she? Finn's heartbeat pulsed in panic mode.

As passengers fanned out from the train cars, Finn started jogging, then running down the platform, calling out "Bridget!" at each open door. No sign of her.

A voice called out behind him. "Oi! What's the fuss?"

Finn whipped around. "Did you have an American woman on this train? Traveling alone and headed to Killathay?"

The conductor cocked her head to the side, considering the question. "Not that I recall. Mostly folks going all the way to Dublin on this train."

Finn felt a clenched fist of worry in his stomach. "And there was no trouble at the Condalk end?" The conductor shook her head.

"Thanks." He raised his arm in a feeble gesture of acknowledgment. He pulled out his phone, dialing Bridget's number.

Voicemail.

Voicemail.

Voicemail.

He began texting, his hands shaking in the sting of the wind.

Bridget where are you? I'm at the station.

It's Finn.

Were you on the train?

Bridget, please pick up!

All his messages were marked *Sent*, not *Read* or even *Delivered*.

The chill that ran through him had nothing to do with the weather.

The last train from Condalk to Killathay was set to arrive around 9:45 p.m. For the next two hours, he scanned the schedule, tried to call the Condalk station (bleedin' recording), texted or called Bridget every 15 minutes, and tried to distract himself from the increasingly desperate scenes he created in his mind. *What if something happened to her?* He didn't even know who to call on her behalf. Sure, he knew that she had a doctor roommate named Tran, but that wouldn't get him far in a city like Chicago.

He got calls from Cill and his mother but with his phone hovering at 8 percent battery, he ignored them, wanting to keep enough charge in case Bridget called. *I'm never forgetting the damn charger again.* For nearly two hours, he sat in his car, alternating between fear, anger, panic, and frustration, pretty much in a constant cycle.

If she wasn't on the next train...

He played out the scenarios in his head. He'd drive to Condalk. Call the hospitals. Talk to the Gardai.

Finn was out on the platform, straining to see the lights from the engine at half nine. As the train slowed into the station, he trotted along the train toward the first car, scanning the windows and doors for a glimpse of her. *Be here, Bridget.*

The train groaned to a stop and only a few passengers disembarked. The panic congealed into a cold weight. He'd have to–

"Finn!"

Bridget! He spun around and ran toward her, catching her up by the shoulders as relief flooded through him. "The hell have you been, Bridget? I've been worried sick about you!" Without a thought, he pulled her into a tight hug. "Fool woman, I'm thinking you died out there, dashed against the cliffs or drowned."

Her voice was muffled against his shoulder. "My phone...a seal tried to steal it, and it got wet, and I had to put it in rice. Did Cillian tell you?"

Stepping back from her slightly, he scanned her face, trying to make sense of the random words she was saying. "Start again."

She'd put her shopping bags on the ground, so Finn grabbed them with his left hand, clutching her hand with his right. He didn't want to let her go for a single moment.

She took a deep breath. "I got a ton of video today, like four or five posts worth. While I was waiting for the ferry to come, I walked down to the beach. Two enormous seals were sunning themselves and a group of people were watching, and I thought, 'hey, great video.' One started kicking up a fuss—the seal, not the people—and we all started backing away. Naturally, I stumbled."

"Naturally."

"I didn't fall! But my phone flew out of my hands, almost into the water. I had to get it, but every time I tried, the seal got more aggressive and closer to the phone. But when the waves started going over my phone, I had to grab it before it floated away. And while all that happened, I missed the ferry."

"I'm sorry...seals tried to steal your phone and drowned it?"

"I know, it's bananas. But I was too afraid to power up my phone while it was wet, so I couldn't call you."

She smiled up at him. "The most unbelievable part of the whole story is I didn't have your number in my binder."

He shook his head somberly. "Your binder failed us. Truly disappointing."

"But at least I had Cillian's number from the reservation. I left him a message."

Should've taken his call. "He called, but I didn't answer. My battery's nearly dead and I didn't want to miss a call from you. He texted for me to call him immediately, but he's always like that."

Bridget stopped at the passenger door. "I'm sorry you had to wait." The little wrinkle on her forehead furrowed. "I wasted your time. Ruined your night." Her voice cracked a bit.

He didn't think, he just leaned forward, kissing the top of her head. "Attacked by seals. Jesus, Mary, and Joseph. I can't let you out of my sight in this country, Boss Lady."

His heart swelled at her response: "I suppose you shouldn't."

Bridget spent the trip home describing the people and places from her journey, and Finn couldn't help feeling that he missed out, a bit jealous he didn't share her experiences. At the cottage, she pulled out a plastic bag that held her phone and a half-pound of dry rice, setting it on the table with a worried expression. "One of the people on the train–the one who let me borrow her phone to leave a message for Cillian–told me to keep it in rice twenty-four hours to dry out. The longer, the better, but it's not a foolproof fix."

"What does that mean for tomorrow?" No phone meant no footage.

She bit her lip in thought. "I have some older video I could use, I think. I downloaded it to my laptop already. My old videos are backed up on the cloud but my backup runs at night, so it won't have anything from today." Bridget began scrawling out a to-do list on the back of a sheet of paper. "This is so frustrating. If I lose all the footage I shot at North Dun, the whole day is wasted."

Again with wasted time. "People have gone to the islands for centuries, and most of those trips weren't memorialized for all time with social media."

She sighed. "You're right. But I'm here to do a job too."

As if struck by a thought, Bridget bolted up from the sofa. "I got you something!" She pulled out a deep green jumper from one of her market bags. "I had to guess your size, but I thought the green of this sweater would really be nice with your eyes."

He picked up the jumper slowly, turning it over in his hands. It was expertly handmade with a soft graded wool that felt sumptuous and expensive. "It's far too dear of a gift for me."

She laid a hand on his arm. "Don't be silly. After I made you wait for hours for me, it's the least I can do. See if it fits!"

He pulled the green jumper on, tugging it down to his waist. It was buttery soft and heavy enough to feel like a warm embrace. It was probably the nicest gift he'd ever been given.

"Thank you, it's grand."

Her face lit with joy. "And you have to see this." Bridget popped up again, pulling out five skeins of hand-dyed wool colored a bright sapphire blue. "I thought this would make something gorgeous, but I'll have to wait till I get home to try it —no knitting needles. Though I did buy a pattern." Her cheeks colored a bit at the mention of the pattern.

"Hold on." Finn opened the deep drawer of the end table by Gran's rocking chair. He rifled around a moment, pulling out Gran's yellow knitting bag.

He hesitated a half-second before offering the bag to Bridget. "Can you use these?"

She opened the bag, full of needles, notions, and ends of yarn. "Are these your grandmother's needles?" She looked up at him, searching his face.

He cleared his throat. "They're not doing her any good. You take them."

She laid the bag down and rose to stand in front of him. Without a word, she threaded her arms under his and leaned in for a hug. "Thank you," she murmured.

He wrapped his own arms around her, holding her close. Holy hell, she felt right in his arms. They stayed like that a beat too long until she disentangled herself.

"Sweater is really soft," she murmured. "I should get to sleep, I'm exhausted."

Finn ran a hand through his hair as he turned away. "Sure and goodnight." He watched as she slipped into the hallway toward the bathroom.

Careful. You're slipping into trouble here.

The next day brought more dripping, sniveling rain. When Finn woke in the early morning hours, the house was colder that it should be. *Bleedin' stove.* He flipped the covers off, stomping to the back door to pull up a stack of logs and kindling into his arms. Like as not, he'd have to start it all from scratch to get the place warm. He bent down to get a twist of paper to light the stove.

"Need help?" A sleepy-eyed Bridget turned the corner from the hallway, the quilt from the end of her bed draped across her shoulders. "Freezing in here."

"Stove went out, must be the heating oil. I'll have this fired up in two shakes."

She shuffled to the kitchen. "I'll put on the kettle."

Soon the room was glowing from the rosy blaze in the stove. Bridget snuggled into the corner of the couch, tucking her feet underneath the quilt as she held the toasty mug to her chest.

"You going back to sleep?" he asked.

"I think I'll just stay out here. It's pretty cold in my room. And we don't have to go anywhere today."

He thought about several ways of keeping her warm. Instead, he grunted. "I'll tend to the donkeys and be back in a bit."

When he returned, she'd switched on the television, with characters from a children's cartoon speaking in Irish as they bobbed on the screen. "Getting a lot out of this, are you?"

She looked up at him. "Do you speak Irish?"

"*Is féider liom.* Sure. Learned it in school, but I don't use it all that often. My Gran would sometimes watch the news in Irish."

"That's wild. I took three years of high school French but can only say 'where's the bathroom' with any conviction."

"Critical information. Here, shove over. Barn's as cold as this room" Finn flopped onto the opposite end of the couch as she offered him a corner of the quilt to get him warm. "Is this what you want to spend the day doing?"

She arched an eyebrow. "At some point I have to edit and post, but until my phone dries out..." she trailed off. "A day off for both of us."

She snuggled back into the cushions of the couch, pulling the quilt up near her neck. "If I wasn't here, what would you be doing today?"

He thought for a moment. "Working, I guess, but that was derailed before you came."

"No, for fun."

'Well, if I wasn't working...I'd be puttering about the place, fixing things up."

"Is there something that needs fixing?"

"It's a 150-year-old cottage. Something always needs fixing."

Bridget scooted herself upright. "I can help, if you need an extra set of hands."

Finn cocked his head toward her. This could be fun. "And if I say I need help mucking out the donkey stalls?"

Her gray eyes twinkled. "Then I will help by making sandwiches when you're done."

He laughed, setting down his cup of tea. "Fair enough."

Neither was in a great hurry to get the day started. Bridget turned up the volume on the television and burrowed beneath her blanket, her feet gently nudging under Finn's leg. "Sorry, I'm still cold."

"Here." Finn flipped the blanket off her feet, pulling them onto his lap. Her thick socks were pink with white polka dots, and fuzzy to a degree that was impractical for anything other than relaxing on the couch. He began to gently rub them, just enough friction to increase blood flow. Finn pressed his fingers firmly into the arch of her foot. Bridget squeaked and pulled them away. "I'm ticklish!"

He arched an eyebrow. "That's dangerous information."

"Just my feet," she said. "But it feels good when you rub them—I walked so much yesterday."

He was struck by how comfortable it all was. Natural, like he was meant to be here, with her. They were quiet together, with the lulling drone of the television.

"What if we just vegged out, watching tv or napping all day?" Bridget wiggled her toes in his palm. "I think we deserve a break...and I know you didn't get a real day off yesterday."

"Is that what you do back in Chicago, lay about all day?"

"Worse," she grinned. "Sometimes I'll spend a whole weekend not leaving my apartment watching old movies and eating Spaghetti-Os and Cherry Garcia."

"Spaghetti-Os?"

"And Ho-Hos."

"Sounds nutritious. Your doctor roommate was ok with that?"

"Oh, this was well before Tran was my roommate. I had a tiny studio apartment in an old building, and during the winter months, I used to hibernate. It's when I learned to knit." She pulled her feet off Finn's lap. "Oh! Hang on, I want to show you."

She returned with her arms full of yarn and paper.

"Ta-da! I got three rows knitted on your grandmother's needles with my scarf pattern last night!" Bridget snuggled back down in the couch and started her next row, checking her pattern several times.

Something caught his eye.

"Does that pattern say Malloy?"

Bridget reflexively grabbed at the paper, but not before

Finn snatched it up. "Malloy family pattern," he read aloud. "You bought this?"

She turned a bit red as she replied. "I thought, since I'm staying in a Malloy cottage."

"Technically, Gran's family was Stack."

She snatched the pattern back. "I liked the way it looked."

Finn smiled in response to her huff. It was easy to get her dander up, but as she began to knit, the slow ticking of the needles made his heart ache the tiniest bit. In the last few months when Gran was sick, he'd leave her bedroom door open, in case she needed him. Many a night he'd wake to the clicking of her needles.

For several hours, they puttered around the house. An old '90s romcom on telly took up the better part of the morning. When both bags of Tayto crisps were empty, Bridget read a book for a while, then cobbled together some cookies from oats, peanut butter, and sugar. It might not be Spaghettio-s or Ho-Hos, but they were decadent and delicious.

As the movie credits rolled, Finn flipped the channel to the middle of the lunchtime news.

"Want anything while I'm up?" Bridget called.

"Another cuppa?"

"On it."

Getting up to put another log in the stove, Finn kept an eye on the news, hoping to catch the weather report. He heard the clatter of the kettle in the other room as Bridget pulled a fresh pot of water.

"And for the lighter side of news, a woman in North Dun battled a harbor seal yesterday over a cell phone..."

Finn froze, his mouth agape. It took him a few seconds to form words. "Bridget! Get in here!"

Her voice was muffled from the kitchen. "Gimme a second."

"Right now! Hurry!"

When she walked into the room, he was pointing the remote at the television, turning up the volume to cinematic levels. "What's so..." She caught a glimpse of the screen and her mouth dropped open. "Oh my God."

The presenter's voice came over the video. "Watchers from the pier got a view of this wild standoff as a young woman tried to retrieve her cell phone from the shore." Finn watched in horror as the video showed Bridget perilously close to the beast, edging toward it to get her phone.

"Now, we remind our viewers that while you might have an important call, seals have been known to be less than friendly. But this story ends well." On the screen, a tiny Bridget lunged for her phone and began to run back up the beach, to the cheers and encouragement of the person who filmed it.

"Maybe we can recommend a waterproof case for next time. And now, the weather."

Finn rounded on her. "You could've been killed!"

Bridget's hands covered her mouth in shock, his words barely registering. "Oh my God, I have to call Mary." She turned, as if to look for her phone. "Ugh! Can I borrow your phone, Finn?"

"I can't believe you did that!" His stomach churned at the close call she had, but he was more impressed than angry.

"Please, I just need to call Mary."

With a mix of irritation and exasperation, he handed over his phone as the kettle began to wail. Did the woman have zero regard for her health and safety?

He walked into the kitchen but kept an ear on her phone call. He caught her side of the conversation as she left a voice mail.

"Mare—It's Bridget. Sorry, I'm calling you from my driver's phone. You're not going to believe this. I was just on TV in

Ireland. Long story, but I was in a standoff with a seal while my phone got washed away. Someone filmed the whole thing, and they just ran the video on the local news. I'm guessing they posted it on social, so I don't know if we can use it, or leverage it. I'm around, so give me a call when you can."

She hung up and stood motionless.

"Bridget?"

She didn't reply.

"Bridget. What's going on?"

She turned toward him, brow furrowed. "This could be something really big."

"What could?"

She ignored him, going to her laptop and logging on. He stood behind her, getting a bit irritated at her preoccupation. She pulled up a browser and searched 'woman seal Ireland phone.'

Immediately, the search bar filled with the video of Bridget, posted all over the Internet. "Viral. I went viral!" Her voice was just above a whisper.

She turned to him, her face alight. "Viral!"

"What the hell are you talking about?" Finn knew he sounded resentful, but her tone reminded him of the times when his sisters spoke of things, telling him that he was too young or stupid to understand.

"Mary might be able to use this and launch me as a major influencer. I could get the Container Corner Ambassador gig! A viral post like this...I have to move fast. Hang on, I have to email her these links." She sat back at the laptop and began to type furiously.

Finn waited a few minutes for her to finish typing and fill him in. Instead, she was completely engrossed in her efforts and ignored him. Feeling the tiniest bit put out, he came back to the table with fresh cups of tea.

Bridget didn't even look up. "Can you grab me some cookies too?"

Guess the hired help wasn't needed for this part.

Chapter 17

Opportunity Knocks

The afternoon was a whirlwind.

Mary called her back almost immediately on Finn's phone, bubbling with ideas of how to make her viral moment benefit HouseHijack and (as an afterthought) Bridget. By the end of the day and a dozen phone calls later, Mary emailed her the plan.

From: Mary D'Esposito
   To: Bridget Kolodziej
   RE: TV Pitch

Ok—I think we've got it. If you can get the footage from your phone, make a post, then tag the anchor and the news show in your caption. We'll pitch them and see if we can get an interview.

Before we do, I need to do a quick media training session with you, but we can do it virtually. How easy would it be for you to get to Dublin?

—M

Bridget stared at the bag of rice that housed her phone. It all rested on this: could she boot it up and salvage the footage from yesterday? She'd told herself to wait until the full 24-hour mark, but the need to know was overriding her normal rule-following behavior.

Glancing at her watch, she was shocked it was already 4 p.m. She'd spent hours on this—so much for a day off and rest.

Opening the bag, she pulled the phone out of the rice, blowing gently into the charging port. Closing her eyes, she whispered, "please." She held her breath and pressed the power button.

Her heart nearly stopped beating when the power light flashed on.

"Yes! Finn! It worked!" She rose from the chair with a clatter, knocking into the table. "Finn!"

He was nowhere to be found.

She hadn't even noticed he left.

The phone vibrated in her hand as it began to receive all her missed calls and messages. Immediately, she synced it to the cloud, backing up all her files. She hovered over the photo button, increasingly nervous as she opened the files from yesterday. The video with the seal was nearly 12 minutes long. Biting the edge of her thumb, she pressed play.

It was gold. Fucking *gold*.

The video started with filming the seal at a distance, but somehow she captured all of the seal's antics and her own commentary, even capturing the seal's face peering at the camera. It was the perfect formula for a viral video, even filming as the water washed over the lens before going dark.

She opened her email, writing a quick note to Mary and attaching a link to the video.

This was going to be big.

Without thinking, she turned to show Finn. *Still gone.*

She'd been immersed in her calls and emails with the Chicago office most off the day. She peeked out the front window. The car was still here, so Finn must be in the barn. As she headed to the back door, Finn's phone rang. She picked it up without thinking. "Hello?"

A woman's voice with an Irish lilt replied. "Oh, I was looking for Finn Malloy."

At once, Bridget transposed into a more formal tone. "Sorry, yes. May I tell him who's calling?"

"Claire."

She didn't physically flinch, but her stomach clenched. "Of course, Let me see if I can find him. One moment."

Bridget gauged the weather before deciding to grab her coat. It was already twilight, and she picked her way carefully down the stone path. Leaning against the large barn door, she pushed it open.

Finn was at the lathe, his back to the door, sanding what looked to be a pillar candlestick. His arms were covered in a fine haze of sawdust, and he was hunched over, focused on his work.

"Finn?"

"Jesus fucking Christ!" He switched off the lathe and grabbed at his chest. "Giving me a fucking heart attack, are you?"

"Sorry, sorry!" Bridget tried to look appropriately apologetic. "You have a phone call." She looked down at the phone, which was blank. Claire had hung up.

"I guess you *had* a phone call. It was Claire." She handed him the cell, schooling her face to keep it clear of any emotion. "Thanks for letting me borrow it. Mine is working now."

Almost on cue, her own phone began to ring. Mary. She walked to the far corner of the stalls to answer.

Mary's voice was giddy. "Bridget, this video is amazing. How quickly can you get it edited and ready to post?"

"Maybe an hour, two at most?"

"Great. Once you post, I'll put a pitch together. We've got to be fast. This will be yesterday's news in no time. Are you around if we get a hit?"

"Wherever you need me."

An hour later, Bridget posted the edited video to her socials, tagging the reporter and show as Mary instructed. She stretched, placing her fist in the small of her back to release the tension of her day at the computer.

Still no sign of Finn. She peered out the back door toward the barn, but the lights were off. At the front door, the car was not in the driveway. She felt a flash of hurt, that he didn't bother to tell her he was going out. The name 'Claire' echoed in her brain, and she closed the door softly. Did he go out with her while she was in North Dun?"

Don't be stupid, Bridget. He's a grown man and can see whoever he pleases.

Except...

Except she didn't want him seeing people.

She sat down at the kitchen table again, idly tapping the keyboard to wake the computer again. She typed "Claire" into the search bar. The results were less than encouraging. Queen of the faeries. White shoulders. Fair and lovely.

Hmph.

This was getting her nowhere. She needed a serotonin boost. With a click, she was back on her social pages, basking in the dozens of likes and the flurry of comments her seaside disaster video was racking up.

. . .

@costycapybara: I can't believe you fought a
seal for your phone!

@JuttsnGutts: <3 <3 <3 you rock!

Blip. Her eyes darted to the corner of the screen. One direct
message.

@ITMElizabeth: Hi Bridget! I'm Elizabeth, a
producer from Ireland This Morning. Would
you be able to come to the station this week
to talk about your video? If your phone is
working (ha ha) you can give me a call.

In her mad scramble to dial her phone, Bridget knocked over
her old cup of tea, spilling clammy brown water all over her
jeans. Didn't matter. "It worked!" she squealed into the
phone.

She was still on the phone half an hour later when she saw
headlights through the front window. "I've got to go, Mary.
Thank you!"

"Brought you some takeaway," Finn said, a paper bag in
hand. "Shepherd's pie." He closed the door behind him and put
the sack on the table for her. "Don't know if you ate."

"Thanks, I didn't eat much." Bridget rose from the couch,
turning off the music. "Finn, I'm sorry about today. I kept
thinking I could wrap up much earlier, but..." She trailed off.

"You were busy," he shrugged.

"Did you go out with...your friend?" *Friend.* That's what we're going to call it.

"No, went into town for some food. Figured you didn't need me mucking about while you were trying to get work done."

"Speaking of that, I have some news," Bridget clasped her hands at her chest, grinning nervously. "I'm going to be on TV!"

Finn's head popped up. "What do you mean?"

"Ireland This Morning has asked me to come on Thursday to do an interview."

He looked shocked, then smiled. "That's grand. Well done, you!"

She exhaled shakily. "That's what took so long, Mary had to get special permission from the client for me to go on camera, then she put me through my paces doing a media training session."

He crossed his arms. "What time do you go on, then?"

"Early...like 6:50 a.m."

"And how're you getting there?" Was he fishing for an invitation?

"I guess I could take a train, or it's about a four-hour drive in." She added the last bit with a casual air. After all, she did hire him as her driver for the duration of her stay. It wasn't a weekend, so he would be on the clock.

"Four hours with a 6:50 a.m. start?"

"Earlier, probably. We could go in the night before, stay in a hotel and have a nice dinner. Mary said she'd give me extra budget to cover expenses to make this happen." She put a hand on his arm. "Please? Let me make it up to you for being so preoccupied today. I'm already nervous, and if you could be there..." She trailed off, leaving the rest unsaid: *Having you there would help.*

"Wouldn't miss it," Finn said. "We'll leave at noon tomorrow."

Why didn't she bring better clothes? Or shoes? Or makeup? Bridget tore around the room the next morning, scrounging through her suitcases to find the right outfit for her interview. "Why can't I dress myself like a normal person?" she wailed, flopping onto the bed with such vigor that her makeup bag clattered to the floor, scattering its contents everywhere.

From the hallway, Finn called, "Are you going mad? What's the ruckus in there?"

Bridget threw open the door to her bedroom. "You have to help me." Whipping around, she pulled him towards the bed, where two blouses and pants were laid out like Flat Stanleys. "Which of these say 'this person is an influencer?'"

"You've got to be kidding me."

"Finnnnnnn!" She pulled on his arm in desperation. "Please! It's too early to video call Tran or Mary, I need someone's opinion!"

He looked over at the bed, fingering the embroidery on the yellow blouse. "This one's pretty."

"Not too yellow?"

"No, but it might be too fancy for an interview. But what do I know?"

"And the pants?"

"Are they even going to see your trousers?"

Bridget wailed, "I don't know! I'm so bad at this part."

"What part?"

"The part where influencers and content creators are supposed to know what to wear and how to look. I wore a school uniform for 12 years—I never learned anything about putting outfits together!"

"Then do your influencer thing."

She stopped short. "What do you mean?"

He gestured to the bed. "Post the two outfits and let your followers decide."

Who was this man? "That's fucking brilliant."

Finn gave her a smug grin and tapped his forehead. "Not just sawdust in here."

"Here." Bridget fiddled with her phone and pulled up the video settings. "Film me?"

"Can't you just take photos of them here on the bed?"

She gave him a look of disdain as she stepped around him toward the window. "The light's good here." She pulled him bodily to standing in a spot just next to the windowsill. "Gimme two seconds."

Walking to the bed, she paused for a moment. They were really running out of time. Screw it.

She peeled off her t-shirt and threw the yellow blouse on over her bra. Slipping out of her joggers, she pulled the black ponte pants on and ran her hands through her hair at the vanity.

Behind her, Finn cleared his throat.

Bridget froze. "Oh, sorry...I hope you don't mind that I changed in front of you. I just...we have to leave soon and I'm in a hurry."

"It's fine."

"Ok, record."

She broke into a huge smile. "Hi guys—I desperately need your help! I'm going to be on Ireland This Morning tomorrow—Thursday—talking about my oh-so-elegant encounter with the harbor seal who tried to steal my phone. But I am the worst when it comes to fashion. So this is like a 'get ready with me' video, but more like Choose Your Own Adventure. Tell me in the comments which outfit works best. This is option A." Bridget spread her arms wide and pivoted from side to side. At the very end of her pivot, she jumped up and down, putting a piece of paper on the floor where she landed.

"Ok, hit stop."

"What was with the jump?" Finn gave her a perplexed look.

"Don't move—you'll see."

She went over toward the bed, tossing the yellow blouse over her head and pulling on the baby blue sweater. In a fluid motion, she shimmied out of the black pants and pulled on the houndstooth trousers.

Bridget quickly moved back to the piece of paper on the floor. "Ok, hit *Record*." She pasted on a smile and once again jumped up and down. "And this is outfit two. Which of these will be best for tomorrow's interview? Leave a comment below to let me know your favorite!"

She remained in place with her wide smile for a few seconds, then said, "Ok, stop."

Bridget snatched the phone from him and sprinted into the front room to begin downloading to edit. With her attention was focused intently on the edit, she didn't notice Finn coming up behind her.

"Where'd you learn to do all this?"

"YouTube, mostly. Lots of tutorials. And watching other content creators. But a lot I've had to learn on the fly, as I was never in my videos until I came here." A few more edits, and the video was done. The final format was seamless, as Bridget hopped up and down, instantly changing outfits with her jump cut.

"That's cracking. I'm impressed."

"I posted another video from North Dun last night, and a

shop owner I met named Aoife emailed to say she's already had five orders since I posted."

She couldn't stop the smile spreading across her face. "I know it's really no big deal," she began, but Finn cut her off.

"Don't say that. You're good at this. Own it."

She felt her stomach get wobbly. "Thank you."

"Now, post it and let's get out of here. I need to swing by Olive's on the way. She's been on me to drop off that candlestick."

"But I don't know which outfit to pack until people vote!"

He cocked his head at her as if she had three eyeballs. "You know you can pack both outfits and just wear the one they choose, right?"

Death by embarrassment is not the best way to go. "Right. Give me 15 minutes."

Olive's shop was bustling with two customers when they dropped in. "Just a mo, you two!" She called from the back room. "Getting something!"

Finn took his large parcel wrapped in brown paper through the small door into the back room. Bridget smiled as she eavesdropped on two older women commenting on the artisanal pieces in the shop in distinctly Bostonian accents.

"These are nice, Kathleen. Maybe something for Joe?"

"He'd kill me if I spent that much on a bowl."

Bridget eyed the back room. No sign of Finn. She tapped the long charcuterie board, the most expensive of Finn's wood pieces. She lowered her voice and spoke as if sharing a secret. "This artist has been featured on TikTok, you know. All one-of-a-kind pieces that take hours to make by hand. Not some cheap tourist souvenir, and the owner will ship it for you. Totally worth it. Underpriced if you ask me."

The two women shared significant glances and began to chat animatedly over the board as Bridget moved to peruse Olive's watercolor prints. When Olive emerged from the back room, she led Finn out as he carried a large cardboard box at her behest.

"Sorry ladies, I didn't have that jumper in blue in XL, but I do have one in cream and one in gray."

"I think we'll get this board instead." The taller woman made eye contact with Bridget, who gave a slight nod and a wink. She caught Finn squirming out of the corner of her eye. *What he doesn't know won't kill him.*

"Marvelous." Olive briskly began ringing up her patrons and they departed in short order, Finn's board in a lovely bag.

As the bell from the door faded away, Olive rounded on Bridget, enveloping her in a tight hug. "Bridget! So good to see you! I hear you have a big day tomorrow."

"How'd you—?"

Finn made a great show of his innocence. "I didn't say a word."

"No, not him." Olive whipped a bright blue and green hand-painted silk scarf from the wall display, catching up the scissors from the counter to snip the tag. "This is going to look lovely with the blue jumper, which is clearly the right outfit" she winked.

"You saw my video?"

"Of course I did! I've been following you since you first walked in two weeks ago. Your shoutout that day brought in half a dozen customers already. The blue jumper is well in the lead, as far as I can tell."

Bridget pulled out her phone. Sure enough, votes for the blue sweater were beating the yellow blouse two-to-one. "I'm useless when it comes to scarves," she said, looping the delicate fabric around her neck limply.

"Come here." Olive expertly tied the scarf in an artful knot that somehow looked casual, yet intricate. "Leave it like this, and just put it on over your head. It'll be perfect. Can't have you disgracing the family now."

Finn piped in. "Speaking of family, cousin—can you come by the house tomorrow morning to feed the donkeys? They'll be fine in the barn, but they'll need fresh food and water."

"Just what I need," she muttered. "Anything I can pick up from your workbench while I'm there? I need something to replace that board that just sold."

"I just brought you a candlestick. Stop your fussing, Ollie. We need to get on the road."

Olive dismissed him with a roll of her eyes. "Fine then. I'll do it." To Bridget she added, "He sells one piece of fancy wood and he's king of the schedule now."

Bridget grinned. "Well, he's taking me into the city."

"Being paid well for it, too." Olive leaned in. "A word of advice, Bridget. Don't let him think he's doing more than he is. That one was born to be a martyr."

Chapter 18

Dublin Down

After Olive's and a quick stop for petrol, they were on the road.

"How often do you go to Dublin?" Bridget asked, working her way through a bag of crisps at a steady pace.

Finn arched his eyebrow. "Honestly, can't remember the last time."

"Really?"

"Who has eight hours to waste driving there and back, only to pay twice what they would at home for the same?"

Bridget's mouth dropped open. "I can't believe you don't go there for concerts or museums or even the airport."

"I've only flown out of Ireland three times in my life, and two of them I flew from Shannon," he said. "Are you in the habit of driving about on holiday? What would be four hours by car in Chicago?"

She thought for a moment, cocking her head slightly to do the mental math. "Maybe Indianapolis? Or Des Moines?"

"Do you drive to Indianapolis often, then?"

She gave a half-laugh. "Point taken."

He was quiet for a moment, the video of her city apartment flashing in his mind. "Not a big fan of cities, generally. I went to Boston to visit cousins once as a kid, and my family went on holiday to Spain one year when my sister was at uni. There was no place to escape from all the people."

Bridget was thoughtful. "Sometimes I think it's easier to be alone in a big city, surrounded by people. I can grab a coffee and bagel, wander out to the lake front, watch the waves, or read a book. Nobody bothers you; they're all busy on their own."

He couldn't imagine being in Killathay for an hour without at least a half-dozen people coming up to him. "Unfriendly, then."

"No, it's really not. It's just that everyone is..." She searched for the right word. "Self-contained."

Finn felt his tension rise the closer they came to the city. Once the farms disappeared into row houses, he felt his shoulders hunch as he gripped the wheel. He navigated them to the Padraig Hotel, a four-story brick building a block away from the River Liffey. He stopped short at the entrance to the parking garage. "Fifty quid to park? They've got to be mad." No way was he going to be part of that kind of robbery. He threw the gearshift into reverse, popping his arm behind Bridget's armrest, preparing to back out.

She put a hand on his leg. "It's ok...Mary gave me an extra 250 euro for expenses, and she's put the hotel on her card. Just park."

Finn looked at her skeptically but proceeded into the garage. "Fine, but make sure you save some of that to cover the petrol," he groused. His stomach was growling audibly, and the sooner parked, the sooner at table.

"Whatever money we don't spend on food and drink tonight is yours—a bonus," she said. "You decide if we just go to the chippy or we splurge and eat at a nice restaurant." She turned a smile on him that brightened his mood.

"Nothing in the binder, then?" The dank and dark garage was nearly full, but Finn spotted an open space and squeezed the car in expertly.

"Nope. No plans at all, except getting me to "Ireland This Morning" by 5:45 a.m. tomorrow morning for my 6:50 a.m. segment."

"In that case, let's leave the luggage in the boot and grab a bite before we check in. I'm famished."

Bundled up, they set off walking toward the river, the festive glow of the holiday lights drawing them in. Across the river, a red-walled pub looked cozy and inviting, with the warm glow of lights illuminating the evergreen wreaths on each window. They took a seat at a pockmarked wooden table near the front door, braving the draft to dine in the glow of the river lights.

The chill night air brought out a healthy color in Bridget's cheeks, and Finn found himself staring at her face. Her eyes were bright, illuminated by the twinkling lights along the river, and her hair was wild and windblown. She tucked into her sandwich with vigor, taking in the buzz of the city in stride.

"You know, at home, there's an Irish pub about three blocks away from our apartment—Duffy's," she said, dabbing at her mouth with her napkin. "But it doesn't look anything like this place. This is perfect."

"You go there often?"

She shook her head. "I don't go out a lot."

"Not a boyfriend back home then?" Was he holding his breath waiting for her answer?

She gave a little laugh. "Nope. Tran has a hobby of trying to fix me up every few months, but I'm a homebody."

"How does Miss Kolodziej spend her evenings, then?" He

leaned forward on the table, propping up his chin with his hand, a pose of rapt attention.

Bridget met his tone. "Oh, it's very exciting. There's usually a puzzle on the table."

"No theater openings, galas or soirees?"

"I did go see Hamilton, does that count? But it was a 2 p.m. matinee on a Wednesday."

"Not rubbing elbows with high society, then?"

"When I started out, I wanted a job that was steady and predictable, not like my parents' jobs. But there's not a lot of jobs for people with degrees in medieval European history."

"Medieval history. You're kidding."

"I know, I know. When I was little, I was fascinated by the bubonic plague. My grandparents had an old set of Encyclopedia Britannica. When my mom would be working, she'd watch 'Wheel of Fortune' and I'd flip through all the volumes. The Black Death hooked me."

"You were a weird kid."

"I was a lonely kid," she said, shrugging. "My mom was a late-in-life child for her parents, an only child. They were in their seventies when we moved in. My mom worked a lot of nights and weekends in real estate before she met my stepdad, so I was alone a lot of the time." Her voice took on a wistful tone.

"I can't imagine a quiet house. Mine was always full to bursting with people coming and going, always noisy. Only when I moved in with Gran did I have a moment's peace."

"How long did you live with her?"

"Almost four years, but the last few months she'd been pretty much homebound."

Bridget reached out her hand to hold his. "I'm sure you were a huge comfort to her."

He gave a snort. "She used to say she had three mules – Tim, Tom, and me. Stubborn fools, all of us."

After dinner, they walked back to the hotel. Their steps fell into rhythm, a steady metronome keeping them in sync. As they crossed the bridge, the lights of the city twinkled brilliantly on the water. Bridget touched his arm. "Hang on. Let's do a selfie." He reluctantly stopped and she moved in toward him, sliding her arm underneath his open jacket, pulling him close to her. She held the camera high in front of them. "Now smile!"

She took two shots, then reviewed them. "Finn—you didn't smile. Come on!" She tucked in close again, but as she took the photo, she tickled his ribs. He flinched with a laugh.

"Aha! The man is ticklish, too."

"Am not."

"Ok, if you say so." She looked down at her camera. "Pictures say different." She held up her phone and showed him— somehow she captured him mid-laugh. He couldn't remember the last time he'd looked so joyful and carefree.

"Can you send me that?"

She looked mildly surprised but pleased. "Of course."

At the hotel lobby, Finn hung back while Bridget strode purposefully across the caramel-colored marble tiles, leaning on the counter with confidence as she checked them in. He settled himself into one of the low armchairs that flanked a fancy blue-tiled fireplace, a far cry from his own sooty stove.

Over the hubbub of the various conversations, he heard a change in the pitch of Bridget's voice. Glancing toward her, he saw she had leaned over the counter, peering at the clerk's monitor. Without realizing it, he was on his feet and moving toward her.

"No, you don't understand...the reservation is for two people, but it's two separate rooms."

"I'm so very sorry, ma'am, but the hotel is booked up solid, and we only have the one room reserved for you."

Bridget put her hand to her forehead, closing her eyes. "It's a double room at least, right?"

"Oh yes, it's a double."

Turning to Finn, she asked, "There's only one room on the reservation and the rest of the hotel is sold out. And we're past the time where we can cancel it without paying." Bridget pinched the bridge of her nose. "Do you mind sharing? Otherwise I'll have to pay out of pocket."

"I'm sure we can manage."

Bridget turned back to the counter. "Fine, we'll take it."

On the fifth floor, Finn carried the bags while Bridget walked ahead to open the door and flip the light switch.

Well, this was going to be a problem.

"But where's the other bed?" Her voice sounded strangled.

"Did they say there were two beds?" The room held a dresser, desk, and bed –barely big enough for two people –and the narrow desk chair did not look comfortable enough to sleep on.

"They said double...like two, right?"

"Like two people. One bed."

She stood at the foot of the bed, processing. "It's not even a king bed!"

"Welcome to Ireland, or frankly, most of Europe. I suppose we're lucky it's bigger than a twin."

Bridget looked horrified. "We're going to have to get another room."

He swung her suitcase up onto the top of the dresser. "Look here, it's already half ten, you need to get some sleep if you're getting up at the devil's own hour tomorrow. I'll go scrounge about for a room and leave you to it."

"Hang on." Bridget sat down on the bed and pulled out her

phone, biting her lip as she scrolled through her travel apps. "I'm not seeing anything nearby for less than 300 euro...and if you're too far away, you might be late picking me up."

Was that all she cared about? "I won't be late."

She dismissed his reply with a waving motion. "It's not feasible." She put her phone down and stared. "We're going to have to share the bed."

"Share this bed. You and I. Sleeping together." Did he hear her correctly?

Her cheeks flamed up as her eyes darted around the room. "Not *sleeping together* sleeping together," she said. "Like, slumber party."

His face must have expressed his doubt.

"We already sleep twenty feet apart at your house," Bridget said. "It's not like we're strangers."

"With two doors between us! Locked doors, by your request."

She frowned. "Think of me like one of your sisters, and you're stuck sharing a bed on vacation."

The mention of his sisters made him groan inwardly. If they were to catch wind of this, it'd be the end of him.

"I didn't bring anything to sleep in but my pants." Now it was his turn to try and avoid blushing.

"That's fine!" she said brightly. He gave her a searching look.

Finn placed his suitcase next to hers on the dresser. "I guess we're in for the night then."

"I'll get ready in the bathroom." Unzipping her suitcase, Bridget rifled around for a few items, clutching them to her chest as she scurried to the jacks.

Here goes nothing.

Finn plugged his phone charger in on the nightstand and set his alarm for 4 a.m. The things he did for this woman.

With a wary glance at the bathroom door, he took off his shoes, socks, shirt, and trousers, then slipped beneath the covers, placing one pillow under his head and one as a buffer between them.

Christ, this was going to be hard.

Shifting, he flipped onto his stomach, praying that his mickey would lay quietly. The thin fabric of his underpants wasn't going to be much of a defense.

He tensed when the door to the bathroom opened and turned his head toward the window. Give her a bit of privacy.

Every tiny noise she made echoed in his mind. Each zip, click, snap and swallow was like a gong.

"Finn?"

"Yes?" He tried to make his voice sound muffled and drowsy, as though he was already close to drifting off to sleep. Nothing was farther from the truth.

"What time do we need to leave?"

"Er, 5:15 should be safe. I've set my alarm for 4, so you'll have time to get yourself in order."

"I'll set mine for 4:15 then. Backup. I took a sleeping pill, so if I don't get up, you're good to splash water on my face."

"Right."

A few moments later, she flipped the security lock on the door and shut off the lights, and Finn opened his eyes. A glow from the street seeped in from the crack in the curtains. He felt her sit down on her side of the bed, the mattress settling around her.

Why wasn't she laying down? Should he say something?

He felt the mattress move again as she rose and went to the window. In the faint glow from the street, he saw she was wearing a skimpy tee shirt and thin short-shorts. As she reached up to pull the curtains together, it was obvious she wasn't wearing a bra.

That mental image certainly wasn't going to help his body behave.

Bridget struggled a bit to pull the drapes closed as best she could and the near-darkness of the room made him feel a bit less predatory. She returned to her side and slid in beside him. He felt her knee brush against his thigh, then jerk back. Bridget popped up to a sitting position. "I thought you said you had pants to sleep in!"

"I'm not naked - I'm wearing my pants.."

"Underpants." She tucked herself into a tight ball. "I thought you meant pajama pants."

"Here then." Finn pulled the extra pillow from underneath his head and stuffed it between them, giving them both even less space. "Better now?"

"Yes, thanks."

She tucked into bed, pulling the blankets around her, but not infringing on his half of the covers. A few turns for comfort, and she gave a sigh. "Goodnight, Finn. Sorry about this."

"My pleasure."

Really? We're going with pleasure? He was acting like a schoolboy, no hope of either governing his thoughts or his appendages.

It was going to be a long night.

He kept his body very still, willing his heartbeat to stop thumping so quickly. Every hum from the heater, every noise in the hallway pricked him back to full consciousness. Even as he listened to her breath become slow and shallow (that sleeping pill must've kicked in quickly), he was fully awake.

He tapped his phone briefly to see the time. 11:42. He closed his eyes again, willing himself to fall asleep. Of all times to have insomnia. He was going to be a mess at 4 a.m.

"Finn..."

His eyes flew open. What did she say?

"Mmmnf." She rolled toward him, throwing an arm over the pillow that divided them. "Sheffer. Min. Mummaaaa."

Carefully, he rolled to face her. In the faintest of the shadows, he saw she was still in deep sleep.

"Bridget?"

"Mmmmm." She snuffled into the pillow, her mouth dropping open slightly as she gave a half-snoring inhale.

There was just enough light in the room for him to see the inviting outline of her shoulder and hips. He shut his eyes tight. She didn't ask for him to be ogling her in while she slept. *Be a gentleman.*

Even with his eyes shut, he listened for the sound of her soft, rhythmic breathing. She gave a sigh, then a soft moan.

"Finnnnn."

That one was clear as day. My God, he was in her dreams.

She mumbled something else, but he couldn't make it out. It sounded vaguely like "cheese."

He propped himself up on his elbow, careful not to disturb her. In the lowest whisper, he said, "Bridget?"

With another breathy sigh, she said, "Please."

His mouth went dry. Why did they have to share this bed on a night where he absolutely, one-hundred-percent should not wake her. Every atom of his being wanted to call her name, to watch her wake up and come into his arms.

He didn't think he ever wanted anything quite as much as he wanted her right that moment.

With his own moan, he turned softly away from her, stretching the taut fabric over his crotch to make it a little less painful.

"Goodnight, Bridget," he murmured into the pillow.

Chapter 19

Star in the Making

The green room at the television studio was a clinical beige, with a two-seat couch, fake plants and a television tuned to the program she'd soon be on. Bridget reached for a bottle of water from a half-empty pack atop an old file cabinet. The lavaliere microphone on her collar was threaded through her clothes and clipped to the back of her waistband so she couldn't lean back comfortably in a chair. A litany of advice played in her brain as she paced the small room, flipping through the notes from Mary: *Remember to mention HouseHijack. Talk about how you've been documenting Ireland. Smile. Don't nod your head every blessed second.*

Finn stood in the doorway. His eyes were bloodshot, and he was on his third cup of tea. "I don't know how you're going to go on and remember all that," he muttered, waving toward her notes.

"Thanks," she said, a deep note of sarcasm in her voice. "I wasn't nervous before."

A young woman with a headset opened the door. "Hi

Bridget—just a mo before we bring you on. You'll be speaking with Nancy at the desk, and we'll cut to your video about thirty seconds in. Don't worry, Nancy will keep you on track."

"Great, thanks." Bridget smiled weakly, resuming her pacing the minute the assistant cleared the doorway.

Finn sat down, rubbing the stubble on his cheeks. "My nerves are wrecked."

Really? "Good thing you're not the one going on!"

He looked dubiously at the door. "I can have the car at the back door in four minutes if you want to bug out of here."

Thwap. She swatted him with her papers but matched his grin, a bit of her tension diffused. "Mary would be on the next plane out to murder me."

The assistant appeared again. "Ok, Bridget. Ready for you!"

Both Bridget and Finn began moving toward the door. The producer put her hand up, "Just Bridget. You can watch from here."

Finn cocked his head to the side as he looked at Bridget.

"I'm fine." She forced a deep breath and tried to smile authentically.

Finn gave her hand a squeeze. "Do us proud."

The studio was dark and cool, with just a handful of bright lights shining around the presenter's table. Three robotic cameras in the studio moved smoothly around thickly wrapped cords, getting into position during the break. The producer walked her to the table. "We're doing a live story right now, but they'll come back to us in about a minute. Nancy, this is Bridget."

Nancy Walker was like a tiny doll, beautifully made up and impeccably coiffed. She reached a hand to Bridget. "You're the seal phone lady. Loved your video!"

"Thank you!" Ok, at least her voice didn't come out as a squeak. That's progress.

"How do you pronounce your last name?"

"Kuh-LO-jay."

Nancy nodded, making a note in her stack of papers. "Just remember to look at me, not the cameras. You'll be great."

Bridget's heart was pounding so loudly, she wondered if the microphone could pick it up. This wasn't like her videos, where she could edit, crop, hide her mistakes. This was live. If she was a disaster, worst case was she'd leave the country in two weeks. Even if she screwed up so badly that she had to retire from society, all evidence would stay in Ireland.

Don't be stupid. The internet is everywhere. Everyone will see this if you screw up.

Bridget shook her head. This internal monologue wasn't doing anything for her nerves and confidence. She perched on the edge of the seat, ramrod straight, trying to school her face into some expression that looked remotely normal.

At once, Nancy's head popped up with a winning smile. *Oh shit, here we go.*

"Thank you, Molly. And now, we have a treat for you in studio. You might remember a few days ago, this video of the young woman who battled a seal at North Dun for her cell phone. Meet travel influencer Bridget Kolodziej. Hello Bridget."

"Hello Nancy." Her mouth felt like it was filled with cotton. Were her lips stuck to her gums?

"Bridget, what brings you to Ireland?"

"I'm here with House Hijack, which manages holiday rentals around the world. I was lucky enough to get a wonderful cottage in Killathay, and I've been touring all around the west coast of Ireland, documenting my travels and meeting wonderful people." Yes! Got the message in right out of the gate. Now I can relax.

"And you met one of Ireland's natives at North Dun, did you not?"

Breathe. Blink. "Yes, in addition to the wonderful people who ran knitting shops and things, I had an encounter with a harbor seal at the ferry who wanted my phone."

"Let's take a look." Nancy stared at the camera, then gave Bridget a quick thumbs-up when the audio from Bridget's seal video started playing before reviewing the printed copy of her scripts. Bridget glanced toward the camera facing her, and she saw the words "QUITE A SCARE" on the monitor above the camera At the end of the video, Nancy's head popped up again.

"That must have been quite a scare." Nancy commented.

"I don't think I realized how dangerous it was until it was over. I got an earful about it from my HouseHijack host." Ok, got that second mention in and a laugh from Nancy. Mary will love her.

"Tell us a little about where you're staying." Bridget's stomach dropped. She didn't prepare for this question. *Shit.* "Um, it's called Red Door Cottage in Killathay, and my host's family has owned the cottage for more than 150 years."

A flash of inspiration. "My host is also a skilled craftsman who makes spalted beech bowls that he sells through a little shop called The Olive Branch in Killathay. I've been so impressed with the artistry of the Irish people."

"Anything else surprise you so far—aside from your encounter with our seals, that is?"

"Waking up every morning with Tim and Tom." Nancy's eyes got slightly wider. *Wait for it.* "The resident donkeys at the cottage, who are particularly fond of waking people up first thing in the morning." Nancy's laugh might have been a bit forced, but Bridget plowed on. "You can see more of the cottage and my adventures by following me on social media at @Cabi-netsCountertopsClosets."

"Well, it's been lovely having you Bridget, and steer clear of the seals in the future." Nancy turned to face the center camera. "When we come back, what the EPA needs householders to know about septic inspections." Nancy stayed fixed with a tight smile until the full studio lights came on. "Commercial. You're all set. Nice job, Bridget. You can give Ellie your microphone on your way out."

Bridget couldn't stop smiling as she edged off the chair. The adrenaline was still chugging through her system, and it felt good. She'd have to call Mary right away and let her know how it went.

Ellie, the producer with the headphones, walked Bridget back through the labyrinthine hallways and dark offices at a brisk pace. Bridget couldn't resist. "How'd I do?"

Absently, Ellie answered, "Uh, great. Especially for a first timer."

"Thanks, I was nervous at the beginning—my mouth was so dry!"

"Happens to most people. We keep a little bottle of water under the desk for that reason." *Gee Ellie, that would've been nice to know in advance.*

Finn was waiting in the green room, facing the TV with his arms crossed.

"So?" Bridget smiled, a tiny waver at the corners of her mouth.

He whipped around, startling her. "The hell was that?"

Bridget's heart dropped. "What do you mean?"

Finn glared at a spot somewhere to his left. "You'd no business bringing me up."

"I was careful not to even say your name!"

"But you said to buy the bowls at Olive's, and the whole town knows you're at mine."

Now she was getting pissed. "Um, *you're welcome*. People know you make and sell amazing bowls. Tragic. You know, having them in your cousin's store might be a clue to people that you sell them too."

He yanked his jacket off the back of the chair, making it rattle as the legs teetered off balance. "Let's go."

This was some bullshit. She caught at his arm. "Wait a second, I did you a favor!"

"Some favor."

"Normal people who sell things generally like people knowing they have things for sale. It's literally a whole industry called advertising."

"You should've asked me first." He yanked his arm away from her grip and stalked down the hallway.

Bridget's mouth hung open and she shook her head in disbelief. What a mammoth asshole. Grabbing her bag and a bottle of water, she felt the adrenaline previously circulating in her system metastasize as a red-hot flame of rage.

"Hey! Finn!"

He didn't even slow down as he approached the door to the parking garage. *Rude.*

"Finn!" Her heels ticked out a sharp staccato on the tile floor as she rushed after him. He threw himself against the metal crash bar of the door and strode through, forcing her to dodge to the side as she followed him through to the garage.

"Goddammit, stop!" She was literally shaking at this point. "You work for me, you know!"

He stopped in place, not turning around. Bridget's temper was wound tight, and she didn't bother to hold back as she continued walking up behind him. "You think I planned to say that? I didn't. I was fucking nervous, okay? Terrified! I came back to the green room, looking for a kind word and all you can say is that you're pissed that I mentioned your work. Like it was some kind of crime I committed. I thought we were past this bullshit. You know what? I won't make that mistake again."

Finn didn't say anything, but resumed his pace toward the car, slower this time. Bridget threw her hands up in the air. "Really? Nothing?"

He turned toward her, focusing his eyes at something over her shoulder. Even in the dim lights of the parking garage she could see his jaw tensing. "You did a good job," he bit off. "You just...I wasn't expecting that, and it took me by surprise. I'm sorry."

To her horror, she began to tear up. "I've never done anything like this before, and I was so nervous and I–" A sob escaped her. *Why do I have to cry?* She rustled in her bag, looking for a tissue. "I didn't think it would make you a-a-angry," she hiccuped.

Finn closed the distance between them, pulling a napkin from his pocket. "Here. Take this. I'm sorry, Bridget. I know you tried to help me, I do. But every time you talk about my pieces I feel like a gombeen, a fraud."

He tipped up her chin with a gentle caress. Through her tears, "I feel guilty every time Olive sells one of my bowls or platters to some unsuspecting tourist, knowing they will realize it's shite when they get it home. And I worry that you'll realize it too."

She blew her nose. "Finn, that's ridiculous. You—"

Without letting her finish, he enveloped her into a tight hug, kissing the top of her head. "You were really good in there. I'm sorry I rained on your big moment. No excuse."

She relaxed into his embrace, pressing her cheeks into the rough wool of his coat. She snuffled into his shoulder. "Thanks."

Her phone buzzed in her pocket. She disentangled herself and saw her text from Olive.

Our own Killathay celebrity! AMAZING JOB!
Tks for the callout! <3 <3

She tilted the phone so Finn could read too. He kissed her softly on her forehead. "C'mon, let's get on the road. I'm sure everyone in town will want to talk to you about your interview."

Finn wasn't wrong. They arrived in Killathay in time for an early lunch at Tommy Malone's. Immediately, a cry went up as they entered. Several of the locals came up to pat her on the back and congratulate her, which seemed to be required viewing among most of the town residents. People asked about Nancy Walker, what the station was like, if she met any of the TV stars from their shows. The attention and buzz re-inflated her flagging ego.

The owner of the pub comped her lunch, saying she helped "put Killathay on the map." Such a claim sparked an animated debate among the locals about which former residents and favorite sons and daughters did more for the reputation of the town. Finn and Bridget exchanged grins, tucking into their meals as the conversation grew louder around them.

"Do you have enough footage to make your next post?" Finn asked, setting down his pint. "Or do we need to head somewhere? Does the binder have suggestions?"

"I figured I'd use the footage from the interview as part of it. I've been waiting to see if the station shared a clip. But if not, hopefully I can screenshot it. And we have our selfie."

"Don't post that." He caught himself. "I mean, please don't post that."

She quirked an eyebrow. "Fine. I should have enough."

"Good. I barely slept last night." Finn gave a heavy sigh.

"Oh God, did I snore?"

"No...or at least, not much. But you do talk in your sleep." Finn gave a crooked grin as Bridget's face went slack in horror.

"What did I say?"

"Not too much."

Oh God. "What did I say?" she wailed, gripping his wrist and pinning it to the table.

"Something about cheese, I think?"

She covered her face with her hands. "This is so embarrassing," she moaned. She uncovered one eye. "Is that what kept you up?"

Finn blushed a little, but said, "No, I don't sleep well in hotels as a rule."

There was probably more to it than cheese, but to save her pride, she wasn't going to push it. "Should we head back home then?"

Finn smiled wearily. "That would be grand. I could use a nap."

Chapter 20

Secrets of the Dolmen

Finn woke from his nap but remained in bed, picking at the coverlet and staring at the ceiling in his room. His temper tantrum that morning played on repeat in his mind.

It was a reflex, the desire to be protective about his wood-working. From his earliest days when his pieces were rough and primitive, his family would smile indulgently or dismiss them out of hand. Gran had given him space to create and been his biggest supporter. He suspected she strong-armed Olive into taking them into the shop, too.

But Bridget had done nothing but support his work and believe in him. Other than Olive, she did more to sell his pieces than anyone. How did he repay her? By berating her at a TV studio. He groaned and covered his head with a pillow.

He was a first-class arse.

Rolling out of bed, he rubbed the stubble on his cheeks as he walked to the front room. Bridget was lying in a deep sleep on the sofa, her lips slightly parted, and a novel resting on her stomach.

Taking pains to be quiet, he opened the grate on the stove and added another stick of wood. Straightening, his eyes rested on one of the photographs on the end table: he and Cillian side-by-side standing on an enormous rock in the summer sun.

Epiphany. He knew how he'd make it up to her.

A snuffle from the sofa, and he turned to see Bridget sitting upright, stretching and rubbing her eyes. "Time is it?"

"Nearly supper. I have a proposition for you. If you let me take you someplace off the binder tomorrow morning, I'll get takeaway tonight."

"Deal." Bridget said, flopping back down. "I'm starving and exhausted."

The next morning, Finn was the one up in darkness. He rapped twice on her bedroom door. "Up, you. Big day," he called through the door.

A noise that sounded like Bridget gave a low moan. "It's 5:30 a.m." Her voice was thick with sleep. "Are you insane?"

"Early bird and all that. You promised I could plan the morning, and we need to leave in an hour or we'll miss it."

He heard a thump as her feet hit the floor. The door swung wide and a disheveled and sleepy Bridget leaned on the door-frame. "You know it's almost midnight in Chicago."

"You're not in Chicago, you're in Kildunne. Get showered and we're in the car by half six. Wear your best shoes for a hike."

Was it petty to smile at her groan? A bit of payback for her early mornings.

To be fair, Bridget was ready to leave ten minutes early. Finn made a great show of putting away his teacup and wiping down the counter as she tapped her foot near the door.

"So today we're..."

"Nope. Not today, Boss Lady. I'm calling point of privilege and taking you somewhere you're not going to read about in your travel guides."

She folded her arms. "Will we have time to hit the Rose Garden in Tralee?"

"Another day for roses." He paused. "Do you trust me?" *Why was her answer so important?*

She frowned, but a moment later she huffed. "Sure. Let's go." With a turn of her heel, she walked to the door, sweeping up her bag.

"As you wish."

"Can you at least tell me what direction we're heading?" It had to be killing her, not being in control of the day.

"If the sun's in your eyes, we're heading east."

"It's Ireland in December. There's no sun." Reaching into the back seat for her knapsack, she pulled out an old-school folded map, making a great show of snapping it open and smoothing it out.

"Are we headed toward Shannon?"

"Nope."

"Dingle?"

"No."

"Galway?"

"That's the same direction as Shannon." It was beginning to hurt, this keeping from smiling. She peered out the windscreen at the night sky.

"I saw the stars the other night. They were beautiful—I've never seen the sky look like that. The glow and color of the galaxies." Her voice was soft, rounded out by her dreamy expression.

Finn felt pride of place swell in his chest. "I don't think I could live anywhere else. It doesn't happen often, but you can sometimes see the borealis on a clear night."

She was quiet for a moment. "I've never seen the Northern Lights. I remember being in maybe fifth grade, and we were on an Alaskan cruise. When my mom married Dennis, she joined his travel agency. Sometimes they'd get incentives to travel, and if the school calendar worked out, they'd take me. One morning at breakfast, they saw the northern lights but they never woke me. They spent an hour watching it up on the decks, and I was asleep, alone in the cabin."

"Did they do that often?"

"Do what?"

"Leave you alone."

She hesitated. "They worked a lot and traveled a lot too. I stayed with my grandparents a lot, or my aunt Judy." He kept his eyes on the road, but he caught her looking down at her binder.

"Where are they now? Your mum and stepdad?"

She smiled faintly. "Somewhere in the Aegean, I think. They booked a 21-day cruise for Greece, Turkey, and Egypt and all kinds of Mediterranean destinations. They aren't going to be back until after Christmas."

His knuckles turned white as he clenched the wheel, a stab of anger coursing through him. "They left you alone for Christmas?"

She gave him a thoughtful look. "I know it sounds bad, but it's not. After mom married Dennis, we moved out of my grandparents' house and I was allowed to be home alone after school and every day during the summer, pretty self-sufficient for someone that young. Now I'm a homebody, but I have my friends, and my roommate Tran. Her family has me over all the time, and their Christmas is something to see!"

He couldn't even fathom not being around family at the holidays. "My mother would probably excommunicate me from the family if I missed ten minutes of my niece's nativity play, much less an entire Christmas."

Her voice was soft. "There's something nice about having no drama, the food you want to eat, everything in its place without the chaos. Tran's family is a free-for-all, with dozens of presents and wrapping everywhere. I love it, but I also love getting back to my room afterwards."

They were silent together for a while, and the gray shadows of the predawn sky began to turn pink. Finn leaned forward to squint at the sky. "We've got to hurry then."

Another half mile and he pulled the car off on the soft shoulder of the road, quickly hopping the stone fence to begin walking up the hillside. The pre-dawn sky was brightening to the point where it would make an easy path up. Bridget stepped out of the car and called after him. "Where are we going? Do I need my equipment?"

"Just bring your phone," he called over his shoulder. Come on, now!"

The ground was soft and spongy, but Finn made quick time moving up the hill, picking out the easiest path for Bridget to follow. At the halfway mark, he turned back to see Bridget picking her way through the squishier parts, a good ways behind. Finn cupped his hand to shout. "Your backside still sore from the waterfall? Giving you trouble is it?"

"My. Backside. Is. Fine." Each word was clipped as she stepped carefully around rocks, gorse and grassy patches. "Are we going to the top?"

Finn grinned. "Not far now. Let me know if you need help, Boss Lady."

Another thirty meters and he arrived at the crest of the hill.

He walked eastward along the flat peak for a few moments as he waited for Bridget to join him.

"Hold up a minute," she huffed. Turning back, he saw Bridget struggling to make it to the top, her yellow wellies slipping on the slick flora. "Is nothing dry in this country?"

Finn trotted back down to help her. "Here now, take my hand." She reached up to him, and despite the cold, her hand was warm in his. With a steady pull, he brought her to the top.

Head down, she focused on brushing the mud off her jeans. "I hope there's something up here worth—oh!"

The rosy glow of the sunrise was beginning to burst into full glory, and from their view, the entire sky was alive with color. Every bird in the valley had erupted with chattering, providing a crescendo backdrop to the breathtaking palette of pinks and purples.

He watched as Bridget took it all in, her face transfixed as she absorbed the beauty of the moment. He half-expected her to reach for her phone, to look for the best angle. But she simply stared at the vista before her, her curls whipping in the wind. In the distance, the valley dipped down into the bay, the reflection of the sunrise shimmering with the waves.

I don't want to break the spell.

He leaned over to whisper. "Worth the trip?"

Without breaking her gaze, she nodded.

"Just wait now."

As the sun finally rose over the mountain in the distance, the pink tones dispersed into bright light, illuminating the entire countryside.

Without a word, she reached for his hand and squeezed. He felt a lump form in his throat, but he forced it down to quietly say, "I once told Father Tim I saw more of God from here than from St. Brendan's. I think he understood what I meant."

"Beautiful isn't a big enough word to describe it."

"I'm glad you got to see it." There was that lump again. His voice sounded gruff, even to him. "My dad would take me up here on days when I'd be up at the crack on the weekends. Being the baby of the family, I think he wanted to make sure I wouldn't fuss and wake the whole house, because I was an obscenely early riser."

"How things have changed," she murmured.

"He'd tell me old stories about his family. Malloys have lived around these hills and mountains since the 1100s at least."

Bridget smiled. "Where I grew up, we'd take field trips to a schoolhouse built in the 1860s. It was barely 100 years old when they made it a museum, and it felt like it was ancient. Now you're talking about tracing your family back almost a millennium. It blows my mind."

"You ready to see something else?"

Chapter 21

Take a Bite

Bridget stumbled along behind Finn's surefooted hiking, but he didn't drop her hand once. "I can't believe I didn't even pull out my phone to take a photograph," she said. "I'm literally the world's worst influencer."

"Don't think it would've translated anyway." Finn glanced back at her to wink but didn't stop his careful progression down the back side of the mountain.

"Are we even supposed to be here?"

"Technically, no. But the land belongs to a friend of my father's, and I'm sure he wouldn't mind. He leaves it for the sheep, mostly. Er, mind where you step."

Bridget immediately took a greater interest in where she placed her feet.

About halfway down the hill, Finn pointed out an immense flat stone laid out on the ground, as long as a dining room tabletop but more narrow, and thick as a tree trunk.

"Here," Finn said, dropping Bridget's hand and jogging

ahead a few paces. He brushed off the surface of the stone and gestured for Bridget to sit.

"Is this it?"

"You mentioned your hundred-years history. This stone was likely placed here thousands of years ago."

"Thousands?" Bridget ran her hand along the rough, weather-worn surface of the gray stone. How many hands had touched this stone before?

Finn sat beside her, close enough so their legs touched. The cold from the stone was permeating from the damp chill of her jeans, and she shivered slightly. The bright sun that had momentarily illuminated everything was now slipping behind a stretch of thick, murky clouds that promised foul weather later that morning.

"Are you too cold?" Finn asked.

There was no way she was going to put a damper on this moment, even if she was near frostbite. "No, I'm fine."

Without a word, he put his left arm around her as he pointed with his right. "My dad said that at one time, there were three of these stones, put together like a doorway. There's an old carve-out behind us, not quite a cave, and it was likely where it led. They call it a dolmen, and my da said that the giants put them here."

"Giants," Bridget said flatly.

"I thought you said you did your homework on Ireland?" Finn gave her a sideways look. "All sorts of giants in these hills."

"So where are the other stones? The ones that made the doorway?"

Finn dropped his arm and slid around, bringing his legs to the other side of the stone. She swung around a bit less gracefully, already missing the warmth of him.

"You can see parts of the other rock there." He pointed down the hillside, where a pile of rocks clustered. "It either fell or slid down and cracked into pieces. Or the giants stepped on it."

"You said there were three?"

"No one knows where the last rock is. I've seen other dolmen like this—there's one on a golf course in Dundalk, even. Their stones are a bit smaller, and they weigh 40 tons. It's not as though someone could pick it up and walk away with it."

"Perhaps it's the fairy folk." She felt him stiffen beside her. "What's wrong?"

"I keep telling you, don't say that out loud."

She looked at him skeptically. "You don't really believe..."

Finn got to his feet. "What did Shakespeare say? 'There are more things in heaven and earth than are dreamt of in your philosophy.' And he was *English*. We Irish have a healthy respect for the Others on this earth. A dolmen is likely a thin place, where the boundaries between what we know and what we don't can be crossed."

Almost on cue, a deep roar of thunder rolled across the sky. Finn arched his eyebrow. "You see?"

Bridget rolled her eyes. "Oh, come on," she laughed. Immediately, fat, stinging raindrops began to pelt down from the skies, and Bridget gave a squeak and fumbled with the hood on her jacket.

"Jesus, we're in for a lashing. That came out of bleedin' nowhere!" Finn pulled her up from the stone and put his arm around her again, trying to walk her closer to the mountain's side. "This way."

Bridget held her hood in place as the wind whipped around them. Finn began to pull on a tangle of vines and branches climbing up the side of the hill. "Come here."

He held back the vines, revealing an alcove carved into the rocky side of the hill. He pulled her toward the hidey hole. "Go on, get in!"

Willing herself not to think of bugs or other creepy crawlies, Bridget ducked into the alcove, tucking herself into a tight sitting position, knees up against her chest. Finn did the same, and they watched the rain flood down in relative protection.

"How did you know this was here?"

"My brother and I, we stashed a bottle of Bushmill's up here when we were younger," Finn said. "One night, we got so drunk we dared each other to sleep on the dolmen stone all night."

"Your mother let you stay out all night?"

"Course not. Snuck out the window while she was sleeping and rode our bicycles to get here."

Bridget shivered again. Finn untucked his arm from his folded legs and wrapped it around her again. She couldn't help it, she leaned into him. Her head fit perfectly, nestled into the crook of his neck. She could feel the rough fibers of his wool sweater pricking at her cheek as she relaxed her body to form to his. "What happened?"

"You're going to think I'm telling tales."

Bridget pulled her head up slightly to look at Finn. "You drag me to the top of the mountain where otherworldly forces try to drown us, and you won't finish your story?"

He grinned. "You won't believe me anyway, but I'll tell you." He adjusted slightly, leaning back against the hollow, wincing slightly as he tried to find a comfortable position, never once losing contact with her.

"We decided to sleep head-to-toe, so each of us could have eyes behind us if something happened. It took us a while to sleep, despite being fluttered with four fingers of whiskey in each of us. It was July, so quite warm that night. Not a breeze to speak of. Cill tells it different, but I'll tell you my version."

Bridget snuggled back into the crook of his arm, dispelling all pretense that it was purely for warmth. "Story time. Go on."

"It was after midnight, I know that. But it was fairly bright, with an almost full moon above us. I had curled up with my arm beneath me, trying to get comfortable on that rock. And I felt it begin to hum."

"Hum?"

He nodded. "Years later, when I visited my cousins outside of Boston, we walked under some great metal towers for the electric power lines and I could hear the air crackling. It was just like that."

Bridget tried to keep the skepticism from her voice. "What happened then?"

"I was terrified. I kicked at Cill with my foot but couldn't get him to wake up. I felt like I couldn't sit up, like I was held to the rock."

His arm tightened around her, and his voice got rough. "I'm telling you, it's crazy, but the next thing I remember, I woke up in my bed, Cill in the bed next to mine."

"How did you—?"

"Damned if I know. To this day, Cill doesn't like to talk about it."

The clammy alcove seemed somehow more sinister, and Bridget felt the hairs on her arms stand up. "There has to be a logical explanation, though."

She wouldn't call his expression patronizing exactly, but he looked down with an indulgent smile. "More things in heaven and earth..."

Before she could respond, he kissed her.

It was a soft kiss at first, testing the waters. He pulled away, whispering "Was that ok?"

"Oh yes," she said, surprised at the heat in her own voice.

She straightened, giving her a better angle to return his kiss with intention.

His hand cupped the back of her head, bringing her closer. He tasted of mint. Finn broke from the kiss gently, his fingers trailing around her collarbone. "Not much space to maneuver in here."

"You're doing fine," she answered. She was a bit disoriented, like she'd slipped slightly off her axis. This wasn't in the playbook, not in the plan.

For the first time in her life, she didn't care.

"Fine, is it?" Finn smiled down at her. "I guess I'll need to do better than that."

At once, his mouth met hers, warm and insistent. Her lips parted as he explored, his tongue insistent, teasing.

She reached up to run her hands through his black, wiry hair as he burned a trail of kisses down her neck. She gasped as his stubbly cheek electrified her nerve endings everywhere he touched along her neck. She twitched, her senses overwhelmed.

"You good?"

"Just trying to remember how to breathe."

Finn's eyes sparked with mischief. "I have some bad news for you, then."

"What's that?"

"Rain's stopping."

Bridget blinked several times, reorienting herself to the surroundings. "Oh." She hoped that the disappointment wasn't clear in her voice.

Finn climbed out of the recess first, holding back the wet bramble and vines so she could stand up without additional insult from the rain. "There. Now we have a grand soft day."

The sun seeped through a gap in the clouds, a thin ray becoming a burnished glow. The arc of a brilliant rainbow appeared behind them. "Oh, that's perfect," Bridget exclaimed. "Even if it doesn't come out on video, I have to try."

"There's no leprechauns or pots of gold, you know..." Finn called after her as she trudged up the steep hillside again to get to the crest.

Grabbing hold of a thicket of grasses on the top of the mountain, she heaved herself up to the peak of the hill. Laid out over in the pillowing fog of the valley, the shimmer of the stray sunbeams coated the mountain with a thin veneer of glittering green. The rainbow was crisp and vivid, arching from the hills to the bay. Bridget reluctantly pulled her phone from her pocket, knowing even as she hit record, there was no way she'd be able to capture this with a mere digital image. "Finn, you have to see this!"

With far less effort, Finn skimmed up the side of the hill and joined her. Careful not to disturb the shot as she panned the horizon with her camera, he stood behind her, slipping his hands around her waist. Leaning toward her ear he said, "Welcome to Ireland, Bridget." He swept her curls to one side and laid a gentle kiss on the back of her neck.

She nearly swooned.

After a few more seconds of footage, she hit *Stop* on the phone and put it in her pocket. Swiveling in his arms, she said, "Are you trying to distract me from my video?"

"Is it working?"

"It is." She leaned in to kiss him again.

The rainbow diffused into the sky as the sun slipped behind the cover of the thick clouds. With an eye on the heavy gray sky, they began to make their way back down the hillside, scraping the mud and muck off their boots every few minutes.

As they neared the road, something in a clearing caught Bridget's eye. Four tiny tea light candles were arranged in a circle, with a scrap of fabric and a key. She bent down to take a closer look, reaching for the key.

"Don't touch it!" Finn pulled at her arm, steadying her as she tipped backwards.

"What is it?"

He frowned. "Someone playing at things."

"No, seriously."

Finn helped her stand. "It's a love charm. That bit in the middle is from the object of their affections, and the candles and key are to unlock their heart. It's rubbish"

Bridget cocked her head. "What happened to 'more things in heaven and earth?'"

"This is just foolishness, playing at things they shouldn't. Come on." Finn continued down the mountain, and Bridget stared at the strange assembly for a moment, then pulled out her camera and took a quick photo.

"So what's next?" Bridget sat on the edge of her seat in his car with the door open, carefully clapping her boots together to loosen the mud without spraying it everywhere. Reaching into the back seat, she pulled out a large tour booklet from one of their many historical sites and spread it on the floor, placing her dirty boots carefully on the paper.

"You're not too knackered? Don't want to go home for a rest and a hot shower?"

At face value, his words were normal and appropriate. But there was something in his tone, that made her think he might have something else in mind.

Stop thinking of him like that. Stop thinking of his damp shirt. Think of something else. She paused, weighing his offer. "I could go for a hot shower and dry clothes." *And maybe continue this at home.*

He started the car and headed toward the cottage. "I've been meaning to say, we're invited to dinner at my mum's day after tomorrow. I canceled on her last week, and we don't have to go. I'm sure you don't want to—"

She cut him off. "That sounds wonderful! I'd love to meet your mom."

"You don't have to go."

She couldn't help herself. "Do you not *want* me to go?"

He rubbed the back of his head. "You're sure to get the third degree. My sisters will probably be there too."

That wasn't exactly an answer. Did he want her to go or not? "If it would cause you problems..." she trailed off.

He sighed. "My family always causes problems, but there's probably fewer if we go."

Bridget used the trip home to edit the video of the rainbow on her, and she was right –the images were a weak reproduction of what she experienced firsthand. When she put the phone down, Finn slipped his arm around her shoulders and Bridget snuggled in as much as the seatbelt allowed. This newfound intimacy between them felt just as precious as it did precarious. As her rational side tried to wave a huge, red *"just one more week"* flag, she diligently tamped it down. For someone who generally protected her heart at all costs, this was dangerous territory.

Maybe she needed a little danger.

When they pulled back through the gap in the stone fence at Finn's cottage, she was struck by how much it felt like home. As Finn walked around the car to open her door, she slipped her muddy yellow boots back on for the walk to the house. The rain had, of course, started again.

Bridget rifled through her bags to grab the binder and a few brochures she'd picked up the day before. She hustled to the doorway, shielding her papers as best she could from the rain.

"I'll put the kettle on and get the fire started," Finn called back as he unlocked the door.

That's it? Her heart deflated a little as he proceeded ahead of her into the kitchen. Maybe she was the only one transformed by the events of the morning. A flash of insecurity swept through her. *Did I read too much into this?*

Peeling off her raincoat and setting her boots carefully in the doorway, she headed straight for her bedroom. "I'm going to jump in the shower," she called toward the kitchen, closing the bedroom door behind her. The rain was starting to come down in sheets again, and the noise rattled at the windows. The day was likely a washout, but she could catch up on her work, maybe even curl up with a book by the fire. It was Saturday after all.

Grabbing the towel from the hook on the back of her bedroom door, she shimmied out of her wet clothes wrapped the towel around her body, grateful for something dry and relatively warm. She laid out fresh clothes on her bed, hesitating as she chose a matching black bra and panties set instead of the faded white cotton bralettes and underwear she routinely wore.

A girl could hope, right?

As she entered the hallway, the bathroom door was not quite closed, and she could hear the shower running inside. She flashed back to her first day in Ireland, when Finn drew her a bath. *So nice of him to get the shower hot for me.*

The door was stuck slightly in the humidity, so she gave it a push and went inside.

She froze.

The water wasn't running for her.

Finn faced away from her, head fully under the spray of the

shower head, rinsing a smattering of foam from his black curls. The thin plastic shower liner was fogged with steam, but not so much that she couldn't make out every inch of his form.

She couldn't tear her eyes away.

She didn't *want* to tear her eyes away.

He turned toward her, rubbing his face to clear the bubbles from his closed eyes.

Oh. My. God.

He opened his eyes. Seeing Bridget, he jumped backwards knocking the bottle of shampoo to the bottom of the tub. "Jesus Christ!"

His hands immediately covered his crotch, catching himself as he slipped.

But not before Bridget got a full, robust, impressive view.

They stared at each other for a few moments, neither speaking.

Come on Bridget, for once in your life...take a bite!

Without a word, Bridget dropped her towel.

Chapter 22

Clean and Dirty

It had to be a dream.

There was no way this woman walked into his bath and dropped her towel. Bridget stared at him, looking luscious and inviting and incredibly hot. Finn raised his hands from his crotch slowly, as he wiped the water from his eyes. No point in hiding anything. It was now or never.

"You coming in?"

She began to move toward him, so Finn pulled the curtain liner aside to give her room, extending his hand to steady her as she stepped into the slick clawfoot tub.

Finn moved over to let her under the hot water, awkwardly navigating two adult humans in a too-small tub. It was impossible for their bodies not to touch.

Bridget faced the water, Finn in the cold behind her. She hadn't said a word yet, but when she reached down to grab her shampoo bottle, she edged her backside into his crotch slowly, agonizingly rubbing against the length of him.

Straightening, she turned to face him, water cascading down the front of her body and running down her breasts.

Without breaking her gaze, she squeezed shampoo into her hands. She tipped her head back and began to work the shampoo through her hair, the movement lifting her breasts and driving him nearly mad. Her nipples were only inches from his own chest, rising and falling as her hands languidly threaded the suds through her curls.

"My God, you're beautiful," he murmured. Her eyes opened as she squeezed the last of the foam out of her hair, rivulets of water draining down her curves. She turned and bent over, her backside sliding against him again. This time she came back up with his bar of soap. "Do my back?"

He worked the bar of soap into a froth, rubbing the lather across her shoulder blades and dipping down to the small shallow at the crest of her ass.

With each pass, his strokes became longer, stretching to the outer edges of her back, edging closer to her hips, her lower thighs and even her stomach. He wasn't going to touch anywhere else unless she expressly asked.

"Is your back clean enough?" He could barely trust himself to speak.

"Let me rinse?" She lifted her hair from the back of her neck and turned to face him. "I guess it's time to clean the rest of me."

He moved toward her, eager to touch. She stopped him in his tracks as she held out her hand for the bar of soap.

His disappointment didn't last long. Bridget began to rub the suds in slow, deliberate circles on her breasts. With the tips of her fingers, she made smaller circles on her nipples, bringing each of them to hard peaks.

"Need some help?"

"No."

Never once did she break eye contact. She was putting on a show just for him. And holy hell, it was working.

She set the soap down and began to dip her soapy hands into the patch of curls between her thighs. She shuddered involuntarily as her hand skimmed her mound. How could his mouth be so dry in a steamy shower? Her hand dipped low again, and he heard the softest moan of pleasure escape her.

Two can play at that game.

Finn reached for the soap, worked up a lather and began stroking himself. Bridget matched his pace, dipping her hand between her thighs with the same tempo. She bent her knees, her hips moving slightly as her rhythm became more frantic.

He was getting too close. He couldn't match her pace without exploding. Bridget closed her eyes, tweaked her nipple and gave a cry of release. *Thank God.* With a moan, Finn pumped his hand a few more times, leaning forward to come toward the drain.

She turned around briefly to rinse in the shower stream. When she faced him again, he pulled her close, the heat of her steam-warmed body curved against his, her arms around his neck. He was conscious of every centimeter of her skin that pressed against him. He kissed her deeply, letting his hands skim down her back to rest on the swell of her ass.

When the finally broke away, Bridget leaned her head against his shoulder, tracing patterns in his chest hair. "I guess we're clean now."

"Not sure about that. Some would call us very, very dirty."

"Then maybe we should dry off." She reached down to turn off the shower and Finn slid back the curtain.

The friction from toweling off his ebbing erection made him flinch. Wrapping the towel around his waist, he leaned down to pluck her towel from the floor. "I think you forgot this, Boss Lady."

Bridget wrapped herself in the towel, tucking it high under her arms. She stepped from the tub pink and rosy, looking completely sated. She stepped toward the sink and worked a comb carefully through her wet curls.

"It's a shame, though," he added.

She paused, looking wary. "What's a shame?"

"I watched you make yourself come...and can't take any credit for helping."

Bridget put down the comb, turned and leaned back against the sink. A mischievous glint appeared in her eye as her hand absently trailed along her collarbone. "Agreed—not very gentlemanly to make me do it all myself."

Finn leaned against the doorframe. *Was that a challenge?* "Only fair you give me a crack at it, then."

"What exactly are you thinking?"

Wordlessly, he reached toward her. He kissed her again, but this was not the tender kiss from the shower. These kisses were savage, hungry.

"Follow me."

He backed down the hallway, urging her toward his bedroom. They shuffled together, focused more on the intensity of the kiss than the geography of the room. When he backed up against the bedpost, he gave a sharp tug on her towel, dropping it to the floor. He pulled her close to him, their bodies pressed against each other, feeling water-warmed skin-on-skin.

"Get comfortable. This is going to take a while."

A nervous smile flickered across her face. She scooted up to the pillows at the head of the bed and snuggled in.

He slid into place alongside her, tucking them both beneath the quilt. "I don't want you getting cold."

"The last thing I am is cold."

He grinned. "Perhaps I should see how warm you are?"

He kissed her again, letting his hands skim across the curves and valleys of her body. He could feel the tiny hairs raise on her arms, and watched her nipples tighten as he brushed over them with the lightest touch.

As his fingers trailed across her hip bones, she gasped and flinched away from him.

"And here I thought only your feet were ticklish." He moved his kisses to her neck and collarbone, making her gasp again. Her body was like a live wire underneath his touch. His mouth closed on her nipple and she arched off the mattress.

"Easy there," he said, grinning up at her. "We're just getting started. Don't want you peaking too early, do we?"

She reached up to run her fingers through his still-wet hair, shaking the droplets out of his curls.

"You're getting me wet." She wiped drops of water from her face. His mouth went dry.

"That's the plan." The heat in his voice sounded like a growl.

He moved to straddle her. In a jerky motion, he took her wrists and pinned them above her head. "Be a good girl and leave them here, would you?"

She nodded, then gasped as he began to stroke gently down her arms, kissing at the creases of her elbows, then near her underarms. She flinched as his stubble tickled the sensitive skin, her nerves tight.

"Tsk! Keep your arms where they belong. You don't want me to tie them to the bedposts, do you?"

"Maybe," she whispered, her voice small and trembling. Who was this woman? In the shower, she was in charge, making him watch as she pleasured herself. But now she was giving him control. Giving him everything.

He could barely breathe.

Finn tongued at her underarm, then began to scatter slow, lingering kisses around the edges of her breast. Bridget's eyes squeezed tight, her breaths shallow. "You want me to suck them, don't you," he said between kisses.

"God, yes."

He hovered over her nipple again, only millimeters away from contact. His breath made her nipples tighten. He flicked his tongue at the very tip, then closed over it with urgency, sucking and nibbling. The notes of her sighs rose like a breathy scale, increasing each time his mouth locked on her flesh, swirling the bud of her nipple with his tongue.

He moved to her left breast, leaving her right one exposed and still wet. Again, he teased her. Again, he savaged her. He slipped his hand between her legs, only teasing the outside of her vulva. She trembled beneath him, maneuvering to give him better access to her core.

"Please," she gasped. "Please."

"What do you want me to do, Bridget." He moved up to kiss her, probing the depths of her mouth hungrily. He broke away. "You have to tell me."

"Please fuck me."

After a long, searing kiss, he rolled off the bed, a prayer that his bedside table drawer would have what he needed. He tossed a condom onto the bed next to her.

"At the ready."

"Can I use my hands now?"

"Oh no, *mo stoirín.*" He coaxed her legs apart and knelt on the bed between them. "You'll be keeping those up there. I have work to do."

He slid his fingertip through her cleft with a delicate touch. "You got her so clean for me."

Bridget's eyes were still shut, her head lolling to one side as she was consumed by his attentions. She was slick and eager, pushing up against the pressure of his touch. He dipped into her with one finger, then two. He began a slow thrusting movement, feeling the muscles of her inner walls tighten around him.

"Look at me, Bridget." Her eyes flickered open. In a moment, he covered her mouth with his own, his tongue searching, hungry. He could hear her small cries as he continued to thrust his fingers into her.

She moved her hands to embrace him, caressing down his shoulders and back then up to his neck. He shivered.

She paused. "Are you cold?"

"Cold? Christ woman, I'm burning for you."

With a smile, she moved her hand, encircled him with a feather-light grip. She ran her hand up and down the shaft, gently cupping his balls on the downstrokes.

This was getting dangerous. He caught her hand. "If I'm going to be any use to you, you have to stop now." Finn leaned across her to retrieve the condom, rolled it on, and with one slow, steady thrust, he was inside her.

He waited a moment, concentrating on the feeling of her enveloping him, marveling at their two bodies joining together. Then slowly, he began to move.

"Do you like this?" he asked, picking up his tempo.

"Ye-e-e-s..." she answered, her voice punctuated by each thrust. "Can you...go...faster?"

Finn grinned. He put his hands under her behind, lifting her up a few inches as he began to thrust.

He could feel her tighten around him, so he slowed his pace. Finn braced himself above her, supporting his weight with his arms. He began a rhythm of slow, languid strokes inside her, grinding against her with his hips as they connected, then pulling all the way out. It was fucking fantastic.

"Can you come like this?" he gasped. "Because I'm getting close."

She considered for a moment, then said, "Roll over."

"Whatever you say, Boss Lady." Finn rolled to the middle of the bed, put both hands behind his head. *I'll let you drive from here.*

Bridget positioned herself above him, slowly lowering onto his erection. All smiles disappeared as Finn gave a low moan of desire. "You feel so fucking good."

Bridget began rocking gently, agonizingly slow, then gradually increasing her speed until she arched her back.

"You want me to—"

"Squeeze them. Hard." In seconds, Finn had her breasts in a firm but not painful grip.

It was all she needed. The arc crested, the dam burst. Bridget swatted Finn's hands away and collapsed on his chest. Her heart was beating so fast he thought she would hyperventilate.

"Um..." Finn moved his hips up slightly and Bridget's whole body shuddered with the aftershocks.

"Give me one second."

"You may not need it." Finn covered his eyes with the crook of his arm, biting his lip in concentration.

Bridget angled upright again, her own body squeezing and tightening around him involuntarily so each stroke prolonged her own aftershocks. Ten, maybe twelve strokes were all he needed and he, too, reached his climax. He put his hands on her hips, freezing her in place as he moved a fraction of an inch up off the bed, convulsing within her.

Leaning down, she kissed him. "I take it you're done?"

"I thought you were going to forget about me."

"I'm very thorough."

"Indeed."

She lifted herself off him carefully, letting him attend to the condom while she stretched like a cat on the bed. "I feel like taking a three-hour nap."

Finn laid down next to her, tracing patterns on her arm. "We can stay here as long as you'd like. Maybe never leave this bed again. I could shift you for days. Every last juicy bit of you."

Her eyes flickered. "I wish. Do you do this often?"

A loaded question. "Have my shower interrupted by a gorgeous woman, standing there without a scrap on? No. I have to say that's a first. Except for every dream I had from about age 11 to 17."

"What happened when you hit age 17?"

"Aisling Riordan," he winked. He began to thread his fingers through her still-wet curls, trying to detangle them but getting caught in the knots. "Hang on."

He rolled off the bed and disappeared down the hall. In a moment, he returned with her wide-tooth comb. "Can't let it dry like this. Sit up."

Bridget sat up, reaching for the comb.

"Let me be doing that." He sat behind her, picking up her hair and running the comb through it gently. He detangled her curls from the bottom up, holding the hair so it wouldn't pull or snarl.

"You're good at this."

"I can braid it too, if you'd like."

"A man who can do my hair? That's hot."

Finn tugged twice on her hair. "Just for that, you're getting a ponytail."

He combed her hair far longer than necessary, not willing to relinquish the tempting pleasure of Bridget's backside pressed up against him. "So, do we have to go to work again, or can we take that three-hour nap?"

She turned to caress his cheek, kissing him again. "As much as that sounds amazing, I need to post today."

He slid from the bed and began to dress. "Can't have you

saying I'm a drag on your plans. Wasn't today Tralee? Or did you want to go to Niamheora? Can't have you missing a literal bump in a field."

She swatted at him, and he caught her hand, covering it with a kiss.

Bridget smiled. "I want us to go and see the bump. But I'm starving."

"Can't have that. I'll tell you what—we can swing by a place I know on the way and grab a bite. Now get dressed, Boss Lady."

Chapter 23

Falling Hard

The Ruins of Niamheora listing in Bridget's binder described the site as "a Neolithic Age mystery." If Finn was writing the review, it would read, "dull lumps in the grass." He tried to offer a wide range of alternatives. Granted, most of them involved returning to his bedroom.

The Binder had decreed that Niamheora was important, and The Binder ruled the day. Somehow, that didn't bother him as much.

Set well into an open field, the Ruins were two enormous concentric circles, rising two or three feet above the rest of the area. Covered with sod and grasses, they resembled a gigantic wax seal someone pressed into the ground.

They parked near the roadside, reviewed the historical marker sign fused to a large stone, then set off. The first of the rings was about thirty yards out. Bridget and her yellow boots walked ahead of him, undeterred by the decidedly unimpressive sight. Finn hung back with the bag of equipment.

"See anything exciting to shoot?" He was careful to tamp down any 'I told you so' tones.

"Ha ha," she called back. "The people who built this lived thousands of years ago. They'd probably think we were magic, talking to people around the world with the touch of a button, all the knowledge of humanity accessible on our phones."

Finn kicked at a stone idly. "Probably be more impressed that we live past twenty-five and have jacks that flush."

Bridget walked this way and that, stopping at times to peer at her phone's camera. "You're right, it's really tough to show the scope and scale here." She scanned the area. "It's going to look flat unless we get some perspective."

"What d'ya say I film you now, close up. Then I'll try to get as far back as I can and shoot you at a distance."

Bridget nodded, her hair flying into her face. "Hang on, let me put my hair back. Should have let you give me that pony-tail." She swept up her hair into a clip, baring her neck.

He flashed to the mental image of kissing that neck. *Focus.*

The wind on the open plain whipped around them now, leaves and bramble swirling about their feet. "It's going to be too windy out here to hear you," he said.

Bridget came toward him, hair secured. "I have a lavaliere mike somewhere in here. Hang on." She unearthed a compact black pouch from the equipment bag. After pairing the micro-phone, she handed Finn her phone. "Run a test video to make sure you can hear me?"

She walked about five paces away and gave him a nod. "Testing...testing, this is Bridget, at the Ruins of Niamheora."

Finn gave her a thumbs up.

"Hi friends! One of the amazing things my HouseHijack adventure has shown me is how accessible historical sites are in other parts of the world. I'm standing right now on the ruins of a ring fort wall, or at least that's what archeologists call it. It's a little hard to see, but these bumps are two concentric circles, which have sunk into the ground, covered with grass and dirt. Experts think they were made by people living thousands of years ago during the Neolithic era. And here I am, just standing here. No guardrails or ropes or anything. I have to say, it's pretty cool. Yolo Solo, everyone!"

She paused with her fake frozen smile until Finn put the phone down. "Ok, stay there, I have an idea." He jogged back to the marker, stepping up onto the stone fence that abutted it and carefully climbed to the top. It was only about three meters off the ground, but it gave him enough height to get depth to the picture. He hit *Record* and waved his arm over his head to signal her to start. "Bring it, Boss Lady."

Bridget grinned and launched into another few moments of description.

Finn raised his arm over his head in a twirling motion, and Bridget stretched her arms out to her sides and slowly began to spin in a circle as she talked.

It was camera gold. Her face was illuminated by the silly joy of the spin. Finn raised his hand again, a big thumbs-up.

And promptly slipped off the wall.

Ow. Oh, goddamn it all, that hurts.

Ah shite, I'm bleeding too.

With a groan, Finn lifted his head off the ground slowly, touching his fingers to the large and copiously bleeding wound above his ear.

He'd been knocked cold before, but a chill ran through him as he saw the rough edges of the rock wall only a few inches from where he landed. Gran would've said his guardian angel was working double-time.

"Finn!" The scream came towards him, and suddenly, a disheveled Bridget appeared in view, half-crying as she kept repeating his name.

"Are you ok? Did you hit your head? Oh my God, you're bleeding!" In a flash, she was fishing in the equipment bag, coming up with the soft pouch from the microphone. She pressed it gently against his head. "I hope this is antiseptic. How many fingers am I holding up? I'm supposed to be the one who falls all the time!" Her voice was escalating into panicked tones, and Finn waved off the fingers she was dangling in front of his eyes.

"I'm fine. Just took a hopper. Give me a minute to get back on my feet." He reached a hand toward Bridget, who gently pulled him up to a sitting position.

Never mind, sitting up was a terrible idea. He groaned loudly, leaning forward toward his knees, willing the throbbing to cease.

"Should I call 9-1-1...I mean, 9-9-9? Is that what we call here?"

"Don't call anybody. Give me a good goddamn minute."

Bridget sat back on her heels. "What can I do?"

"Medical kit. In the boot."

She nodded, returning in moments with the same well-used first aid kit he'd used on her at Bernie's cottage. "Doesn't look like there's much in here," she said doubtfully. "Some gauze. I have some gaffing tape in the camera bag, we can bandage you up."

"Give it over." Holy hell, his head was beginning to hurt. He winced in pain as he pulled out the wad of gauze and pressed it on his head.

"We need to get that looked at."

"Would you stop fussing over me?" Ah, that came out a sight too sharp. Bridget recoiled, making him immediately regret his words. "I'm sorry, I'm not used to letting people fuss over me. Side effect of growing up with three sisters. I was mothered to death."

"Of course." But he could see the hurt written plainly on her face.

"I don't think I got anything recorded before I fell..." he said, dabbing at his wound with the gauze.

She grew still. "Where's my phone?"

Finn patted himself down to see if it was in a pocket or on his person. "I think I dropped it."

Bridget got to her feet and retrieved the phone from a grassy patch a few feet away. He could hear her replaying the video: his own voice, then a loud thunk and groaning.

"How'd I do?" he called to Bridget. Ouch. Raising his voice caused his head to throb, and for nothing—she didn't even crack a half-smile as she shoved the phone into her pocket. "Is it broken?"

"It's fine. We need to get you to a doctor." She stood before him, one hand outstretched. "Can you get up?"

He grabbed her hand and with a few stumbles, got to his feet. Was the world supposed to be spinning like this? It wasn't often, but on occasion his stubbornness was outranked by his good sense.

"Do you think you can drive to A&E?" he asked.

It was a tough call. Was his head wound more painful, or did it hurt more watching Bridget try to drive his car? The lurching and grinding as she attempted to shift gears easily shaved a year off his life and his transmission's. He called Dr. Warren on the way and he called ahead to A&E to pave the way for them.

At the clinic, the doctor glued the cut on his head, bandaged it and gave Bridget explicit instructions to watch him for further signs of a concussion. As she left to gather the discharge paperwork, Finn turned to Bridget. "A quiet room and undisturbed sleep was not what I was hoping for this evening," he said, squeezing Bridget's hand. He hoped that she'd read his flirtation as an apology for derailing the day and losing his temper when hurt.

"No strenuous activity, I'm afraid." Bridget said wistfully. The doctor returned with paperwork and a friendly reminder to see Dr. Warren in a week.

In a week, Bridget would be gone.

He cleared his throat. "Now I have to survive you driving us home," Finn said, as he slid carefully back into the passenger seat.

Bridget paused for a moment, hand on the ignition key. "I want to apologize for making you feel smothered before. I tend to panic in situations like this, especially when I travel."

"I shouldn't have barked at you."

"No, you were fine," she said, waving off his apology, her eyes filling. A tear broke away and started streaming down her cheek. "When I saw you there, bleeding, I could barely breathe. I felt like I was choking."

Finn lifted her hand to his mouth, kissing it gently. The cold pack dropped to his lap as he leaned over to wrap her in a tight hug.

She broke away with a watery smile. "If I plan everything, there's less risk of an accident. Then here we are, your head cracked open, possibly concussed —"

"Probably not!"

She ignored him. "When I saw you on the ground, Finn... all that blood. I knew it was my fault that you were hurt."

"Don't be daft. I'm the clod who fell."

"You wouldn't have been there if it wasn't for me. I was so scared you..." She trailed off, her voice cracking.

Finn pulled her back to his chest, rubbing her back as her breath steadied.

She peeled back from him again, brushing her eyes with the edge of her sleeve. "I'm sorry I'm such a mess." She glanced at her watch. "It's almost four, and it's going to be dark soon. We should go -- there's no way I can manage these roads in the dark."

He squeezed her hand. "Lead the way, Boss Lady." Perhaps it wasn't a terrible thing to be fussed over.

Bridget drove them home, aging his transmission by another two or three years. When the headlights shone on the front stoop, a small brown package rested against the door.

"You order something?" Bridget asked.

"No." Finn's brow furrowed, immediately making him wince. That cut and bump were going to be a sight tomorrow.

They walked slowly up the drive, arm in arm. Finn started to bend down and retrieve it before Bridget tugged him upright. "Let me get it. I'll never get you inside if you fall." She plucked the keys from his jacket pocket, opened the door, and ushered him in.

"You're being be ridiculous, woman."

"Lay down, I'll get you more ice for your pack." She placed the box on the table. With a growing sense of unease, Finn eyed the package. No name, post address or stamps. Someone dropped this off.

He sat down heavily on the sofa, the headache throbbing.

When Bridget returned with a handful of ice, she paused by the table again. "There's no postmarks. It looks hand-delivered. Do you know who sent it?"

"I'll deal with it in a minute." Christ, he knew he sounded a grouch. "Sorry."

She raised an eyebrow but didn't remark on it further. "I'll scrounge up something for dinner."

As she fussed in the kitchen, the ice on his head relieved some of his headache.

The box had to be opened. He got to his feet slowly, wary of becoming lightheaded. Slipping off the cover, there was a bit of tissue and a mammoth plate of biscuits. A card sat atop.

So grateful again for your help with Roddy. I'll be at McCann's tonight, if you want to stop by.
— Claire

"Cookies?" Bridget appeared over his shoulder, and Finn closed the card. She handed him a plate of warmed up shepherd's pie and sat down beside him.

"Claire must have brought them by...still trying to make up for getting me fired."

Bridget gave him a level look. "She seems awfully interested in making sure you know how much she appreciates you."

"Is the Boss Lady jealous?"

Bridget didn't make eye contact. "She'll have you all to herself in a week or so, I suppose."

The wrench he felt, hearing her say she was going. How casually she talked about moving on.

They ate in silence for a few moments, every clink of fork against plate ringing out in the uncomfortable quiet.

"I'm not interested in Claire." *I'm only interested in you.* He stared at her, hoping she could detect the depth of his words.

Her eyes flickered toward him. She bit her lip, as if she was considering whether to comment. Instead, she stood, taking up both their empty plates. "Let's get you settled in for the night."

Maybe the headache was a blessing—there was no awkwardness about whether their morning encounter meant sharing a bedroom for the rest of the stay. Still, she was there when he stripped down to his pants to get under the covers, and she didn't look away.

There was likely no way he could repeat their earlier activities anyway, not with his head still aching. She kissed him goodnight, a chaste kiss on the forehead. He caught her shoulders, pulling her back toward him for a real kiss; with the heat and passion of a lover, not a nursemaid.

"You're feeling better," she murmured, placing her hand on his chest. He wanted to pull her down onto him, to feel the length of her body against his. He wound his fingers into hers, wanting to say something but remaining quiet.

"Try to sleep. I'll check on you in a bit." He was surprised by his sharp sense of loss when she left the room.

Chapter 24

Asses and Donkeys

Once she settled Finn in bed, Bridget turned off the lights in the main rooms and retired to her bedroom with laptop and cell phone (with a spiderweb of cracks across the screen) in hand. She sat cross-legged on the bed, pulled the quilt over her lap and quickly texted.

Are you up? Can you talk?

In less than thirty seconds, TRAN HO flashed on her vibrating phone.

"That was quick." Bridget tried to keep her voice low.

"You put up the bat signal, I answer. Besides, I just got finished with a subdural hematoma procedure that took for-ever, so I'm in the cafeteria trying to grab a bite for lunch. What's up?"

Where to begin? "You know how you told me when you talked me into coming here—"

"Are you giving me credit or blaming me?"

"Shush. Remember how you told me to try to experience things, to take a risk and find leprechauns and all that?"

"Oh my god, is this the sexy cab driver?"

Was she that easy to figure out? "I mean..."

"OH MY GOD IT'S THE SEXY CAB DRIVER!"

"Seriously, you are at work, Dr. Ho!" Bridget squinched her face in embarrassment for anyone within earshot of Tran in the hospital cafeteria.

"Who are you calling a ho, Miss Hot for Irishman? Start at the beginning, tell me everything before I get paged."

Bridget could feel her cheeks flaming. "Well..."

"Did you have sex with the Irishman?" Tran hissed into the phone. "You had sex with the Irishman! Who *are* you? I don't even know you anymore. This is amazing." Bridget had a vivid mental picture of Tran in her scrubs shrieking into her cell phone between bites of a clammy Cobb salad.

"I had to put him to bed like ten minutes ago, because the doctor thinks he might have a concussion."

Shocked silence. "What kind of sex are you having that you gave him a concussion? I'm impressed!"

God, she missed talking to Tran. "Stop, you dork. He fell off a stone fence and hit his head trying to film me in a field today. You know I'm not good with blood and stuff, but you would be proud of me. I got him to the ER. I mean, it's called A&E here. But that was after...you know."

"Ok, details. Give. Now."

"I might have accidentally walked in on him in the shower this morning."

Tran gasped; her dramatic intake of breath easily detected over the 2,000 miles.

"He drew a bath for me that first night, so I thought he turned the shower on for me because the door was ajar and I walked in."

"Oh my God, what did you do?" Tran whispered into the phone.

"I couldn't move. I stared at him like I was a statue, and I saw *everything*."

"Was it a good everything? Clinically speaking?"

"Very, very good. Impressive specimen." Bridget felt her heart start to beat faster, even in the retelling. "I don't know why I didn't just turn around and leave. But I just...dropped my towel and got in."

She could hear Tran pound her fist on the cafeteria table, making the silverware clatter audibly. "Yes! Finally! And?"

"And...it was amazing. Like, I-don't-know-what-possessed-my-body amazing."

Tran gave a loud woot. "Girl! If there was ever someone in need of a hot, no-strings-attached vacation hookup, it's you."

No strings attached. Of course, it had to be a fling. Rationally, she understood that. She glanced toward Finn's bedroom. The urge to go to Finn felt like a bungee cord stretched to its breaking point, straining to snap her back.

"You don't think I was stupid?" Bridget chewed the edge of her thumb.

"Not if you don't get attached. He doesn't think it's a long-term thing, right? You won't do something stupid like move to Ireland to have his babies? You're on the lease for eight more months, you know."

"I know, but I kind of think I—"

Tran cut her off. "Ah, crap, that's my page. Bang away, girl-friend. Doctor's orders. Do NOT behave yourself there but be safe. And stop fucking that man into a coma."

"Concussion!" she laughed.

"Coma, concussion...what, you think I'm a doctor or something? I love you, goodbye!"

The line went dead, and Bridget hugged the phone to her chest. Tran was right, she was only here for one more week, no time to be catching feelings for someone she'd probably never see again.

She was playing with fire.

Bridget felt the phone buzz again.

SEND PICS!

She scrolled through her phone photos (careful not to cut herself on the cracked screen), searching for the selfie she'd taken of the two of them in Dublin. Sure, he was handsome. But it was the joy in his expression that melted her. Few people saw that side of Finn, but he shared it with her.

She sent the photo to Tran via text, then got to work. She flipped open her computer and started to download the photos and videos from the day for editing.

Despite the disastrous ending, the video from Niamheora turned out well (with a little editing, captions, emojis, subtitles and other effects). When she pulled up the last clip Finn took right before his fall, she held her breath as she watched. He was right, the perspective gave depth to the video. He had a good eye.

Even when he slipped, he tried to keep the phone aloft, so when his head made contact with the rock, it was captured before he dropped the phone. Thank God the audio was connected to her lapel mike; she wasn't sure she could've handled hearing the crunch of his head hitting the stone. As it was, her own shriek and heavy breathing were clearly audible and traumatizing.

She cropped his fall out of the footage, pieced together the segment and sent it off to Mary just before 8 p.m. Perfect.

A crack of lightning flashed outside, followed by a booming thunderclap. With a jolt, she flinched. *Oh no.*

The donkeys were still out in the field.

Would they be safe out all night in the rain? Probably not. Would Finn be upset that she didn't bring them in? Or worse, would he be furious at himself for not caring for them? She flipped the quilt off her legs, steeling herself for the mission at hand. Somehow, in the dark, she was going to bring these donkeys in. Alone.

Bridget put on her boots, slipped into her coat, and brought her phone as a flashlight to pick her way down the path to the barn. She unlatched the door, turned on the light and barred the door behind her.

The donkeys were laying down as close to the barn wall under the roof overhang as possible, looking balefully at her as she opened the door.

"I'm sorry, I know I'm not Finn. But I need to get you guys inside."

Tim clambered back up to standing and moved toward the barn door. Bridget stepped back, giving him plenty of room to pass, but ventured to pat his hindquarters as he entered the bar. Without a lead, he walked over to his stall and waited for her to open his door. Tom showed no signs of movement, so Bridget opened Tim's stall. Tucked safely into the warm hay, Tim promptly laid down.

One down.

Another bolt of lightning flashed overhead, followed by a wall-shaking boom. Tom stood up with a start and began caterwauling, circling nervously in the shelter area.

Bridget found the lead that Finn used before and walked out to the shelter area. "Come on, Tom." She edged toward the animal, her hand outstretched. Finn warned her that Tom was a biter and had no qualms about kicking as well.

Tom gave a snort and turned away from her. Another crack of thunder and he darted toward the field.

"No! Tom, please!" Running after him, she slid on a slick patch of grass, catching herself with her hand before she fell.

At least she hoped she slipped on grass.

Oh God, it wasn't grass.

The stench of manure violated her nostrils as she stood. Tom snorted and continued circling. "Come on, Tom. Have a little compassion, buddy. There's a good boy."

He backed up a few steps and Bridget froze. If he went out to the field, there would be no way she could get him back alone. "Please, just come into the barn with me? It's warm there, and I'll get you some fresh water?" She tried to whistle at him. The mule stopped short, cocking his head toward her.

She opened both arms, hands outstretched as a supplicant, taking one step at a time. "Nice hay, those pellets you like? I can get them for you. I can hook you up, baby."

Tom huffed again, taking two more steps toward the field.

"No, come on now. Let's show Finn I can do this." At Finn's name, the donkey's ears twitched. Without a word, he moved back through the doorway into the barn. Bridget nearly cried with relief. "Good boy, Tom!"

Closing up the barn door behind them, she opened Tom's stall. He walked in without a fuss and laid down in the hay. "Guess it just had to be your idea. Typical male."

Bridget gave each animal fresh water, a forkful of hay and their pellets in easy reach. She patted Tim's nose, and her hand hovered carefully near Tom, weighing her chances of an amiable truce. The donkey snuffled, then moved his nose into her hand for a pat. She scratched at his nose and ears.

"Aren't you the sweet boy? Finn makes you sound like a demon incarnate." Tom nuzzled her palm, docile as anything. "This might need to be our little secret."

The offending scent wafting around her broke Bridget's concentration and it was clear this was going to require immediate attention. After securing the barn door, Bridget paused at the back door. How did her whole outfit get baptized with that stench?

She peeled off her boots, pants, and socks at the kitchen doorway, parking her offensive boots out on the back step. She padded toward the washing machine bare-legged, throwing the pungent clothes inside. Hesitating, she opted to strip down and add her sweatshirt, bra, and underwear, doused the whole load with soap and a prayer to the laundry gods.

Even naked, she could still smell the manure. Gross.

Though it was not quite 9 p.m., Bridget was exhausted. It would have to be a quick shower before bed. And with the dull ache in her backside, she'd be sleeping on her stomach.

She crept through the parlor to the bathroom, praying neither Cillian or another of Finn's relatives would pop in unannounced. Memories of the morning's adventures played in her mind with Technicolor clarity as she stepped into the shower. Finn's hands, covered with soap, pumping his hand back and forth as he—

What is wrong with you! She turned off the hot water spigot and let herself be jolted back to her senses with the cold shower. But her mind was working overtime, entertaining the idea of seducing a man with a possible concussion.

With a squeak, she hopped out and reached for her towel.

Her towel. She remembered in a flash where she left it. Smack in the center of Finn's bedroom floor.

She checked the cabinet beside the sink for a spare—no luck. She could either dry her entire body with a damp washcloth or retrieve her towel.

Bridget squeezed water from her hair and used her hands to siphon moisture from her as much of her body as possible. She opened the door and shivered in the bracing air. She'd forgotten to add fire to the wood stove, so the frigid air made her teeth chatter.

She tiptoed to Finn's room, turning the knob and easing the door open to prevent any squeak of the hinges. Slipping through the doorway, she dropped to the floor to retrieve her towel.

"Bridget?"

She froze, crouched naked on his floor, just outside the crack of light from the hallway. *Where was the goddamn towel?*

"Sorry—I just forgot something. Go to sleep."

"My ice pack fell, would you get it?"

Something in his voice made her pause. "You saw me walk in."

"Either that, or I'm having a most enjoyable dream." His voice was holding back amusement.

What was she trying to hide anyway? Bridget stood up, standing just outside the light from the hallway. "I left my towel in here this morning."

"And what were you doing in here this morning?"

"You, actually." She placed her hands on her hips, taking a step forward into the light. "Damn shame you had to go and beat your head on a rock afterwards. I have that effect on men."

"I agree with you there. Because right now, there is nothing I want more than to get out of this bed or get you into it."

"The doctor said—"

"Fuck the doctor."

"Make up your mind," Bridget grinned. "If I slip into your bed for one minute, will you be a good boy and go to sleep?"

Finn flipped the bedcovers up on her side. "I'll try."

"Just for a minute...because I'm freezing." Bridget slid in beside him, pressing her cold, damp body against his warm one. He slipped an arm around her as she snuggled into his chest.

"Jesus, woman. You're an icicle. Forget the ice pack; I'll bury my head between your diddies."

"Lie still," she said. "No exertion, remember? Nothing that gets your heart rate up."

"Can't promise that."

"Don't move then." She pressed her ear to his chest. "I'll just lay here for a while, listening to your heart."

"Good morning."

Bridget blinked as her surroundings began to register. Finn kissed her, wincing slightly as he rested his head back on the pillow.

"How'd you sleep?"

Finn touched the back of his head gingerly. "Fairly well, considering. Headache is just about gone."

Bridget rolled over to look him in the eyes. "Pupils look fine too. Not groggy?"

"No."

A horrifying thought crossed her mind. "I didn't talk in my sleep last night, did I?"

"I wish. No windows into your soul that I heard." Finn lifted himself slightly to get a glimpse of the clock behind her. "Have to get up and get the donkeys, the poor things were out in the field all night."

"No, stay. I got them in the barn last night during the rain.

That's why I had to take a shower. And maybe why I have to burn my clothes."

"You didn't." Finn raised himself up on his elbow, disbelief on his face. "Unbelievable. I have two idiot donkeys to thank for the surprise of a naked angel in my bedroom? Extra apples for those boys."

Bridget pulled the sheet around her to sit up. Glancing toward the end of the bed, she gave a small gasp of minor outrage. "My towel was on your bed the whole time?"

His face broke out into a devilish grin. "Mum taught me to pick up after playtime." His expression changed to a look of flat horror as he groaned. "Dinner at my mum's tomorrow. Thank God I have a concussion so we can beg off."

"You just said you're fine."

"They don't know that."

"Stop that. I want to meet them."

"Don't say I didn't warn you." He shuffled to a sitting position. "Where are we off to today?"

She rolled onto her side, "You're off the clock today, so I can't tell you what to do."

"Does that mean I can give the orders?" He traced along the hollow of her throat with his finger, easing the sheet down to reveal her breasts.

"Within reason." She began to kiss a trail down his chest. "I might have some ideas of my own."

Chapter 25

New Habits

They moved through the morning routine with a comfortable ebb and flow of activity. She stoked the stove and set the kettle while Finn made a pot of real oatmeal, not that package porridge Bridget purchased her first day here.

Hard to believe that was almost two weeks ago.

"How long until breakfast? I can turn out the donkeys while we wait."

"A quarter hour or so," Finn answered, reaching past her for the small bowl that Bridget had salvaged from his workbench discards. While sanding it, he'd discovered a weak spot in the wood, which made it unsuitable for sale. Bridget claimed it, blowing off the sawdust and filling it with lemons, apples and oranges.

He plucked two of the apples from the bowl. "Give those good boys their treat." Her eyes flashed with humor, but he appreciated the blush that rose in her cheeks.

A bit of salt, a bit of milk, a sprinkling of cinnamon and

brown sugar. Amazing how having a stocked refrigerator and cupboard made it easier to cook.

"I had an idea for today," Finn brought the bowls and spoons to the table as Bridget returned from the barn, bringing the wind in with her. "It's a grand soft day out there, isn't it?"

"It's gorgeous out."

"Then I want to take you to the seaside. Not to work, just to enjoy."

It didn't take long for him to convince Bridget to wander the streets of Mayflin, a fishing village along the peninsula about three hours from the cottage. He dangled descriptions of rows of houses painted in pastel colors and quaint fishing boats and the tourist in Bridget could not resist.

Mayflin served his purpose as well. It was far enough from home that it was unlikely they'd encounter anyone from Killathay. No meddling, no neighbors reporting back. The absence of prying eyes lifted a huge weight from him and he filled the empty space with Bridget.

She delighted in the smattering of wreaths, light strings, and the bustle of locals with parcels and bags that gave a holiday shine to the town. Over the last two weeks, she'd gained an air of confidence as she shot her videos. Mayflin buzzed with activity as many of the locals were making the most of the weather chatting up their friends and neighbors.

Even though they were supposed to be tourists, Finn found himself pressed into duty as cameraman. Bridget had a way of asking questions that made every person feel like they were a minor celebrity. Not that it took much to make an Irishman share the craic.

She was careful to take several breaks to ensure he wasn't overexerting. They sat together on a small bench overlooking the harbor. She snuggled into the crook of his arm, but she started up to make sure she wasn't too close to the cut on his head. "Am I fussing over you too much?"

He threaded his fingers through hers. "You know I'd hate it from anyone else, but I quite like your bedside manner."

"Have you done any Christmas shopping yet?" Bridget peered toward the window of a toy shop.

"Are you fishing for a Christmas present?" he teased.

She responded with a tight smile. Instantly, he knew she was thinking the same thing. *She'll be gone by Christmas.*

He'd always imagined that heartache was a flowery term, but the pain her words caused in his chest was no metaphor. For a moment, the unsettling ache made him wonder if he was truly ill.

He cleared his throat. "With four siblings each with partners and nine nieces and nephews, it would bankrupt me to buy them all gifts. I give toys to the wee ones and 20 quid to the teenagers. And I buy for my ma."

"What's your mom like?"

Finn exhaled. Where to start? "She's in everyone's business. When I was little, if I got into trouble on the way home from school, she'd hear about it before I got home."

"How often did you get in trouble?"

"Oh, daily." He kissed the top of her head. "But there was no one better if you were hurt or upset. She'd put you up on the stool in the kitchen while she made dinner and listen to whatever injustice you suffered. Especially after my father passed. She worked days as a waitress in Killathay. My sisters would get me out the door for school, but she'd be off at three when I walked home."

Bridget squeezed his arm.

"The woman has never told a story in a straight line in her life. If you ask her what she's bought at the market, you'll end up hearing a story about the shopkeeper's sister's boyfriend, who holidayed in Malta and lost his luggage. And you're just along for the duration."

"That's not so bad, she's interested in people."

Finn shot her a dubious look. "We'll see how you feel after you meet her. And you should probably stop eating now, because she will stuff you to the gills, given half a chance."

"Should I offer to make a dish tomorrow?"

"Not unless you want to make her think we're getting married." His voice caught slightly on the last word, but Bridget didn't seem to notice. "But we'll bring a box of something to be sociable."

The sun was setting as they arrived back at the cottage.

"Should I get something started for dinner?" Bridget asked, setting down a box of pastries bought as a hostess gift for Noreen. She nestled into the sofa and picked up her knitting.

"Don't you worry about that."

She shot him a querulous look, raising her eyebrows as she picked up on his intent. "Something else then?" Without breaking her gaze, she moved the knitting back onto the table.

In one fluid motion, he slid into place next to her, covering her mouth with his. All day, he'd been in her orbit, holding her hand, sharing kisses as their only intimacy. Instead of inoculating him against desire for her, it had inflamed him.

He felt a desperate anxiety at their time together ticking down. She'd be leaving in a week, and that wasn't anywhere near enough time. Greedily, he wanted to spend as much time with her with the four walls of the cottage. Not sharing her with the outside world.

With an urgency that bordered on desperation, he tugged up the hem of her blouse, burying his face in the swell of her breasts. Bridget's head tipped backward as he pulled the cup of her bra aside, swirling his tongue around her nipple.

"Let me help." She sat up, pulling her blouse off and reaching back to unclasp her bra. As she shrugged it off, Finn slid to his knees in front of her.

"All of it."

Her eyes clouded with a heat to match his. She unbuttoned her jeans, lifting her hips to ease them down and off. She sat before him wearing only thin cotton panties, pink and white flowers, a tiny ribbon bow centered at the top. He placed his hands on each of her upper thighs.

"All...of...it."

She hooked her thumbs into the scrap of fabric that separated him from what he most desired. Slowly, she raised her hips again. Before she could peel the panties off, he leaned forward, capturing the tiny bow between his teeth. Her scent filled his senses, and he felt a wild desire that bordered on despair.

With a guttural sound, he tugged them gently down to her knees . He couldn't wait any longer. He pulled back, releasing the bow with a snap of the elastic against her thighs. He grabbed at the impeding garment pulling it down to her ankles. He coaxed her knees apart, pulling her down to the edge of the cushion.

Without preamble, he fixed his mouth to her core, the gasp of ecstasy driving him to frenzy. He moved one, then two fingers inside her. Her low moans turned to chirps of pleasure as he increased his tempo. He caressed the length of her with his tongue, blindly reaching up with his free hand to find her breast.

Her cries changed to incoherence as she neared her climax. Finn stopped. Bridget was panting with exertion, pleasure-drunk from his attentions. He looked up, a wicked grin spreading across his face. "Do you want me to keep going?"

"I may murder you if you stop."

"Allow me to propose an alternative." It took him less than 10 seconds to pull the condom he'd optimistically tucked in his wallet that morning. He unbuckled his belt and unfastened his jeans, bending forward to accommodate his forged steel erection.

Dragging her to the very edge of the sofa, he moved to dip inside her, then pulling out to rub against the length of her. Holy hell, she was wet for him. In one slow motion he buried himself in her, ripping a groan from his throat.

The basest instincts took over. *Pleasure. Friction. Building. Release.* As she squealed her peak, he grunted his own, shuddering as he came inside her.

He collapsed on the sofa beside her, both of them in dazed recovery. Finn grabbed a tissue to clean up. "You were...saying about...dinner?"

"I'm starved. Let's get carryout tonight. Would you get it while I download the video from today?"

"Sure then." Finn watched with appreciation as Bridget rose to clean up, watching the sway of her hips as she padded to the bathroom.

Chapter 26

Dinner at Noreen's

The car lights faded in the distance as Finn left for the takeaway. Bridget swept up her phone and dialed Tran.

"Bridge! Twice in two days? What's up girl?" Bridget could barely hear Tran over the noise of a crowd. "I'm at the airport in pre-check, so I might have to call you back."

Bridget pinched the bridge of her nose. *Of course.* Her first leg to Fiji was today. "Sorry, I completely forgot with the time change."

"What's wrong?" Tran could always tell.

"Nothing, it's just…"

"Is it the guy? Is it weird now? Is he still in a coma? Is he ghosting you? How can he ghost you in the same house?" Tran's rapid-fire questions somehow made her feel worse.

"Nothing like that. He's been amazing. You'd really like him."

"Hang on." Muffled voices came through the phone as Tran. "Sorry, I have to run, Bridge. I'll call you back when I'm at my gate."

He'll be back then. "No, don't worry about it. It's fine. Have an amazing time in Fiji. Tell everyone Merry Christmas for me!"

"Love you. And keep it casual with the coma patient. I need you back here."

Leave it to Tran to zero in on the problem.

It wasn't that she was nervous about leaving Finn. It was her absolute terror at not *wanting* to leave him.

Staying with Finn was like playing house. None of it was real. Ok, the sex was very real. The attraction, the connection... those were real. But she was a practical woman. Finn said he'd only left Ireland a handful of times in his life. This was Bridget's first trip overseas in nine years.

Long-distance was one thing. A relationship that only existed on video calls...that wasn't enough.

She couldn't settle for crumbs.

When she woke the following morning, Finn's hand was resting on her hip. Even as they slept, their contact was unbroken. Rolling over carefully to release the strands of her hair captured under his arm, she nuzzled up to his spiky cheek. "Good morning."

Finn stretched, his muscles twitching as he hyperextended. With a satisfied exhale, he turned back to Bridget. "Good morning to you."

She traced a pattern in the whorls of his chest hair. "I have six more days here and only three more posts I have to make. That means I've got a little—" She leaned forward and kissed his lips. "—flexibility—" She kissed the hollow of his throat. "—on how we spend our time today." She kissed the juncture of his neck.

In a singular movement, Finn whipped the coverlet off them, rolling until his full weight was pressed atop hers.

"As your tour guide—" He kissed her, his tongue insistent and searching. "—and your host—" His mouth was at her ear as he whispered, kissing just beneath her earlobe, devouring the distance to her clavicle with a ravenous trail of kisses. "—I am duty-bound to show you the best our country has to offer." Finn dropped his head to capture her nipple in the warmth of his mouth. He broke away only to fumble in the nightstand.

With a gasp, she bent her knees up, reaching down to guide his penis into her. He fell upon her in a frenzy, jackhammering until her thoughts were reduced to simply *more*.

With a shudder and a few grunted words in Irish, Finn fused her body to his, an unbroken connection of bone and sinew and skin. She felt every quiver in his body echo in her own.

Bridget's mind began to reassemble, as they lay side by side, chests heaving from exertion. *Six days.* She was so greedy for his touch, desperate for every opportunity to entwine her body with Finn's.

The post-sex clarity kicked in. Not just sex. She was starved for all of Finn, the banter, the boyish grin, the tenderness he hid from everyone else.

Forget any warnings about playing with fire; she was already watching her skin blister.

Finn's mother lived in a row home painted a cheery robin's egg blue with a faded yellow door. After a quick spin around the town square, Finn parallel parked in a spot across the street. Another reason Bridget was thankful that Finn was back to driving—parallel parking with a stick shift would've taken her hours.

Bridget hung back respectfully as Finn rapped at the door. "Remember, the cookies are from you, not me," he whispered.

Muffled voices rumbled inside, then a woman with close-cropped salt-and-pepper hair and thick eyebrows came to the door, smoothing the front of her blouse. "Come in, come in! No need to stand on formalities."

Finn stepped back, allowing Bridget to walk in first. "Mum, this is Bridget Kolodziej."

"Thank you for inviting me, Mrs. Malloy. I brought cookies!" Bridget handed the string-wrapped box to Finn's mother and stepped awkwardly to the side.

Finn gave his mother a quick kiss on her cheek. "The good ones, mum. From Farrelly's."

"Now, you shouldn't have gone to such trouble," his mother replied, stopping as she caught sight of the shaved spot on the back of his head. "Finn! What happened to you?"

He touched the wound on his scalp carefully. "Nothing to worry about. Hit it on a rock a few days back but the doctor said I'm fine."

"And not even calling to tell me." She swatted at him with a tea towel. "Good thing you've such a hard head."

She ushered them into the compact parlor, where two smaller children watched a cartoon and two pre-teens fixated on their phones. "That's Ciara, Michael, Aisling and Rowan. This crew belongs to Maggie, who's in the kitchen."

Finn leaned in to give her a clue. "Maggie's my second-oldest sister. It goes Mary Kathleen, Maggie, and Fiona, then Cill, then me."

Louder, he added, "You lot, this is my friend, Bridget." A series of half-waves came from the kids.

"Hello! Bridget!" A woman in her early forties popped out

of the doorway of the kitchen. "I'm Maggie, come on in the kitchen. Ma, the pot's boiling."

Noreen shuffled back to the kitchen.

"Go on then," said Finn. "After you."

Maggie and Noreen fussed over several pots and bowls in varying states of heat and completion. "Can I help with something?" Bridget asked.

"Aren't you a love. No, I think we have it all to sorts." Noreen skittered between the pots, pressing down on the roast with her finger and stabbing the potatoes with her pinkie. "We'll eat in two shakes. Ah! There's the bell. Get that, Finny?"

"Finny?" Bridget smirked the tiniest bit.

"Careful Boss Lady." Finn winked back at her. "I'm Finny to my mother and mother alone."

Before they could answer the bell, the front door opened and a heavily pregnant woman entered carrying two covered casserole dishes. "Ma, is there room in the oven to heat these for a few? Jerry, come on, don't let all the heating out!" A man quickly followed, ushering in a toddler in a bright red coat.

"Are you Bridget? I'm Fiona, this is Jerry, and the baby's Ursula—Sula for short. Coming through!" Fiona heaved the casseroles over her head to make it through the tight room to the kitchen. The compact house was now full to bursting, and after a jerk of the head from his wife, Jerry ushered the younger children to wash up in the bathroom.

The table was set for eight, so Finn pulled out four tray tables from the hall closet and set them up around the television. "How long till dinner, Ma?"

"Quarter hour until we're all set."

One of the teenagers looked up from her phone to stare at Bridget. "You're the social media lady, aren't you? An influencer?"

"Yep, call me Bridget." Bridget smiled uneasily. As an only child, this gaggle of children of all ages was a bit unnerving. Nothing made her more insecure than the absolute judgment of a thirteen-year-old.

"Who are you on TikTok?"

"Ciara, leave her alone, you menace," called Finn. Ciara ignored him, and put a hand on her hip, waiting for Bridget's answer.

"I have an account called @CabinetsCountertopsClosets," Bridget said, peering over the girl's shoulder as she typed in the first part of the name into the app. "There, that one" she added, pointing at the tiny logo that marked her account.

Ciara tapped her icon to see more. "Ooh, you've got a lot of followers!" The grudging teen admiration was like winning the lottery. Ciara scrolled through her content thumbnails. "And they just watch you walk around Tilleen and Killathay? That sounds boring." Ciara hit the "follow" button but was clearly losing interest.

A parade of dishes came out to the table, followed by Finn's sisters making plates for their little ones and placing them in front of the television. Maggie leaned over and confided, "We'd have been murdered in our beds if we suggested eating in front of the television when we were kids, but this one's gone soft." She waved a fork at Noreen.

"A good thing for you I have," Finn's mom replied.

The conversation ricocheted between plans for Christmas shopping, talk of a new owner for the local football club and gossiping about Cillian and Mary Kathleen. It seemed if you weren't present, it was open season to analyze your social life.

After polishing off their heaping plates, Maggie cleared the table, Fiona put on the kettle for tea and Noreen passed around the cookies along with a warm spice cake. The children were ushered upstairs, and the real purpose of the evening began: her interrogation.

"So, Bridget, I understand you're on the social media?"

"Do you come from a large family, Bridget?"

"Where did you go to school?"

"We saw you on 'Ireland this Morning.'"

"Did you always live in Chicago?"

It was like being on the receiving end of tennis practice. As soon as one question was volleyed away, another came over the net.

But they saved the ace for Noreen. "Father Tim tells me that you're renting out my mother's cottage through Christmas then."

Bridget took a sip of the scalding tea, flinching slightly. "Just another week. I leave on the 22nd. It's such a lovely place. The other cottage I had booked was not in any state for renters. Or humans of any sort."

Noreen turned to Finn, and both his sisters swiveled their heads in turn.

"You're also staying there, Finny?"

"You know I am, Ma." There was a warning in Finn's voice, but it was still respectful.

"Is that really something you should be doing?" his mother tsked. "So hard on poor Bridget here. Come stay upstairs in your old room while she's letting the cottage. Or stay with Cillian."

"Ma, I told you. It makes more sense for me to be there since I drive her every day. You want to add two hours to my workday?"

Noreen drew the napkin from her lap and laid it on the table. "Work, is it?" she asked primly.

"He's driving her all over the county, isn't he?" Jerry interjected. A level look from Fiona cut off that line of support in an instant.

Bridget jumped in. "Finn has been very helpful. I don't know what I would have done without him that first day."

Fiona quirked an eyebrow but buried any retort in her napkin.

"It's causing a lot of gossip in town, Finn. It's not right to have two single people under the same roof. No offense to you, Bridget. But people at church were talking," said Maggie.

Finn leaned over his plate, his expression inscrutable. "And what are they saying, Mag?"

"I won't repeat it."

"You wonder why I don't go to church anymore," Finn muttered.

Noreen pursed her lips. Fiona reached across the table, placing her hand on Finn's arm. "What about Claire? She'd be heartbroken if she knew you were stepping out on her."

While Fiona was fixated on Finn, Bridget sensed Maggie had eyes on her. She schooled her expression to be as neutral as possible.

"Claire?" Finn gave an exasperated laugh. "Is that what you're after? Claire is not interested in me, nor I in her."

"Roddy's bloody nose would beg to differ, Finn." *Bloody nose?*

"He earned that."

The Malloy women exchanged glances, and it was obvious that a silent decision was made to change the subject. Bridget was left with her mental image of Finn punching someone.

"Bridget, where have you gone in your travels here?"

Bridget shook her head slightly to dispel her thoughts. Finally, a safe topic. "All over the county—I think Finn is getting tired of gardens and shops and historical sites."

All the heads swiveled toward Finn. "You? Going to museums and the like? And shopping?" asked Fiona.

Maggie snorted. "What sort of spell is he under, Bridget? Finn Malloy, willingly going shopping? Get that, Fee!"

"She pays me well." Finn cut in. Bridget could feel him tensing beside her. Almost without thinking, she slipped a hand under the table to squeeze his thigh. A little moral support.

"I'm sure she does, Finn. I hope you're showing her the best places," Fiona said archly.

Another raised eyebrow from Noreen, and the sisters dropped their line of questioning. The conversation turned to the nativity play, destinations still in Bridget's binder, and Mrs. Plover's long-standing grudge against Mr. Benjamin, the organist at church.

As the sisters cleared the table and began the washing up, Bridget leaned toward Finn. "How am I doing?"

"You survived. But don't go into the kitchen." Finn cocked an eyebrow at her as she rose from the table, dishes in hand.

"I'll be fine," said Bridget. "If there's one thing I know, it's cleaning up."

"You've been warned."

Fiona was at the sink, her burgeoning belly pressed up against the edge. Maggie was drying the dishes when Bridget walked in. "Can I help?"

Maggie tossed her damp towel to Bridget, saying, "I'll put away if you dry."

"Deal."

Fiona looked over her shoulder at the kitchen doorway, then leaned into Bridget to speak with a lowered voice. "Bridget, if you're at all uncomfortable with Finn staying at the cottage, you've only to say something. I know there's only one more week, but we can make him stay with us."

"No, it's been nice to have someone to show me around."

The sisters exchanged glances. "It must be hard being a single woman in a strange city. Do you have a young man back home?" Maggie grabbed the last of the plates from Bridget.

Tread carefully. "Not at the moment. I live with a room-mate, Tran, who's doing her residency in surgery at Chicago General Hospital."

"But you've not lived with a man before? Other than your father, of course?" asked Fiona.

Maggie added. "He can be awfully stubborn, but we both practically raised him. We can get around the man. Both of us could use the babysitting as well."

"It's really not an issue,"

Fiona heaved a dripping roasting pan into Bridget's hands. "Finn is notoriously difficult to live with," she offered. "Even Cillian couldn't bear to have him at his place for long."

"If he gets out of line, you tell us and we'll take care of things," Maggie shoved the large pan in a cabinet that would have been perfect as a "before" picture.

At that comment, Finn walked in the room. "You'll take care of things, will you? I suppose both of you have been working Bridget over, squeezing more out of her?"

"Don't be rude, Finian."

"We should go now," Finn said, his voice clipped.

With that both sisters turned. "You can't!"

"And why's that?"

The sisters shared a guilty look. "Well, you see —" "Er, well..."

Their explanation was cut off by another bell at the front door.

"You didn't." Finn's expression was murderous.

From the other room, they heard Finn's mother. "Claire! Such a lovely surprise."

Fiona grabbed his hand. "You behave yourself, Finn!"

He wrenched away from her grip and left the kitchen, his sisters following. Bridget hung back in the doorway.

A young woman—Claire, obviously—looked confused as she stood in the doorway with a book in her hands. Noreen was trying to peel her coat off, half-spinning her as she stood.

"Claire's brought me a book from her mother. Come, Claire, have some sweets. We were just sitting down for a bit." She put her arm around the younger woman's shoulder, propelling her into the room.

"I really can't stay..." Claire made eye contact with Finn, and even Bridget could sense her silent pleading for escape.

"Finn, get Claire a cup of tea."

Finn's face was tight, the corner of his mouth twitched slightly, but he turned and stalked to the kitchen, brushing past Bridget. She turned to see him standing at the electric kettle, his shoulders tight and high, and his entire demeanor poised between fight or flight.

Bridget hesitated, not wanting to get into the middle of a family squabble. The urge to comfort him trumped her reluctance, so she crossed the kitchen and put a hand on his back. "Are you ok?"

Finn didn't turn around but continued staring down at the stove. "My family who can't leave well enough alone. Dragging Claire out in the dead of night because they want me paired up with a girl—only because her dad can give me a job I won't lose. I've half a mind to just leave out the back door."

At once it made sense: the cookies, the job interview he missed, the girl he defended. All of them centered on the pretty young woman being fussed over by Finn's family. Bridget stood in stunned silence. She felt the air leave her chest, leaving her hollow. Her arrival had caused these problems.

Finn turned, a bitter expression on his face. "Don't worry,

I'm not going to start a fight." He kissed her on the forehead as the kettle blew. He clattered together a cup of tea and saucer, poured the water and teabag. "Let me bring this out and then we'll get out of here."

Chapter 27

A Date with Claire

Leaving Bridget safely in the kitchen, Finn braced himself to face the united front against him in the parlor. Claire was flanked by his sisters and mother, well-cornered. He held out the cup. "Here. Tea."

His mother's eyes narrowed. Such appalling manners were mortal sins in Noreen's house, but Finn was beyond caring.

"Thanks, but I really should go." Claire swiveled, reaching for her coat again over the protestations of Noreen. "I was just stopping on my way to a friend's house. Can't be late."

"Nonsense. You've only got your tea just now. Can't let it go to waste. Sit, then!" His mother and sisters continued a barrage of protests, urging her to stay. Claire darted a glance toward Finn.

Fiona elbowed her way to Claire's side. "I ran into your mother not two days ago at Tesco, Claire. She's looking well."

Maggie chimed in. "Yes, and I hear you all are planning a holiday in Rome this summer, how lovely."

"I–" Claire stopped short and sipped the tea, wincing at the still-steaming cup.

Fiona widened her eyes in feigned surprise. "Finn's always talked about wanting to go to Rome, haven't you Finn?"

He set his arms tight across his chest. Not a chance he was getting drawn into this. Was it his imagination, or did Noreen's hand twitch as she controlled the impulse to give him a cuff on the ear? About thirty more seconds and he'd be out of there without a goodbye and leave the Malloy women to reap this nonsense on their own.

"And Claire, this is Bridget. She's one of Cillian's tourist customers, and Finn has been driving her around. She leaves on Friday, isn't that right? Back to America?"

He turned as Bridget appeared in the doorway, stepping toward her without even realizing it.

"Nice to meet you, Claire," Bridget offered with a half-wave. "Finn's been very helpful and professional these past few weeks."

For the love.

Claire took another whisper of a sip from her cup, then rose to her feet. "I so appreciate the tea, but I do need to be going."

The protestations began anew but Claire held firm. With a half-apologetic wave, the door closed behind her.

For a moment, there was just silence. Finn's hands clenched and released as he struggled to rein in his anger. "Which of you did this?"

"I don't know what—"

"Finn! How could you think—"

"Her mother asked her —"

All three started to argue, but Finn crossed his arms. "All of you. Fine. All I needed to hear."

He strode to the door, snatching his coat and Bridget's from the coatrack. "Well, that's it then. Thank you for dinner, mum. Bridget and I are leaving."

Bridget remained still, looking as uncomfortable as Claire had a moment before. Finn helped her into her coat.

She smiled weakly. "Thank you for a lovely dinner, Mrs. Malloy."

The low whoosh of air emitting from the car vents provided the only sound for the first half of the way home. Finn occupied himself with mentally totting up the list of wrongs his sisters had committed. Finally, Bridget took a break from biting at her thumb to speak.

"So...Claire."

Here it was, then. "What about her."

"That's cookie Claire, right? The Claire who called the other day?"

"Yes."

"Are you sure there's nothing there?"

Finn huffed angrily. "My sisters and mother are meddlers, trying to bully me into something. As usual. But I told you before, there's nothing between me and Claire."

He stoked his anger towards his family as they drove along the narrow streets of Tilleen until the lights and houses turned into hills and stone fences, with just the glow of the headlights to guide them.

"But *could* there be, Finn?" she asked quietly.

Goddamn it. Her too?

He braked sharply, pulling off to the soft shoulder of the road. He threw the car in park, killed the lights, and wrenched around in his seat to face her.

"I told you that I was let go from my job at Kehoe's Dairy. What I didn't tell you is that a man named Roddy White was a right old pervert. He cornered a new girl in the break room, trying to get her to step out with him. That was Claire."

He paused for a moment to look at her in the slight glow of the dashboard. "I don't have anything going with Claire, not then, not now. But things being what they are in this county, people have me married off to her just because I punched an arse who crossed the line."

"Is that why you got fired?"

"I didn't get fired, I quit. Walked up to my boss, told him I'd laid out Roddy and turned in my ID tag."

"You stood up for her." Bridget's voice was soft.

"I'd have done the same for anyone. In fact, it causes me more trouble than not when I do such things."

"So why are you so upset that she came by?"

He looked straight ahead, tapping his thumb on the steering wheel. Could he trust her with the truth?

"In a week, you'll be gone, I'll be back to where I was the day we met. A string of jobs, all favors called in by family members."

"Is it so bad that they're helping you get a job?" she asked.

Finn shook his head. "It's not that they helped. It's that I get to a place, start feel like I'm making a difference, and the foreman or a supervisor says, "Good job, Finn...good thing your uncle, or your ma, or your brother-in-law put in a word for you. And I realize that position would never have hired me if I wasn't a Malloy. Do you know what it's like to never know whether you're worth hiring or just worth a favor?"

He ran a hand through his hair. "Even this job—driving you, renting you the cottage, it started with a handout from Cillian. When Gran's cottage came to me free and clear, she thought it would help me get on my feet. But there's taxes due, more than I have. Until you came along, I didn't know how I'd manage."

He took her hand. "When I put the listing for the cottage on HouseHijack, I saw money. Only money. I wasn't thinking of helping you. I was only thinking of myself and doing something that didn't have my family's fingerprints all over it. It was selfish and I'm sorry."

Finn paused again, swallowing hard. It could change everything between them. "When you go back to Chicago, I'll be back in the same place I was: no job, too many bills. As much as I might hate it, the job at Claire's father's place is my best chance."

Bridget connected the dots. "You don't think you'll get the job if you don't go out with Claire."

"I don't mean that I'm going to marry her to get a job or anything. But it would probably help if she didn't know that you and me..." He trailed off, searching for the right way to describe things. "That we were involved."

Bridget ran her fingers along the armrest. "Don't beat yourself up about the HouseHijack listing. I'm glad I got the chance to stay with you."

"Go on with you." He put his arm around her and pulled her close across the hump of the center console.

She snuggled in. "I was terrified and feeling helpless, and you came aboard the train and took charge." She looked up at him with a grin. "Not going to lie, it was pretty hot."

"Yeah?"

"Yeah."

She kissed him, deep and devouring. His anger dissipated into a savage hunger for her.

Her hand slipped between his legs. The jolt of her touch made him swell, tight and constricted beneath his jeans.

Bridget moved her hand in a slow, stroking motion up and down the denim with an excruciatingly light touch. He closed his eyes to concentrate on the sensation, tilting his hips forward slightly.

"Is this ok?"

"Jesus, woman. You're going to make me come in my jeans."

"I guess I should make sure that doesn't happen." She popped the button at the top of his jeans, and Finn exhaled shakily. He dropped his hand to the side of his seat, reclining it as much as he could. He lifted his hips, giving her access to unzip his jeans and tug them down a few inches to keep the zipper from any tender bits.

She traced along the underside of his shaft with her finger, then encircled him with a loose grip, barely making contact with his skin. He drew a sharp, quick breath as she tightened her grip, sliding her hand gingerly up and down the shaft.

She took the tip in her mouth, swirling her tongue then dipping lower to take him all the way into her mouth. He moaned, concentrating all his energy on not thrusting deeper. Every nerve ending in his lower region was overloaded as she began to move in a steady rhythm up and down. It wasn't going to take more than a few —

"I'm gonna—" he gasped, moving to try and give her space. She held him in place, and he felt himself jerk against the roof of her mouth as he strangled a cry. She slowed her ministrations until the urgency of the moment abated. Finn didn't know if it was the aftereffects of his head injury, but he absolutely saw stars.

"You are a surprising woman, Bridget Kolodziej." He placed a finger under her chin but she burrowed into his chest instead, not meeting his eyes.

"I'm sorry your family was giving you a hard time. "

"I prefer the hard time you just offered...it's among my favorites."

She didn't reply, only pressed against him. He held her for a moment, kissing the top of her hair.

Her seduction was an offering, a balm for his pain.

But he couldn't shake the feeling that it was a parting gift.

The rest of the ride home was quiet, and when they arrived at the cottage, Bridget quickly hung up her coat.

"You want to watch something on the tv?" Finn asked.

"No, I think I'm going to turn in. I have a bit of a headache." Bridget gave him a quick kiss and slipped away to her bedroom.

For a moment, Finn stood silent. Not like Bridget to retire this early, but after the stunt his sisters pulled, it wasn't surprising she had a headache.

His anger flaring again, Finn headed out to the barn for distraction. Not that he wanted to admit it, but Bridget's callout on "Ireland This Morning" created a surge of demand for his work. Olive was texting him daily to ask for additional pieces and to nag him to pick up his commission check. He'd sold more pieces in the last two weeks–despite it being the slow season for tourists–than he'd sold all year.

It was after midnight when Finn came back into the house, running a hand through his hair to dislodge any stray wood shavings. Bridget's door was closed, no light shining beneath the crack at the floor. Well, she was entitled to a quiet night.

But still, he stood outside her door for a few moments, leaning against the door for any sign she was still awake. He couldn't resist whispering, "Bridget?"

Silence.

Damn. A quick washing up, and he was back to his room

for the night. Alone. After an hour of tossing and turning, he grabbed his phone from the nightstand.

He opened the social apps and it immediately showed him @cabinetscountertopsclosets, probably because it was the only account he'd followed. After a few missteps, he was clicking through her feed with relative ease. Videos of the places they'd visited scrolled past and he felt a bit of pride in how well the ones he shot were received.

While Bridget had edited out his fall at Niamheora, his voice was still in the audio. The comments were a revelation.

> @$teph$cott1977: Who's the guy?? We can hear him but not see him.

> @churchlady1rene: Declare him at customs when you import him!

With a frown, he scrolled through some of the remaining photos. His finger froze, suspended mid-swipe, as a still image of Gran's room came up on the timeline. The silver brush and comb set were front-and-center on the windowsill, glowing faintly pink in the first colors of the sunrise. Gran's book of poems, the one his grandfather had given her while they courted, was open to a page with a pressed flower. His gaze fixed on the square black-and-white photograph, curved with time. It was a picture of him.

He was only about 8 or 9, tucked up in his grandmother's lap as she sat on her rocker. He braced for the pain of the memory, but the dull ache didn't come. Instead, his chest filled with a wistfulness, a sweeter flavor on the normal tang of loss.

The cottage had started to come alive for him in the last two weeks. Brighter, more cheerful. It was no longer a shrine to loss, a place for him to hide from the world. Sharing his home shook off the cobwebs of his grief and anger.

Gran had given him this cottage for a reason. He was beginning to think that the reason was Bridget.

The next morning, she was up well before him by the looks of things. Brochures and papers were in orderly piles around the kitchen table, framing her laptop as she typed. She was in the zone.

He walked up behind her and kissed the top of her head. "Morning."

Bridget jumped. "I didn't hear you get up!" She began to stack the papers into a single pile.

"Don't clean up on my account. Kettle on?"

"Should just need a warmup. How's your head?"

"Barely a twinge."

She nodded. "I fed the donkeys and turned them out to graze about an hour ago."

He looked toward the back field through the kitchen window. The faint outline of one of the donkeys was visible through the early morning mist. Bridget made more progress winning over those creatures in two weeks than he'd made in a year.

"How long have you been up? You were sound asleep when I came back in from the barn around midnight."

She looked back at her computer, avoiding his eyes. "Around 6. I texted with Tran last night and fell asleep right after. I had to get some things sorted. It's supposed to be sheets of rain today and cold, so I was thinking we could stick around here." She rubbed the back of her neck.

Finn rested his hands on the back of the wooden chair. "Everything good? You seem a bit stressed."

"Do you have a second?" She patted the table next to her.

"What's up?" He scanned her face for a clue.

She looked down at her hands. "I got an email this morning from the airline, telling me what to do to prepare for my upcoming flight."

Gut punch. "You still have five days."

"I was thinking about what you said yesterday about your job prospects with Claire's family." She cut off for a moment, taking a deep breath. "Be honest, Finn. If you weren't so mad about everyone trying to fix you up with her, is Claire someone you could be happy with?"

Not her too.

"Claire doesn't want to go out with me, I've heard it from her own mouth. What are you trying to say, Bridget?" His voice was low, wary.

"I don't know," she rubbed her forehead. "Leaving here— leaving you—is going to be brutal. I thought we could keep this a fling, since it was crystal clear from the outset that I'd have to leave. No strings."

It felt like a vise was cranking tight around his chest.

Bridget's chin quivered. "And last night, while we were making dinner with all your family—"

He cut her off. "They were out-of-bounds, Bridget, they—"

She held up her hand. "No, I loved it. Loved being part of that chaos. But I was a problem for them. I'm a problem for you!"

"You don't know what you're going on about." The muscles in his cheeks contracted.

"Even if you don't go out with Claire, why would they want us together?"

"My family doesn't get to decide!" he snapped, rising from the table as the chair skittered out from under him. He strode to the kitchen, snapping on the burner to searing hot for the kettle. It wasn't news that she would leave him, going back to her organized, methodical life. From the first minute he met her, the clock was ticking. Now she was trying to plan his life for him, like his sisters, like his mother. He was so fucking tired of being managed.

"Of course they don't decide, that's not what I meant. But seeing this through their eyes," she trailed off. "I stupidly let myself think that this could be something more." She got up to join him the kitchen, slipping her arms through his to wrap around his chest and pressing her cheek against his back. "We have to be realistic. It's not like you're going to come with me to Chicago, and I can't live here."

"You keep saying that."

"I don't want these last few days to be uncomfortable or weird."

He kept his eyes fixed on the kettle as he extracted himself from her arms. "No, I get it. We should keep to client and customer. Bang on." He moved to the cupboard to get a cup. Anything to put some distance between them.

"We still have five days together," Bridget took a beat. "We can still..."

"You looking to pay me for these services too? Or do those only come with the deluxe HouseHijack contract?" The instant the words slipped out, he regretted them. She drew back, the hurt written plainly on her face. It cut him to the bone. "Fuck, I'm sorry. I don't mean that."

He opened his arms, and after a beat, Bridget moved into his embrace. He kissed the top of her head again, burying his face in her curls. It wasn't a surprise that she was saying these things. He wasn't stupid; he knew this would have to end. But for the moment, with her pressed against his chest, there was a hunger for some way where this could be something that could last.

"So, friends then?"

"Friends. Sure." The word tasted sour even as he spoke it.

The whistle of the kettle made him pull away, turning off the range and making two cups of tea. Like friends.

The rest of their discussion was light and inconsequential, but the shadow of the ending of her time hovered over every word. She returned to the table to finish up her work, and Finn rested uneasily on the sofa.

Another quarter hour passed.

"Can I ask something without you getting mad?" Bridget's voice was tight and measured, trying too hard to be casual. "The job with Claire's family. Is it a good job?"

"Could be."

"And for you to get it, Claire's family needs to think there was nothing between us, right?"

Damn, that hurt.

"Sure." His voice sounded rough, even to him.

She took a deep breath. "You should take her out to dinner or something. Explain things and set a time to talk to her dad about the job. It's been two weeks, and you haven't had a moment to do it, because I've kept you driving me around." She started stacking her papers again, despite their being tidy and in order. "I don't want our time together to hurt you. Hurt your future."

His jaw clenched. "Maybe I will then."

She was silent for a second. "Good. That's good. Right."

"Right." They stared at each other for a moment. Did she regret her suggestion?

"I have a lot of editing to do, so I'll..." she gestured to the computer.

"I have to get three pieces done for Olive by Friday, so I'll..." he gestured toward the door.

Another half beat of silence. He turned on his heel and headed out to the barn.

Chapter 28

Landlord Enters the Chat

The moment the back door slammed, Bridget pushed her laptop forward to rest her forehead on her arms. *Idiot.* Why couldn't she leave well enough alone? Just go away in a week without making such a big deal? This is how it had to be. He'd get his job, she'd protect her heart. Everybody could go back to normal.

It was only five days, right?

The reality of her departure came on in a rush. Soon she'd be back in her apartment, her orderly life ready to resume. No smelly donkeys or smoky wood stoves. A cup of coffee instead of tea. Her carefully curated life back to normal. Maybe even a crack at Container Corner.

And yet...

She picked up her phone and began recording; not to create content, but rather to preserve the cottage in her memory. For her, not her followers. She snapped photographs of the threadbare rugs, the old wooden rocker, the knickknacks on doilies and the ancient kitchenware. Shot video of the view from the windows, the donkeys out in the field. The reality that her time in Ireland was ending drove her to archive everything.

She needed to remember all of it.

At three, Finn came indoors to make a sandwich. She could smell tung oil on his hands and saw flecks of sawdust trapped in his dark curls.

She could take it all back. Tell him she was being stupid. Ask him to forget it all.

"Finn?" She needed him to look at her, to see that she was willing to risk things for him. "About earlier…"

He looked right through her. "Can it wait? I'm going to lay down for a kip."

"Uh, sure."

Finn made a great show of washing up the plate and cup, putting them away in the cabinet, wiping down the countertop and hanging the tea towel precisely on the hook.

Without making eye contact, he said, "If I'm still sleeping at four, could you wake me? I've got a date and need to leave by five."

He gave a nod, sliding past her in the doorway. In a moment, she heard his door shut.

This was what she'd asked for. Why did it make her miserable?

A few hours later, Finn woke and showered, coming out of the bathroom in a cloud of steam, dressed in a dark green flannel shirt and jeans, freshly shaved. He walked past Bridget, his soapy clean scent trailing in his wake.

"I'll be back later tonight to bring the donkeys in. You good for supper?"

"Yes, thanks." Bridget pasted on a cheery smile. She was happy for him, right? Like a buddy or a roommate. *This was your idea, remember?*

He nodded and began to put on his coat. As he opened the door, Bridget couldn't help it. "You look nice, Finn."

He turned toward her, a flash of longing in his gaze, quickly governed into a smooth, neutral expression. "Thanks. Goodnight."

Then he was gone. For a few moments, she stared at the closed door. Claire was a nice girl, maybe she could make Finn happy. Why did she feel someone won the lottery with a ticket she dropped?

She tried to read a book, watch a tv program and get some work done, all in the span of twenty minutes. Bridget gave up pretending that everything was great.

Everything wasn't great.

Everything freaking *sucked*.

She picked up her phone and dialed Tran. Voicemail. But it wasn't like she didn't know what Tran would say. Her voice played in Bridget's mind, echoing the texts from the previous night: "You need to make it perfectly clear that this ends when you leave. Can't start leaving broken hearts all over the world."

But what if the broken heart was hers?

December 22 was coming up quick. She had two choices. She could sit in the house, snuffling and feeling sorry for herself, or...

She picked up the phone to dial again.

"Olive? What are you doing tonight?"

Visiting a pub with Olive was a different experience than visiting one with Finn. Finn routinely pulled them toward the quiet corners away from the crowd, but Olive perched on a stool at Tommy Malone's bar, bantering with Tommy and Joe and engaging everyone in conversation. Olive was good craic, as they say.

Evening Olive looked different than Daytime Olive as well. Her eyes were lined in thick black streaks, with sparkly pink eyeshadow all the way up to her brows. She was a jumble of bracelets and necklaces, and she crossed her long legs carefully in a very short skirt and spiderweb stockings.

For every new patron that sauntered up to the bar, Olive cracked a joke and gave a compliment or a bit of grief, depending on how well she knew them. As each person engaged with her, she made it a point to introduce Bridget.

Nearly everyone seemed to know of Bridget. Some asked if she was "that social media person," "the one with the phone," or worst of all, "Malloy's American."

Olive introduced her to every handsome, single man in the county, drawing them into prolonged conversations. Each made a point of flattering her, asking her questions, talking up the local sites she hadn't yet seen or laying on compliments. Most amusing was hearing each of them in turn running down their friends, giving her a laundry list of why their faults should exclude them from Bridget's attention. They called out to the barman to buy the ladies pints and shots of whisky, but Olive was equal parts host and watchdog, keeping Bridget from overindulgence.

After a quick trip to the bathroom, Bridget returned to see Olive texting furtively. Olive slid off her stool and said in a low voice, "We need to get going." Her eyes darted toward a squat man with a shock of red hair chatting up a few people by the door.

Bridget couldn't hide her disappointment and confusion. The attention had been good for her flagging ego, and the petty part of her wanted Finn to come home to an empty cottage. "What do you mean?"

Olive knocked on the bar to get the attention of the barman who was engaged in deep conversation at the other end of the bar. "Nothing to worry about but a few minutes ago, that man by the door came in and he's...." She cut herself off as the man in question approached them.

"Oi! Olive."

Olive took a step forward to face him, her arms crossed. "And what do you want, Bernie Coughlin?" Her voice dripped with disdain. Bridget shrank back at the name, trying to make herself disappear behind Olive.

"Hear you've got the American with you." Bernie said, craning his neck around Olive to look Bridget up and down.

"What do you need to know about that, now?" Olive placed her large handbag on the empty stool beside her, a clear signal that he was not welcome to join them.

Bernie gave a huff of laughter, his eyes narrowing. "Been soaking the boys for drinks, have you? That bird of Malloy's should be buying *me* a drink."

Olive snorted. "Off with you, Bernie. We're well enough without your presence." Olive gave another sharp rap of her knuckles on the bar, signaling again for the tab.

Bernie slid around Olive and thrust a meaty hand toward Bridget. "Since Olive here isn't showing her manners, I'll introduce myself. Bernie Coughlin."

Everything in her being wanted to turn away from him, but years of conditioning made her reach out and shake his hand. "Bridget."

Instead of releasing her hand, he held on tightly as he pulled her in to speak. She could smell the tobacco and sour drink on Bernie's breath. "I finally meet the tourist Malloy poached from my cottage. Not good enough for you, was it?"

Stay calm. Bridget schooled her expression to not show her unease, but her heart was racing. "Sorry it didn't work out."

He gave a bark of a laugh and dropped her hand. "Sorry, she says. She's sorry." He turned to the crowd in the pub and raised his voice. "Stole 5,000 quid right out of my pocket, and the bint says she's sorry."

A few of the voices in the room started to rumble in defense of Bridget. "Leave off, Coughlin." "Go sit down, Bernie." In one smooth motion, Olive snatched her bag off the stool, swinging it up to clear space between Bridget and Bernie. Bridget gathered up her coat and began to follow, but Olive placed her arm on her shoulder to stop her.

"I've asked you to move along, Bernie. I won't have you harassing my friend." It wasn't a threat, but it carried the weight of a warning. Bridget noticed most of the bar watching the exchange, some men discussing the situation in low voices.

Bernie swung his arms wide to appeal to the crowd. "Is that right? You're taking the side of Miss High and Mighty American, turning her nose up at my cottage, got me taken off the listings."

"Let's go," Bridget said, squeezing Olive's arm.

The barman was suddenly at their corner of the bar. "Go home, Bernie. I won't have you making trouble with these ladies."

Bernie swayed a bit. "Lady my arse. You think the whole town doesn't know what she's doing with Malloy at his place?"

Bridget recoiled as if struck. Several of the men in the pub rose angrily to their feet. They paused when a loud shout came from the front of the pub.

"Coughlin!" Finn stood stone-still in the doorway, his

expression twisted with fury. A bewildered Claire stood half a step behind him. Even from where she stood, Bridget felt the heat of Finn's anger radiating toward Bernie.

Bernie's eyes shifted toward Finn. "There he is, the poacher. Are you startin' then? A nice deal for him, getting paid for the driving as well as the riding!"

It was over in a second.

Finn crossed the room in a flash, and Bernie was splayed on the floor, moaning and holding his hands to his face. A few cheers went up in the room, with a smattering of applause. Tommy came out from behind the bar, a few cubes of ice wrapped in a questionably clean bar towel. Bernie reached up to take the pack of ice from him, but instead, Tommy handed it to Finn for his fist.

Turning to the man on the floor, Tommy prodded him with his shoe. "You're done here, Bernie. Next time I see you, I call the Gardai."

A few patrons in the bar gathered around Bernie, manhandled him to standing, then pushed him toward the doorway. Olive and several others gathered around Bridget to offer support and apologies.

Finn stood apart, icing his knuckles and avoiding eye contact with Bridget. Claire stood behind him, asking to see his hand.

Bridget was torn; more than anything, she wanted to take Finn's rough hands in hers. But after that, the last thing he needed was her making a spectacle in public.

She stepped back, bumping into Olive.

"You good, Bridge?" Olive said in a low voice.

"I think so."

Olive called out to Finn. "You ok, cousin?"

Finn gave a curt nod, then met Bridget's gaze. The light in

his eyes had turned ominous and dark, and she flinched at the pain in his expression. He didn't speak but stared right through her. Claire dipped a paper napkin in a glass of water, dabbing at Finn's bleeding knuckles.

"Finn, I..." She felt like she needed to apologize, but the words wouldn't come.

He turned away. "Later." He brushed past the gathered crowd, sending a barstool toppling. Bridget watched as he stalked to the door, hesitated for a moment, then held it open for he and Claire to leave.

Olive took a long, last swallow of her pint, emptying the glass. Tommy swept up the empty glass. "Sorry for the trouble. Your tab's clear."

Olive gave him a weary smile. "Thanks Tommy." To Bridget she added, "Let's get out of here."

At the car, Olive sighed as she fastened her seat belt. "Not the evening out I hoped we'd have, Bridge. I'll take you home."

Home.

In that moment, home was a cottage in an Irish hillside, not her orderly apartment with every drawer, cabinet, and surface set to her exacting specifications. Home was the creaky door and floorboards, tiny bathroom, and kitchen. It was the photos of Finn's family, the well-worn table and chairs that bore witness to generations of meals and homework and laughter. It was the quiet beauty of the sunrise from her bedroom and curling up by the stove in the evenings.

Home was Finn.

Bridget stared out the window into the darkness of shadowy hills. Even as Finn spent the evening escorting another woman out on a date, she couldn't help wanting him. She wanted *this.* Despite every rational cell in her body screamed that it was impossible.

She had to rip off the bandage and make a clean break.

She turned to Olive, then hesitated. Would she be her accomplice if it meant hurting Finn?

"Olive, I need your help."

Chapter 29

What We Keep

As they walked back to his car, Finn scanned the street for any sign that Bernie Coughlin was lurking, every fiber of his being longing to get one more punch on the weasel. His knuckles throbbed and he was grateful for the distraction of the pain.

"You've gone round the bend for her, haven't you?"

He turned with a start, almost forgetting Claire was next to him.

She smiled as she kicked idly at a stone as they walked. "The biddies in town would give up on trying to link us together if they saw your face back there."

"Don't know what you're going on about."

"Oh, you do know, Finn Malloy." Claire laughed and poked him on the shoulder. "That American girl has turned your head. A big reason why you and me...it was never going to work. That and a whole lot of other reasons."

Finn started to protest, but Claire raised her hand. "I told you last week. I'm grateful for your help at the dairy, but I'm not interested in becoming a couple. I couldn't take the pressure from my ma anymore, and figured if we went out, she'd leave me in peace. But I won't get between you and Bridget. You'd be doing me a favor to go out with her more often."

His thoughts churned like treacle. "But you wanted to go out tonight."

"You asked, I said yes. That way, my ma can't hold it over my head that I refused to go out with you." She shrugged. "You're a nice guy, Finn, but I'm not interested in you like that. Which is good, because if I was, that scene back there would've broken my heart."

If he was a man of any sense, he'd give in to his family's prodding and make something with Claire. She was pretty and smart and good craic. But he didn't want Claire, not like that. "Let's get you out of here before you freeze to death."

She gripped the top of her coat, then stopped for a moment, turning to look back at the bar where Bridget was. "Unless you want to go back to Tommy's? I can call my brother to pick me up," she said.

"No, I'll take you home, Claire. I'm sorry I ruined your evening."

"Stop it, you fool." She swatted at his coat. "But if you want my advice, tell Bridget how you feel."

As he pulled up in front of her house he asked, "You want me to walk you up?"

"God, no. That'd be worse for you than me. Don't worry though—when your Bridget goes home, I'll have you meet with my dad about the job." She slipped out of the car and walked round to the front of the vehicle. Standing in the glare of the headlights, Claire cupped her hands to call out, "Tell her, Finn!" then slipped away to her duplex.

He could imagine the third degree she'd be getting inside. Sure enough, his mother would probably be calling him with her own interrogation in the morning.

As he pulled off the curb, he rang up Olive.

"Finn!"

"You two still at the pub?"

"No, in fact, I dropped Bridget back at your place not five minutes ago."

He was silent for a moment, half of him wanting to ask how Bridget was, the other half not wanting to expose his concern. Especially not to Olive. "Good," he forced out. "I'll be another twenty minutes. Was she mad you texted me?"

The line was quiet for a moment. "She understood why I did it. But she's pretty shaken up, Finn. Bernie scared her, I think."

Again he felt the urge to pummel that twisted beast of a man. He gripped the steering wheel so tightly that one of his knuckles began to bleed again.

"I wish I'd gotten there faster. We were only two doors down at the Goose, but I had to settle the tab before I could get over there."

"You got there when it mattered. How's the hand."

Finn looked down at his fist. "I'll be fine."

"And your heart?"

"What do you mean by that?" He tried to keep his voice steady.

"Finn Malloy, if you don't think I can't tell from miles away that you are wild for Bridget, you're mad."

The tangle of emotions tightened again in his chest. What if he admitted it? Said the words out loud. Meant it.

"I...care for her." The knot in his chest began to unravel, and for the first time in years, he felt something akin to relief.

"Jesus, Mary, and Joseph, it's a bloody miracle. Now tell her, will you? Don't wait. Tell her tonight."

"I will."

"I'm serious, Finn. You need to talk to her. Tonight. It's important."

"Thanks for tonight, Ollie. I owe you."

"Like I'd let you forget it."

He pulled off to the curb along a quiet street. He was slightly stunned by the effect his own words had on him. "I care for her," he repeated in a whisper.

A quick glance at the clock: 11:15 p.m. Most everything in town was closed up tight. He couldn't buy her flowers or chocolates or whatever it was a man did when he professed his feelings. It would just have to be himself.

He hoped it would be enough.

As he pulled up to the cottage, he could see the lamp on Gran's piecrust table glowing in the window. His heart leapt a bit as he threw the car in park.

He fumbled with his keys in his rush to open the door. "Bridget?"

The room was quiet and still, all other lights in the room were out. A folded note was propped up on the lamp.

> Finn—
>
> I'm so sorry about what happened tonight. Olive tried to say it's not my fault, but I know it is.
>
> I refuse to be the reason you miss out on your chances for a good job and a happy life.
>
> Again, I'm sorry.
>
> —B.

Ridiculous. How could she think that? He walked to her bedroom door and knocked. "Bridget? You awake?"

No answer.

He knocked again. "I need to talk to you."

Should he dare? He reached for the handle but stopped himself. He'd no right to open a closed door.

He stood still, then leaned his forehead against the rough wood of the door. There's no way she could sleep through his knocking and calling. This was on purpose.

In a low voice, he spoke toward the door. "Listen, Bridget. I don't know if you're awake or asleep or angry...but we need to talk."

Silence.

Deflated, he wandered back to the parlor, slumping on the couch. This was his fault. If he'd done a better job of protecting her, if he hadn't gone out with Claire...the list went on.

The last thing he wanted to do was entertain these thoughts. He'd take care of the donkeys, wash up and go to sleep.

In the morning, they'd talk.

Sleep eluded him for hours, his mind racing through how to tell Bridget that he cared for her. That she meant something to him. That he didn't want her to leave. He didn't yet know how to solve for the problem of living 2,000 miles apart, but they could figure that out together.

He woke with a start, his alarm clock rattling at 7:30 a.m. With barely four hours of sleep, it was going to be a rough morning.

But the first priority was Bridget.

He heard rustling noises in the kitchen. He weighed whether to skip the shower and tell her how he felt, but a quick sniff of his own breath convinced him that his romantic profession would go over better if he was washed and fresh.

He showered, shaved, and took pains to make his hair behave. Slipping out of the bathroom, he dressed quickly in a pair of jeans and a button-down shirt. He flipped the covers up to make his bed, his heart beating a staccato tempo as he dared to entertain the possibility of bringing her back to bed with an honest and open heart.

A deep breath. He was ready.

He walked into the front room. "Bridget? Do you have a minute to talk?"

No response. The front door was ajar, two suitcases standing on the front stoop. Olive's car was parked behind his in the drive. His cousin was standing next to it, lips pursed and shaking her head. "Bridget?" His heart began to beat faster, panic setting in.

"Sorry, be right in." Bridget closed the boot firmly and came into the cottage slightly out of breath.

He was trying to make sense of things. "What the hell are you doing?"

Bridget didn't quite meet his eye. "You got my note last night, right? Finn, I'm so sorry about what happened yesterday."

"Don't worry about it. In fact, it's all good. You see—"

She cut him off. "No, I can't be responsible for ruining your prospects here. I'd never forgive myself. So, I'm going to take the train up to Dublin today."

"What are you talking about? No!" His heart began to race.

"I got on an earlier flight. I stripped the linens from my bed —they're in the washer. I'll pay you for the full amount, don't worry."

"I don't care about the bleedin' money!" *This was insanity.* How was this derailing so fast?

She ignored him. "But it *is* about me messing up your future. You have a life here, and I'm complicating things."

"No! Bridget, I...you don't have to do this."

Her voice was thick with emotion. "Yes, I do. This has been amazing—*you* have been amazing. But I don't belong here in this life." She pressed the base of her palm against each of her eyes in turn, smearing her mascara. "I came here because I wanted to be an influencer, for real. And you helped me find my voice. Mary might have something else for me, maybe Container Corner, and it's not like they have any locations in Ireland." As her rambling words spilled out, Finn struggled to keep up.

"You're not making sense." *Leaving?* "We have four more days!"

"Every minute I stay here makes it that much harder to leave. I need to go. Today. Thank you for everything, Finn." She choked back a sob and moved to the door.

He grabbed for her hand. "Please don't do this. Bridget. Please. We need to talk. Let me take you to the train at least!" He felt his body go cold with distilled panic.

She slipped out of his grip, turning away. She couldn't even look at him.

And then she was gone.

Finn dropped down on the sofa, stunned. *Gone.* He should have known better than to open his heart to someone who was only passing through. Someone who had an entirely different existence, who thought of him as a distraction.

He rubbed his eyes, ignoring the sting of his raw knuckles. Did it scare her, to see his brutish behavior with Bernie?

And Olive, the traitor. Making plans to sneak away with Bridget, take her to the train. After telling him last night to open his heart and tell Bridget—

Fuck. He never told her. Olive's insistence made sense now.

The madness of the morning's scene derailed his plan to share his feelings for her. If she knew how he felt, maybe he could convince her not to go. In one fluid movement, he grabbed his keys and coat.

He could catch her at the train.

A handful of people gathered on the platform at Killathay station, most clutching paper cups of coffee or staring at phones. Finn raced up the ramp and scanned the area desperately for Bridget.

He spotted her mountain of luggage at the far end of the platform and relief swept through him. He didn't miss her. She was seated alone on a wrought-iron bench, staring off into the distance.

"Bridget?"

She turned, and he watched surprise, joy and pain flicker across her face. "What are you doing here?"

"Can I talk to you for just a minute?"

Bridget glanced at her watch. "The train arrives in eight minutes. I don't know what else there is to say, Finn." Her voice sounded wrung out.

He took a breath. *Now or never.* "I know it doesn't make sense, and I know you have a life in Chicago. But I...I care for you. More than I thought I would. When I saw you the other night at the bar, Bridget..."

"Finn, I—"

He took her hand in his. "Please, let me finish. In that moment, I knew it was no accident that you were stuck with me for three weeks. I should have hated you, hated the disruption to my life, for complicating everything." He tipped her chin up gently, bringing her gaze up to meet his eyes. "But it's been the best weeks of my life."

She pulled away. "I care for you too, Finn. But this isn't going to work. I'm going home in the morning and things will just go back to the way it was."

All the hope he'd pinned on her response began to splinter and crack. He had to try. "Could you...stay? Stay to the new year? Spend Christmas with me?" He tried to force a grin. "Wouldn't even charge you for the room."

She pulled her hand back to her own lap. "It would only make things worse, Finn."

Panic flooded him. This couldn't be the last time he'd ever see her. "Tonight then. Let me take you home and I'll drive you to Dublin tomorrow." His voice grew louder and more urgent. She got to her feet, stepping behind her stack of luggage.

"It doesn't make sense, Finn," she said, her voice rough with tears. "Why would we put ourselves through that?"

"Because I love you, you daft woman!"

She stopped short, whipping around with a look of shock. "What?"

"I love you. It makes no sense, I know. But you've carved a Bridget-shaped space in my life, and there's no one else able to fill it." There it was. He laid himself bare for her, and he waited, stomach tight for her response.

A tear slipped down her cheek as she offered him a wobbly smile. "I don't know if that's enough to make this work." The train whistle sounded in the distance. "You asked me to stay here. But if I asked you to come to Chicago with me—right now —would you come?" Her words were hopeful, but wary.

Chicago. A litany of reasons why he needed to stay in Ireland cascaded through his brain. The cottage. The donkeys. His mother. His family. His woodworking. Olive's shop. The reality of picking up his life and joining her in a big city, completely out of his depth. The weight of it brought his dream back in check.

Before he could respond, her face fell and she blinked back tears. "See? It's not something either of us can do. These last few weeks...I will never forget them, never forget you." She took a shaky breath as she bit her lip. "That's what we keep."

They were silent together as the train slowed into the station, the roar of the hydraulics too loud to continue. When the train gave its last hiss, she took up her bags. "I'd better give myself enough time to get these in, you know me with luggage and trains." She gave him a watery smile, then kissed him quickly on the cheek. "Goodbye, Finn."

All he could do was watch her leave.

Chapter 30

Change of Plans

Trains are not the ideal place to have a breakdown, but Bridget didn't have a lot of options at the moment. The first leg of the journey she alternated between sobbing in the toilet compartment and mentally berating herself for letting things get out of hand.

The hurt in Finn's eyes haunted her. It felt like a betrayal to leave him. Pair that with a healthy dose of self-loathing for running away to stability and predictability like a coward and she was in utter misery.

Ireland was like a dream. You have to wake up from dreams.

Olive's parting words echoed in her mind as well. *"I won't talk you out of going. But don't give up on Finn, ok?"*

Bridget dabbed her eyes with a handful of whisper-thin toilet paper she cobbled from the bathroom compartment. She was trying to do the right thing, the rational thing. And it was tearing her to pieces.

After changing trains in Mallow without incident, she arrived in Dublin at lunchtime, careful to have all her luggage at the door as the train came to a complete stop. She'd booked a small hotel room about three blocks away from Heuston Station.

Her insistence on leaving today was a little white lie to both Olive and Finn; her plane was scheduled to depart the next morning. Once she'd made the decision to leave, she didn't trust herself to stay in Kildunne any longer. This break would give her time to recalibrate before heading home, to finish up her content with Mary and tie up all the loose ends she could.

She rented a cozy room at an older hotel about four blocks from the River Liffey. Not a planned expense, but necessary. The Shea Hotel was much more rustic than The Padraig where she'd stayed with—*stop*! *Stop thinking about Finn.*

The distant professionalism of the hotel staff was comforting, and they promised her room by three and offered to hold her bags. She felt invisible, and it was exactly what she needed.

Bridget slung her knitted crossbody bag from North Dun across her jacket and headed out to wander Dublin in search of a meal. After a vinegar-soaked lunch from a chipper, she browsed through shops like a tourist, purchasing small gifts for her mom, Dennis, Tran, and her boss, Carl.After all, she needed to get back in good graces with Carl, as her chances of getting the Container Corner gig were almost nil. InfluenCZA tended to frown on broken contracts.

She owed two more videos to Mary, so she half-heartedly captured a smattering of footage of the Christmas decorations along her path.

At three, Bridget collected her belongings, grateful for the peace and anonymous solace of a hotel room. With her now-practiced cyc, Bridget edited together the Dublin video and packaged it up for Mary. To be fair, this assignment had pushed her to learn more about her craft, challenged her to develop her own eye and perspective.

. . .

TO: Mary D'Esposito
FROM: Bridget Kolodziej
Hey there—winding down on the content, and by my count, I have 2 videos remaining. Here's the first one, from Dublin. I'll get you another video tomorrow. Let's meet for lunch when I get back to Chicago!
-Bridget

She turned on the television, hoping to find a sitcom she'd seen a million times. Something to occupy her brain so it couldn't slip into thoughts of Finn. When that failed, Bridget perched on the edge of the windowsill, peering through the curtains at the lights and movement of the city. *Go out. Explore. Do something.* Her mind railed at her to escape from the room, to embrace the waning hours of her time in Ireland. *You were supposed to do this by yourself anyway!*

Maybe this influencer life wasn't worth the heartache.

She ordered room service for dinner—a cheeseburger to get her palate back to American food. Before bed, she laid out her clothes for the next day, set an alarm for 5 a.m., spread a cloth on the sink to organize her toiletries in order of how they would be used in the morning, and turned down the covers at a 90-degree angle. It was barely 8 p.m., but the events of the day had drained her of energy. She slid between the covers, willing herself to sleep without running through the litany of ways she'd screwed up in the past 24 hours.

As she began to drift off, her phone buzzed with texts from Mary.

Video is approved. Dublin's great, but you
need to make the last video about the rental.

Get your host to let us add the link this time.

HouseHijack could use the bookings!

Bridget pinched the bridge of her nose as she put down her phone. That was going to be a problem.

Reluctantly, she pulled up her videos and skimmed the footage she'd taken at the cottage to remember. Surely she could cobble something together from her spare footage, if she could handle her emotions. She hit *Play*.

The montage of shots from the tiny cottage overwhelmed her. The half-drunk teacup at Finn's spot on the sofa. The stack of firewood he kept piled high so she wouldn't have to go out at night. The knobby rocking chair with its threadbare cushion. His Gran's knitting needles, with a few rows of yarn that she'd cast on from her trip to North Dun. The yarn that matched his eyes.

And now that yarn is wadded up in my suitcase. She'd slipped the yarn off his grandmother's needles that morning, returning them to the yellow yarn bag. She considered whether the few rows she'd knit were worth saving, but in the end, she tugged the yarn and watched everything she'd created unravel into a mess. The universe was not subtle.

Bridget closed her eyes. She had enough footage to create the last video if she could bring herself to do it, but not tonight. She curled up into a ball, tucking the pillows around her, and begged for sleep to come.

Chapter 31

Out of Last Chances

Long after Bridget's train departed, Finn stood on the platform numb and dazed. His thoughts were thick, churning like concrete. He began to text her.

> Don't go. The next stop is Cul Cuinne.

> Get off and I'll meet you there.

> Please.

His fingers hovered over the *Send* arrow. Instead, he arrowed back until the whole appeal was gone. Why would she get off the train to have the same conversation? Nothing had changed. She wouldn't stay and he couldn't go. He felt his heart began to thud, like his blood had turned thick. They'd talked about her leaving a million times, but the staggering pain at her actual absence...there were no words large enough to contain it.

Olive. Olive would know what to do. She'd needle him to make amends, bully him into calling Bridget or going after her.

He sat down on the bench, imagining that it still held a trace of warmth from Bridget and dialed his phone.

"Finn." The resignation in Olive's voice squelched any bit of hope.

Finn chewed the inside of his cheek. "She's gone then."

"I tried to have her talk to you. And told you to talk to her." An undercurrent of '*I told you so*' filtered through her words.

"I did talk to her. I'm at the train station." He half-laughed, bitterness setting in. "Fool that I am."

A pause. "Come over to the shop. I have someone coming by in a few minutes, but they won't be long."

Finn rubbed the back of his neck. The shop was too public, held too many memories. "No, I'm not fit for company. I'm heading home. Thanks, Ollie."

Before she could protest, he rung off.

He spent the morning wallowing, checking his phone every few minutes for texts from Bridget. His despair curdled into anger, at himself, at Bernie Coughlin, at his family for their stunt with Claire.

He checked his phone again. More likely, any texts would be from his sisters or his mother. Sure, they wouldn't be able to leave well enough alone. But so far, radio silence.

He tried working in the barn, but his hands felt clumsy. Rather than jeopardize the works in progress with a careless effort, he gave up in frustration. Heading into the house, his phone rang. After a brief leap of hope, he saw it was Cillian. *Figures.* His sisters likely drafted him to ring, since he was a neutral party in their scheming.

A rush of noise in the background, then Cillian said, "Mum's having trouble with her Wi-Fi. You think you could swing by and help her out today?"

Sly, this one. "What, is there going to be an intervention there? Room full of everyone telling me what I'm doing wrong?"

There was a pause. "The hell are you talking about?"

"Very smooth, Cill. And here I thought you'd be on my side in this thing."

"It's the fucking Wi-Fi, Finn. If you're going to be an ass, forget I asked. I'll do it." With that, he rung off.

So transparent. Probably part of their strategy to have Cillian soften him up. Finn waited for the next sibling to try and press him for information, cajole him into visiting his mother's house or dropping by for no reason.

None came, called, or texted.

The lonely afternoon crawled into a silent night. For such a tiny house, it felt cavernously empty. At one point, he swallowed his reluctance and walked again into Bridget's bedroom, a lingering scent of lavender the only clue of Bridget had been there.

He'd have to give her 5 stars as a guest.

Back in the kitchen, he reached to the top of the cupboard and pulled down a dusty bottle of Jameson, downing a shot with a grimace. He didn't want to spend another night chasing sleep, and the whisky would help drown out the voice in his head. He put his head down on the kitchen table and closed his eyes.

Out of nowhere, his jacket was thrust into his hands, Cillian standing in the open the doorway. "Olive told me. And after you sounded daft, I figured you needed to talk. C'mon, let's get a drink." Cill pulled him up from the table, stuffing him into his coat.

Cillian propelled him into the cold night air, walking in unison to the car. In no time, they pulled up to Tommy's. Sitting at the bar, Cillian called for two shots of Jameson instead of their usual pints. When they arrived, Cillian pushed them both toward Finn. Wordlessly, Finn knocked them back.

Cill studied him. "Olive gave me the short version. You want to talk about it?"

"No."

"Suit yourself." Cillian turned on his barstool, making a great show of looking at his phone.

Finn sighed. "She's going back to Chicago tonight."

"Wasn't that always the plan?"

"Shut up then."

"You can't be thinking she'd give up her influencer lifestyle and move in with you after a few weeks? Sure, if she was staying with *me*, then I could see how it would happen, but *you*?" Cill elbowed him in a teasing way, but Finn's eyes remained fixed on the empty shot glasses.

Cillian tried a different tack. "You can't expect her to stick around if you don't tell her how you feel."

"I did tell her," he muttered.

Cillian swung around on his stool to face him. "You told her what exactly."

"I told her that I loved her. And I wanted her to stay. She still left."

The shock on Cillian's face would've been amusing at any other time. "But you went out with Claire!" The Malloy News Network, alive and well.

"Bridget's idea. She didn't want me to lose the job with the McKibbons."

Cill stroked his chin. "You told her how you felt and she... what, walked away?"

"She asked if I'd go with her to Chicago."

"What did you say?"

Finn looked up at Cillian, the answer clear in his bleak expression. "Not the right thing."

Cillian sighed. "Another round, then."

They closed down the pub well after midnight. Cillian's girlfriend Mairead collected them with a tone of disapproval, but drove Finn home.

The cottage was cold, dark and starkly empty. Finn switched on the television, a visceral need to fill the room with something resembling people. The effects of the alcohol were wearing off quickly, leaving him with a headache and a morass of regret.

A screech rang out from the back pasture, and he groaned. The donkeys were still out in the field, and from the sound of things, quite irritated. They could join the club.

Before he could get himself out to the barn, he felt his phone vibrate in his back pocket.

New Post from @cabinetscountertopsclosets

He sat down heavily on the rough wooden stool. Did he even want to watch it?

Who was he kidding? He clicked the link.

Bridget was in a hotel room—*hotel room?*—with her face scrubbed clean of makeup, eyes a bit puffy. The glare of her ring light was too bright, but Finn was fixated.

"I'm about to leave for Dublin airport, heading back home

to Chicago," she began. "I wanted to reflect on what this trip, this adventure, has meant to me. For those of you who followed my posts back in the US, my content centered on organizing things, making them neat and sensible."

Bridget gave a soft laugh, looking up at the ceiling briefly. "When I came to Ireland, I thought I could put those skills to good use. I'd show where I was staying. I'd have an orderly plan to show what living in a rental home was like, the sights of rural Ireland, that kind of thing."

She paused again. "What I didn't expect was that my trip to Ireland, and Kildunne and Killathay in particular, would change me."

She took a sip from her water bottle. "The very first day I arrived in Ireland was such a run of bad luck it was comical. But that was the day I met someone who not only helped me, but became my personal guide. He showed me so much more than the tourist books ever could, even though he doesn't even use social media. He introduced me to his friends, his family, and was by my side at every turn. He's incredibly talented and kind...once you get around his rough edges."

Bridget took a deep breath, her voice shaking a bit when she resumed. "And one of the hardest things I will do is leave him," she said, blinking back tears.

"I thought my first big assignment as a content creator would be straightforward, easy-peasy. But I'm not sure..." She cut herself off, biting her lip. "I'm not sure this is what I want to do anymore."

She took a breath to steady herself. "I'm going to be silencing my notifications for a while, taking a little break. I need to think about what I want this account—this career—to be. My next post is my final installment in this project, a love letter to my time in Ireland and my House Hijack cottage in Kildunne. Don't worry, I won't be deleting anything, mostly because I'm contractually obligated to keep this account live for the next twelve months at least." She smiled faintly. "But I need to clear my head and return to my real life."

She wiped a tear off her cheek. "Thank you, for following me, for sharing this adventure. And Finn, I love you. Thank you..."

He caught his breath, watching her chin tremble. *She loved him.* The force of her words smashed into him, bringing him to shocking mental clarity.

"...this is what we keep."

Chapter 32

Sweet Home Chicago

Chicago snow turned to gray slush almost as soon as it fell, as cars and buses churned the foulness onto the sidewalk from pothole puddles. Bridget braced for impact, tightening her hood around her head as she trudged to her El stop.

In the week since she returned to her empty, tidy apartment, she'd done her laundry, finalized her expense report for Mary, did her invoicing and wrapped the presents she'd bought for her parents, Tran, and her boss. She'd called her parents on Christmas Eve to listen to them rave about the new on-board pickleball courts. They asked a few half-hearted questions about her trip, and she replied with equally neutral answers. She could tell they never even glanced at her posts.

Tran had been a rock; since the day Bridget decided to cut her losses and come home, she'd carved out time to video call her daily from her beachfront villa. On Christmas, the whole Ho family serenaded her with "We Wish You a Merry Christmas," before disintegrating into loud debates on pitch and harmonizing.

But the expanse of lonely, quiet, organized space of their apartment gave her brain ample bandwidth for regrets.

She'd been true to her word. She deleted the Instagram and TikTok apps from her phone and blocked her notifications on email. By the time she boarded her plane, her life as an influencer was unplugged. Once home, she banished The Binder to the lowest shelf of the bookcase, tucking all the notes, ticket stubs and receipts from the trip in its front pocket.

Out-of-sight, still very much on her mind.

Luckily, Mary was out-of-office for the week of Christmas. Bridget had deliberately "forgotten" to include the HouseHijack links to the cottage on her last video, which probably put her in bad graces with the client. She lived up to the spirit of the contract, if not the letter. Another few weeks and she'd have the final installment of the contract in her bank account.

Her boss Carl closed her office between Christmas and New Year's, but Bridget decided to go in anyway, catching up on her backlog of assignments and giving her something productive to occupy her time.

She shivered as icy wind stabbed at the backs of her legs between her boots and her coat. Around her, the winter worker drones hunched over to protect their faces from the biting wind, most headed to the El platform.

An approaching train rumbled as she neared the station, and she fumbled with numb fingers for the Ventra app on her phone. An "Unknown" call flashed on the screen and Bridget hit the "X" to decline the call.

Lurching through the turnstile, her phone rang again. Still "Unknown."

With a sigh of frustration, Bridget answered it as she began to climb the stairs to the platform. "Hello?"

"Bridget." She froze on the staircase, the person behind her knocking into her then moving around her with a muffled curse. The voice on the phone was hardwired in her memory.

"Finn?" Even hearing herself say his name created a sweet and precious ache.

"I need to know one thing, Bridget."

"Finn, I can barely hear you. This isn't a great time—"

"Tell me right now. If I had said yes to Chicago, would you have said yes to me?"

The overhead speakers blared out the approach of the next train, and Bridget covered her exposed ear with her gloved hand to muffle the noise. "I don't know what you mean."

"If living in Chicago was not an issue, if I said I'd come with you...would you still be with me?"

"Finn, I ..." Crying on an El platform in negative four degree windchill was not a great plan. "I can't do this again with you. What's this all about?"

"Where are you right now?"

"What? I'm on the El platform, going into work. Why?"

"Which El platform?"

"What?" His questions made no sense. "I'm on the Belmont El platform, about three blocks from my apartment."

"Belmont is in three stops."

Bridget pulled the phone away from her head to look at the screen again before putting it back to her ear. "What do you mean?" Her voice was barely a whisper.

"Bridget, I realized that when you left, the...never...hurt... before. Mum...sorry" The rumble of the approaching El train broke into everything that Finn was saying, chunking his words into unintelligible fragments. With a squeal of brakes and hydraulics, it came to a stop, the doors yawning open.

"Hold on, please. I can't hear you!" Bridget turned away from the train and moved to the farthest corner of the frigid platform, huddling in the cold.

"Stand clear of the doors," the speaker announced, and the train rumbled away, as Bridget curved her hand around the phone to create a cave of muffled silence around her microphone. "Finn, I couldn't hear you."

This time, she heard him loud and clear. "I said, when you left, I blamed everyone for my being miserable, Olive, my sisters, even bleedin' Bernie Coughlin. Ma gave me holy hell for wallowing. But I was stubborn, and for that I'm sorry. In the last few days, I figured I might be an idiot, and the consensus from every relative is that I am. My sisters got tired of hearing me go on about missing you, so they put me on a plane last night."

Bridget wiped her eyes with her gloves, smearing the tears across her face and making her nose run, even as she couldn't stop smiling. "And you're here?"

"Next stop Belmont," he said. "I can't believe it, but I'm here."

Her head was spinning. Finn was here. In Chicago. Bridget's heart was thrumming in her chest. "I can't believe it either," she said, her face splitting into a wide smile.

Her stomach dropped. "Wait—you said you came in from O'Hare?"

"Yes, and we're now pulling in, do you see the train?"

She groaned. "You're at the wrong Belmont station. My train line doesn't go to O'Hare. There are two Belmont stations in Chicago."

"Are you bleedin' kidding me? What kind of city has two train stations with the same name?"

Bridget shook her head, trying to come up with a plan. "It's only three miles away. Get off there and I'll take a cab over to meet you."

"Don't make me wait too long, Boss Lady."

Boss Lady. How could two silly words make her heart melt?

She inched along Belmont in her cab, trying to make the cab faster by sheer force of will. When they pulled up to the corner station of the subway line, she flew out of the cab, scanning the area for a man with wild black curls. Finn was nowhere to be found. She frantically pulled out her phone to call him.

"Disastrous train trips are kind of our thing."

She spun around at the sound of his voice, the burst of joy at seeing him erasing the memory of the last hollow, lonely week. She propelled herself into his arms, hugging him as tightly as her thick parka would allow. The scent of him, even dulled by a day's worth of international travel, made her feel whole again.

"Do I not even get a kiss then?"

She turned her face up to him, and he kissed her with the strength and desperation of a starving man.

"I can't believe you're here," she whispered again.

He took her hand. "Let's get out of this fucking cold, and then we'll talk."

They navigated to a pancake cafe a block away. The wind whipped around their legs as they entered the diner through the flimsy plastic-and-metal windbreak doors. In moments they were seated at a booth, curving their hands around brown ceramic mugs of coffee.

When the server left with their orders, Bridget leaned across the table. "I still can't wrap my mind around you being here. In Chicago. Why didn't you call?

"I didn't want to give you the chance to say no," he said. "Would you have told me not to come?"

Bridget started to answer but paused. "I don't know. These past few days haven't been great. But it doesn't change the fact that you have a life in Ireland and I have a life here."

"I know. It was wrong for me to expect you to stay. That was never in your plan. But there have been a couple of things that happened."

He pulled out his phone. "I know you're taking a break from social media, but —"

She looked confused. "Wait, you saw my post? You don't have social media."

Finn winked. "Good thing I did. But I was interested in your thoughts on this video reply." He handed his phone across the table, cued up on the account @FinnLovesBridget.

Instantly, Bridget recognized the setting for the video. The Olive Branch was lit and lively, with voices in the background. She hit play, and watched Finn step into frame, wearing the sweater she gave him.

"Hello, Internet. I'm Finn Malloy, and if you've been following Bridget's posts, I'm 'that Finn.' Posting like this is the last thing I want to be doing. But it took a beautiful, sexy, stubborn, set-in-her-ways woman from Chicago to make me realize that sometimes, a stubborn, set-in-his-ways Irishman needs to be dragged into the 21st century."

Bridget's eyes flickered up to meet Finn's, but he motioned to her to keep watching.

"Bridget turned my world upside down, in the best possible ways. Her belief in me forced me to do things I'd been too much of a coward to do. And every day that passed, I fell in love with her a bit more."

In the background, someone erupted with "awww," and was shushed.

"It's Christmas Day, and my family has given me a ticket to Chicago, leaving in two days. I'm not sure if they want to be well rid of me, or if they think I've got a shot at convincing Bridget that she and I are worth fighting for."

"So, Internet, I'm off to surprise her and will let you know what happens." In the background, she heard Ciara's voice say, "that's it!" and the video ended.

Finn said nothing as Bridget sat staring at the phone for several seconds.

"Hang on," she said, pulling out her own phone from her backpack. Her fingers flew over the screen as she redownloaded her TikTok. Opening up the app, she clicked on notifications.

"Oh. My. God." Her post—with Finn's stitch—was doing numbers. Thousands of likes, hundreds of shares. Notifications that she was being featured on accounts everywhere. Her direct messages were flooded with requests, interview opportunities and unsolicited advice about her love life. She clicked to the @FinnLovesBridget account and looked up in shock.

"How did you get more than 50,000 followers with one post?"

It was Finn's turn to be aghast. "What? I just posted it yesterday! Where do I see the likes?"

She pointed to the spot on his phone so he could see for himself how popular his post was. He ran his hand through his black curls as he processed this information. "I suppose that makes my plans here in Chicago pretty straightforward," he grinned.

"How's that?"

"Your Mary will be breaking down my door, trying to get me for her clients."

Bridget laughed, giddy at the feeling of being with Finn, setting aside all her anxiety and fears. "Imagine what we could do together."

Finn set down his phone, reaching across the table to hold her hands. "I wouldn't want to do it without you."

Bridget couldn't stop smiling. "The man who despises social media is now a content creator."

"And a short-term rental owner. As part of my Christmas gift, Cillian said he'd oversee the rental of the cottage, and my nephew is taking over the donkeys while I'm gone. I opened the HouseHijack calendar for the Red Door Cottage, and already have three weeks rented before April."

"Your family wanted you to come? To be with me?"

He rolled his eyes. "Meddlers, all of them. We had quite a blowout after you left, but once they saw what your leaving did to me...they scrabbled up the funds and bought a ticket."

She almost didn't want to ask, but she needed to temper her emotions. "When do you go back?"

Finn paused. "Not sure yet. I'm trying not to take it personally that they got me a one-way ticket. I suppose I should make sure you are interested in having me stay. But I have a hotel for tonight."

Bridget took a deep sip of coffee. "That hotel you booked... is it refundable?"

"Until noon."

"Cancel it."

"You sure?" He cocked his head to the side.

The tentative hope in his expression broke through her last cowardly instincts. She reached for him, curling her hand around his. "You never asked me who I dreamed about."

He furrowed his brow. "What's that?"

"When I drank the water from Eirhann Waterfall...that night I dreamt of you."

Finn said nothing but slid out from his side of the booth, offering his hand to help Bridget to her feet. Threading his fingers into her curls, he pulled her toward him, kissing her with a gentle intensity that felt like a promise. "More things in heaven and earth, *mo stoirin.*"

Finn reached into his pocket and dropped a crumpled $20 bill on the table. "Does that cover it?" he asked, his eyes dark with desire. "Because if I can't get you alone soon..."

"I think it's time I give you a tour of my apartment."

"Lead the way, Boss Lady."

The End.

Acknowledgements

Books often take a convoluted path to publication, and this one is no exception. So many people helped make it what it is today. Special thanks to my beta readers, Sara J. Kader, Natasha Gaubert, Pamela Keating, Susie Dodge and Pamala Knight. Your insight and encouragement helped me to bring Finn and Bridget to the world.

The generous advice, mentoring, and hand-holding by my colleagues at Chicago-North Romance Writers helped this book evolve from idea to finished novel.

I'm so grateful for the unflagging support and encouragement of Jeanne DeVita and Jenny Hooks, both brilliant writers and friends from my high school days in Mr. White's Creative Writing class. As he wrote in my yearbook, "to whom much is given, much is expected." I've been the lucky recipient of a wealth of support from you both over the years.

I am so lucky to have supportive female friend groups, both online and in the real world.

The Circle crew: Shawn, Mary, Sarah, Blair and Jessica, for dragging me into the influencer marketing life. I'm so lucky to work with my friends.

The Cheesecake Girls: Kirsten, Rosemary and Dawn, a standing monthly dinner date that has been the foundation of friendship for a quarter century. And by extension the Salty Gals, my friends for more than two decades both online and in real life. I would be lost without you.

Finally, I have to thank my most vocal and committed supporters: my family.

For my parents, Jerry and Susan, thank you for your unwavering belief that this book would be published. Hope you enjoy it more than the infamous book I wrote with my friends in 5th grade.

My mother-in-law, Nora, who has been with me on every trip to Ireland and who experienced the real luggage-stuck-on-a-train moment with me that inspired Finn and Bridget's meet-cute.

For my children, Brendan, Tim and Katherine, who gamely support my writing. Please skip all the pages I tell you to skip.

And most of all, my husband Patrick. I love you and I would choose you every time in every timeline. You are what I keep. 🖤

About the Author

 Laura Ridgefield is the author of contemporary romance novels that are equal parts wit and warmth (with a healthy dash of spice). By day, she runs a marketing firm that specializes in PR, crisis management and (surprise) influencer marketing. She currently lives in the Chicago suburbs with her husband, with whom she has three grown children. *Under the Influencer* is her debut novel.

For updates on future books and bonus content, visit www.lauraridgefield.com.

Photo credit: Shawn Zurawski